ENCHANTER'S CHILD
BOOK ONE

Twilight Hauntings

ENCHANTER'S CHILD
BOOK ONE

Twilight
Hauntings

ANGIE SAGE

 KATHERINE TEGEN BOOKS
An Imprint of HarperCollins Publishers

ALSO BY ANGIE SAGE

Maximillian Fly

Septimus Heap
Magyk
Flyte
Physik
Queste
Syren
Darke
Fyre
The Magykal Papers

Todhunter Moon
PathFinder
SandRider
StarChaser

Katherine Tegen Books is an imprint of HarperCollins Publishers.

Enchanter's Child, Book One : Twilight Hauntings
Text copyright © 2020 by Angie Sage
Illustrations copyright © 2020 by Justin Hernandez
All rights reserved. Printed in the United States of America.
No part of this book may be used or reproduced in any manner whatsoever
without written permission except in the case of brief quotations embodied in
critical articles and reviews. For information address HarperCollins Children's
Books, a division of HarperCollins Publishers, 195 Broadway, New York, NY
10007.
www.harpercollinschildrens.com

Library of Congress Control Number: 2019944666

ISBN 978-0-06-287514-3

Typography by Joel Tippie
20 21 22 23 24 PC/LSCH 10 9 8 7 6 5 4 3 2 1
❖
First Edition

For Hannah-Grace Strover, with love

Contents

Prologue

It is five minutes to midnight. The last train from the fortress city of Rekadom is full to bursting with Enchanters, Sorcerers, Beguilers and their families, and yet still people are desperately trying to squeeze into its one ramshackle carriage.

In the middle of the crush on the platform is the king's Enchanter, Hagos RavenStarr. He is carrying his baby daughter, and with his wife, Pearl, he too is trying to board the train. They are almost there when a sudden shout rings out from a guard of the city gate: "Hagos RavenStarr! Pearl RavenStarr! Halt! By order of King Belamus the Great!"

Silence falls. Hurriedly, Hagos takes out a small blue leather wallet. Desperate to keep its contents from the clutches of the king, he pushes the wallet deep into the pocket of his daughter's little woolly jacket, telling her, "Poppa will come and find you, sweetheart. I promise." Then he says to his wife, Pearl, "We must give her to someone on the train. It is for the best."

Pearl knows this is true. The previous night, which they spent freezing in a dark dungeon surrounded by rats, terrified their little girl, and Pearl was never going to let that happen to her again.

As two guards grab hold of Hagos, he thrusts his daughter out of harm's way. "Poppa!" She screams out the only word she knows. "Poppa!" But all she sees are her father's hands pushing her away as her mother grabs her from behind and swings her around toward an open window of the carriage, where a woman with two little girls of her own is leaning out.

With tears streaming down her face, Pearl pushes her daughter into the woman's arms, crying out her own language from beyond the Blue Mountains, "Haah-lecks! Haah-lecks!" which means: "Take her! Take her!"

The woman looks down in shock at the protesting bundle she has suddenly acquired. "No!" she yells. "No!" But Pearl is already being dragged away by the guards.

The train whistle blows; clouds of soot-smelling steam

envelop the carriage and cries of farewell ring in the air. As Hagos and Pearl are marched back through the iron gates of the city, the last train from Rekadom begins to move. Their daughter wails in despair and then bites the arm that holds her.

It is not a good start.

Ten years later . . .

CHAPTER 1

The Cards

"MONSTER," ALEX SAID, HER FINGERS fluttering like bird wings above a shimmering hexagon that lay on the dusty ground. Alex, skinny and small for her age, with dark sparkling eyes and a mass of thick black curls held back by a twist of green cloth, was crouching behind a low wall that ran around the edge of the busy marketplace in the cliff-top town of Luma. She was hidden from view behind a friendly seller of spices—a large woman wrapped in a bright yellow jacket and wide pink skirts, who was happy to warn Alex of any unwanted attention from the Sentinels in return for a free reading of her cards, which were always uncannily accurate.

A boy, tall with spikily cropped brown hair and an intent expression, was kneeling beside Alex. He was watching the hexagon with a look of wonder—he had never seen anything like it before. "What do you mean, *monster*?" he asked, feeling a little cheated.

Alex shrugged as she snapped her fingers and the shimmer died away to reveal not one hexagon but seven tiny ones just big enough to sit in her palm. They lay in the dust, wafer-thin tiles of magical mother-of-pearl, each shimmering with a different color that wandered across its surface like oil on water. Alex scooped up the seven hexagons and tidied them efficiently into a slim stack in her hand. "I saw something huge—a monster, I guess—in a cave, with people. I suppose it was going to eat them or something."

"*Eat them?*" The boy looked horrified.

Alex shrugged. "Why else would a monster have people in its cave?"

The boy relaxed. "So you didn't actually *see* the monster eating the people?"

Alex shook her head. "No, I didn't. I must go now. I'm going to be late."

The boy put out his hand to stop her. "Can you try it again? Please. Just one more time?" he asked, trying to pay Alex another silver penny.

Alex pushed the coin away. "It won't be any different," she told him. "It never is."

"Please," the boy said. "It's important. *Please.*"

Alex sighed. "Okay, but you have to concentrate. Think of your question and *nothing else.*"

"I will. I promise." The boy put his hands on either side of his head and pressed hard, as if he were keeping his thoughts from escaping.

Working quickly, Alex placed six hexagons in a circle so that they touched. And then, into the empty space in the middle she carefully placed the last one, which the boy noticed had a swirly number 7 moving inside it. Once again she waved her fluttering fingers and the boy watched, enthralled, as the edges seemed to dissolve and become one big shimmering hexagon with a rainbow of colors washing across its surface. Now Alex began to make swirling movements with her index finger and the multitude of colors spiraled around, following the tip of her finger. In the center of the whirlpool, a dark spot appeared and grew steadily bigger, like a widening pupil in an iris of many colors. Alex stopped her stirring and looked into the darkness, her hands braced firmly on the dusty ground to stop the sensation of being about to fall into a deep pit that always came over her.

The boy, hands still clamped to the sides of his head, watched her intently, holding his breath with concentration. "What is it?" he asked.

"It's the same. A kind of . . . monster."

"What kind?" the boy asked. He leaned over and

looked at the cards, wanting to see for himself. But he saw nothing but a spiral of gently moving colors with a dark spot in the middle. Disappointment overcame him. "It's a trick," he said, annoyed. "Somehow you make a lot of colors move and you pretend to see things in them."

"Well, if that's what you think, you can get lost," Alex told him. "I don't show my cards to people who don't trust me."

The boy did not move. He stayed kneeling, staring into the swirling colors. "I'm sorry," he said. "I didn't mean that. Please tell me what you saw."

Alex sighed. She could understand the boy's concerns. She would feel the same if she'd asked someone what her brother was doing right now and all they would say was "monster." It would be scary and, she guessed, a little annoying too. She glanced over the wall into the market, checking for the telltale orange coat of a Sentinel. It was the end of the afternoon and the market was winding down, which meant there were fewer people to provide cover. Concentrating hard, Alex stared into the black pit once again. "The monster feels very cold. It does not move. Its joints hurt. Its heart is stilled."

"Oh." The boy sounded disappointed. "Is that how it will always be? Can you see if it will always be cold? If its joints will always hurt? Will its heart always be still? Can you tell me? *Please?*"

Alex didn't like using the cards to see the future, but

she was intrigued by the boy's persistence. Placing her hands on either side of the shimmering hexagon to steady herself, she gazed deep into the darkness in the center of the swirling colors until her head swam with dizziness. "Fire. It is eating fire. Its heart is beating. I can feel it." She sat back onto her heels, feeling as though the world was spinning around her. "That's it," she said. "I'm not looking anymore."

The boy was smiling broadly. "Thank you, thank you! That's the best news ever. Jay—that's my brother—he'll be so happy."

People were strange, Alex thought. Why a monster that sometime in the future would eat fire and come alive would be better than a dead monster was a mystery to her. A sudden hiss from the spice seller brought her back to reality. "Hush, child, hush! *Sentinel.*"

Alex swept up her cards and slipped them into their neat little five-sided wallet, which she tucked hurriedly into the broad green sash wrapped around her waist.

The boy seemed not to notice. "That monster you saw in the future," he was saying, "was it—"

"Shush!" Alex told the boy. "Listen, if you want monsters, there's one here right now. Behind you."

The boy went to turn around and Alex grabbed his arm. "Don't look around, you idiot. There's a Sentinel over there. Did you see the tall woman in the orange coat? She's checking us out. Prophecy is illegal, you know."

The boy's eyes widened in fear.

"You'd better go," Alex said.

"No," the boy said. "I'm not leaving you to get into trouble because I kept asking you questions. And it will look suspicious if I just run off, won't it?"

"Okay. So we'll just chat. Like we're friends."

The boy nodded and swallowed hard. "So, um. Do you. Um. Do you come here often?"

Alex laughed. "Like we're *friends*, dummy. I'll do it. You just listen." She raised her voice, "And so I've got to be back by sunset, okay? I promised to look after Louie this evening."

"Who's Louie?" asked the boy.

"Look, if we're friends, you ought to know that. He's my little brother. Well, sort of."

"Sort of?" asked the boy.

"Foster brother. He's cute. Oh, sheesh, she's coming this way. Hey, what's your name? They test you sometimes. I'm Alex."

"Benn."

Alex relaxed and smiled. "It looks like you brought us luck, Benn. She's turned around. Started arguing about the sausages over there."

Benn breathed out a long, low whistle. "Scary . . . ," he said.

"Only if we got caught," Alex said briskly. "And we didn't." And then, with a quick "Thanks!" to the spice seller, she picked up her backpack and slung it over her shoulder.

"Hey!" Benn called out as Alex moved away. "Wait!" But Alex, blending easily into the shadows in her short indigo jacket and faded black pants, was gone.

Benn stared at the warren of alleyways that led off from the marketplace, wondering which one Alex had taken and how she could vanish so quickly. He sighed. He felt unsettled, as though everything was suddenly upside down. Not because of what she had seen, but because he wanted to be Alex's real friend, not a pretend friend just to escape the Sentinel. But Alex was gone, and because he was a market trader from outside the town, he must leave before the gates were closed at sundown.

Benn's hand closed around his day's takings—a fortune of forty-nine silver pennies (one had gone to Alex, but he considered it very well spent) for a cartload of lemons. It made the early morning trudge up the steep track with an unwilling donkey worth every step. He climbed over the wall and spent another silver penny on a packet of hot pepper flakes from the spice seller as a thank-you for keeping them safe. "Tread careful," she told him as she gratefully pocketed the little coin after he had refused the change. "Them Sentinels see more than you think."

Her warning spooked Benn. He hadn't realized what a dangerous place Luma could be. He thought of Alex and it struck him how brave she was—or foolish perhaps, he wasn't sure—to be taking such risks with her cards.

Benn hurried back to his cart and a morose donkey named Howard. He patted Howard's nose, gave him a handful of oats and jumped up onto the driver's seat. The oats and the prospect of going home raised Howard's spirits considerably and the donkey trotted happily across the rapidly emptying marketplace, past a noisy band of musicians who were setting up a line of drums on a platform and headed toward the Sentinel gatehouse, which was the only way in and out of Luma. As they drew near, Benn could not help but glance up at its tower to check if there was a glint of a spyglass watching him, but the little slit of a window looked empty. With his eyes on the thick metal gates that would slam shut as soon as the night bell sounded, Benn waited in the gatehouse shadows to show his trader's pass and be allowed out. His heart was beating fast now. Maybe they could tell he'd bought a prophecy. Maybe he'd never get out of this hot and dusty town. Ever.

Now it was his turn to show his pass, and he held it out, his hand trembling. The Sentinel, an elderly man in an orange coat with dark blue flashes on the sleeves, nodded him through without a second glance, and Benn and Howard were free. Howard set off at a jaunty trot down the Luma Twist—the steep and winding track that would take them to the foot of the cliff from which they would set off home to their farm in the heart of Lemon

Valley far below. As Howard skittered almost joyfully around the hairpin bends, the clop of his hooves beating a jaunty rhythm, Benn thought about Alex and her strange cards. *Those cards were for real. And so was Alex.*

CHAPTER 2
The Pokkle

THE SILVER-TIPPED POINTED ROOFS OF the Luma houses were glowing in the last rays of the evening sun, and the alleyways that wound between them like lazy snakes were already in darkness. But Alex knew every twist and turn and she scooted fast around the winding bends, racing through the spicy smells of the evening meals being cooked and the sounds of children being called home. High above from the little crow's nests perched on the pinnacles of the higher rooftops came the mournful notes of flute players as they piped the sun below the horizon. The excitement of the marketplace and the boy with the fire-eating monster in his future began to evaporate as

Alex ran home to reality and, very probably, to trouble. Her foster mother and her two foster sisters were going out that evening and she had promised not to be late. But she already was.

Every lamppost in Luma had a different carving to help people find their way through the tangle of alleyways, and at last Alex reached the one with the carved lizard curled around it. Here she turned off and headed down a long, echoing footpath sandwiched between two high walls, which led to a door at the far end, lit by a blob of light glowing through its circular window. As she scooted up to the door—proudly adorned with a door knocker in the shape of a fairy—it opened before her and Mirram D'Arbo, her foster mother, greeted her impatiently. "You're late."

Alex stopped to catch her breath and take in the confusion of color shining before her. Her foster mother was dressed in flowing blue and green silks that were bound with glimmering silver cords, crisscrossed in exactly the same way as the cheap sausages (cat meat, so they said) were tied at the market. Emerging at the top of the cat-meat sausage was a small, irritable face crowned with a pile of dark hair, which was held in place by a headband covered in sequins.

The vision brought a wide smile to Alex's face, which Mirram took as approval. "Sorry," Alex said breathlessly. "But I got everything on your list. Even the honey-soaked raisins." And before Mirram could reply, Alex headed past her, off into the dimness of the house.

Suddenly, from right above Alex's head came a harsh squawk: "Wretched girl! Late, always late!"

Alex glared up at the rafters that ran across the lofty room. The pokkle had the run of the house, but it lived mainly downstairs, roosting on a variety of platforms that Mirram had haphazardly hammered to the beams of the ceiling. A scuffle above told Alex that the pokkle was indeed up there. Alex loathed the creature. Believed to be a mix of gecko and parrot, pokkles were a popular pet in Luma, and this particular one was Mirram's pride and joy. The size of a small cat, it resembled a large, multicolored lizard covered in feathers. It had a feathered crest upon its head, one of the finest in the town according to Mirram, and stubby little wings. Like all pokkles, it had the ability to change color at will, but it was not, like most pokkles, silent. Mirram's pokkle had the parrot's gift of speech and mimicry along with an uncanny ability to repeat words just spoken. Alex knew perfectly well who had first said "Wretched girl! Late, always late!"

Mirram walked over to the narrow stairs that led up to the next floor. "Zerra! Francina!" she yelled up to her two daughters. "Time to go!"

Alex heard the sound of her foster sisters' feet flip-flopping quickly down the stairs and politely came out of the kitchen to say goodbye. The sisters shimmered brightly in their own silk tunics, one of red and one of yellow tied in the same crisscross fashion as their mother's. Francina's thin, straight hair was covered in glitter, and Zerra's unruly dark curls were threaded with blue ribbons. With jeweled sandals on their feet and matching pink sparkly headbands, they reminded Alex of the brilliantly colored birds that circled above the rooftops on the early morning thermals and greeted the sunrise with their raucous cawing.

"Cat-meat sausage! Cat-meat sausage!" A sudden screech came from above, much to Mirram's bewilderment. Alex grinned up at the pokkle—every now and then the creature got it just right.

The sisters ignored Alex and headed straight out of the door, where they waited, impatiently tapping their multicolored nails on the doorframe. "Come *on*, Ma," Zerra, the younger but—to Francina's annoyance—taller of the two said.

But Mirram was now issuing instructions to Alex. "Give Louie his supper, then he's to go straight to bed and no stories, he's been a bad boy today. Feed the pokkle. Make the spicebread. Two loaves. And sweep the rugs *properly* this time. Got that?"

Alex nodded. "Have a nice evening," she said.

"What's left of it," Mirram said sourly as she headed out.

Alex watched until the three shimmering figures

reached the end of the long footpath, flickered briefly in the lamplight and then were gone. Alex closed the door and breathed a sigh of relief; she and Louie had the house to themselves for a few hours. Well, almost to themselves, as long as you didn't count the pokkle.

CHAPTER 3

The Naming

ALEX'S FOSTER SISTERS HURRIED ALONG the narrow alley behind their mother, the flip-flopping of their sandals slapping the pressed earth. Zerra and Francina were looking forward to their evening—drummers and a hog roast in the marketplace—and were planning to slip away as soon as they could. But first, Zerra had something to say to her mother.

Their mother was, as ever, striding ahead, expecting them to follow like the well-behaved girls they were supposed to be. Not far ahead now was a bridge between two houses and beyond that the wide street that would take them straight to the marketplace. Zerra could see that already the street was busy with a colorful stream of people in their best clothes all heading for a good night out. She threw Francina a meaningful look—if she didn't speak to their mother now, she wouldn't get another chance tonight. Francina nodded, willing to do her part. Quickly, she and Zerra caught up with Mirram and walked closely on either side of her, boxing her in.

"What are you doing?" Mirram asked irritably. "There isn't room for three."

Zerra began her planned speech. "Ma, it's about Alex. We've got a bad feeling."

"I'll give you a bad feeling, Zerra, if you don't stop treading on my dress."

Zerra hurriedly continued. "Look, Ma, Alex doesn't belong to us. She should be grateful, but she isn't. And now she's putting us all in danger."

Mirram halted abruptly and a wave of annoyance washed over her. She hadn't had a night out for a long time and the last thing she wanted to think about was her increasingly strange foster daughter. "What on earth do you mean—danger?" Mirram demanded, even though with a sinking heart she knew exactly what Zerra meant.

Zerra glanced around to check that the alley was empty. "Alex is doing Prophecy," she said, "with Enchanted cards. You should Name her, Ma."

"*Name Alex?*" Mirram spluttered, shocked. To Name a person in Luma was a terrible thing to do—it meant betraying them to the Sentinels. Once betrayed, they would be taken prisoner and kept in the notorious Vaults beneath the town. Most of those Named never saw daylight again.

But this prospect did not seem to worry Zerra. "Yes, Ma. You should Name Alex before she gets found out and we *all* get into trouble."

Mirram looked longingly at the bright tide of people in the street ahead. She could hear the drumming in the marketplace now, and the excited whoops and calls of the audience. A wave of resentment welled up inside her. Why did her daughters have to be so prissy? Why couldn't they just ignore things like she did? And why bring it up now and spoil a fun evening? It really wasn't fair. "Okay, so we get rid of Alex," Mirram said snappily. "And then who do you suppose would shop, cook, wash and clean, and babysit Louie, huh?"

"You would?" Francina ventured warily.

Mirram gave a loud snort that put her daughters in mind of an indignant camel. They watched her turn on her little pointy blue silk heel and without another word stride off beneath the bridge and into the street where, like a brilliant droplet of water, she seemed to dissolve into the shimmering stream of people flowing toward the sound of the drums.

In the shadows of the bridge, the sisters looked at each other. "I told you she wouldn't listen," Francina said.

"Then we will just have to find someone who will, won't we?" Zerra retorted. And without waiting for a reply, she too joined the flow of people heading toward the marketplace.

Francina dived in after her, and by means of some sharp digs in ribs, she pushed her way forward and joined her sister. "What do you mean?" she demanded, grabbing hold of Zerra's sleeve. "*You're* not going to Name Alex, are you?"

"Well, *I'm* not going to risk being sent to the Vaults just because Ma doesn't care enough about us to do the right thing. Let go of me."

But Francina clung on. "Zerra, you can't do that! Please, Zerra."

Zerra shook off her sister angrily. "It's her or us, Francina. That's the truth of it."

Francina felt like a rock had dropped into her stomach. Shocked, she followed Zerra almost blindly as they were swept along and spilled out with the crowd into the marketplace.

The marketplace was buzzing with excitement. Up on the stage a group of drummers were dancing and whooping, while three flute players shimmied like snakes, their high piping tones piercing the rhythmic bass rumble. It looked carefree and wild, but appearances were deceptive, for up in the gatehouse tower a Sentinel with a spyglass watched for suspicious behavior that might give away secret practitioners of Enchantment.

It was toward the gatehouse that Zerra now made her way, with Francina hurrying after her. "Zerra, please. Think about this a bit longer," Francina pleaded.

"There's nothing to think about," Zerra snapped. She stopped and turned to face her sister. "Unless *you* want to think about which cage you'd like to dangle in down in the Vaults?" Then she turned on her heel and strode off.

Francina felt winded, as though Zerra had punched her. She watched her sister walking away into the shadows of the gatehouse and then hurried after her, while far above, the blind glint of a spyglass followed her. Francina caught up with Zerra by the orange door beneath the arch marked Sentinels Only. Her sister was already opening the little hatch beside it that covered the informer bell. Francina lunged forward and pushed the hatch down. "Zerra, *please*. Think about Ma. This will make her a Harborer, won't it?"

Zerra stared coolly at Francina. "Well, she is, isn't she? She's been Harboring an Enchanter of Cards."

"But she hasn't meant to," Francina protested, quailing beneath the gaze of her sister. Zerra's dark eyes looked cold—and utterly terrifying.

"Oh, *really*?" Zerra retorted. "So how come Alex has those cards, huh? Because Ma has let her keep them, that's why. I tell you, Francina, Ma has known all along, ever since we got Alex. And I reckon that, seeing as you're the eldest, Ma has told you about Alex and her weirdo cards and *you've* known too."

"No!" Francina shouted in a sudden panic. "No, Zerra! I didn't know *anything*. I swear it."

Zerra's answer was to flip up the little hatch in the wall and press the informer bell. High up in the turret, she heard the tinny ping that would change her life forever. Francina heard nothing—she had her hands clamped over her ears in horror.

The bell was answered instantly. The orange door opened to reveal a Sentinel: an officious-looking man with slicked-back hair and a clipboard and pen in his hand. Francina felt panic rising in her throat. *He's been listening behind the door. He's heard me defending Ma*, she thought. In slow motion, as if from a great distance, Francina heard the Sentinel ask, "How many?"

"Three," said Zerra, staring straight ahead. "I Name three."

Francina threw up over Zerra's sparkly feet.

CHAPTER 4
A Knock upon the Door

IN THE LITTLE KITCHEN AT the back of the house, Alex was kneading spicebread while Louie ran his fingers around the dough bowl and licked them noisily. Louie loved the time he and Alex spent together without his sisters making nasty comments and Momma getting fussed over everything. When he was with Alex the world seemed a lot more fun. He watched her put the bread on top of the clay oven to proof and then said, "Can we do the magic color cards?"

"Shh!" Alex hissed, pointing to the front room.

Louie's hand flew up to his mouth. *Sorry*, he mouthed. *I'll get the pokkle bag.*

Alex grinned and gave him a thumbs-up sign. While Louie rooted in the cupboard under the sink, Alex took a handful of honey raisins from the jar and went out to the main room to lay them out in a line, running toward the high-backed chair where Louie always hid with the pokkle bag. It was a well-rehearsed routine and it always worked. The pokkle could never resist a honey raisin, even though it knew it paid for the pleasure with a few hours inside a bag. Which wasn't so bad, especially as it always found more raisins inside the bag.

Alex dropped three raisins into the pokkle bag—a robust little sack lined with sheep fleece for muffling sound. Watched by the pokkle, Louie tiptoed over to hide behind the chair while Alex waited for Louie's yell of triumph. It came soon enough, as the pokkle had not been fed all day.

Alex carefully replaced the bag, complete with its occupant, beneath the sink, and then she and Louie went into the big room and sat on the rug beside the low table. There, watched intently by Louie, Alex took her cards from their wallet and began to shuffle them. It was something she had done many times with Louie, but tonight it felt different somehow. As the little hexagons grew warm in her hands, Alex got up and began to pace the room. She felt uneasy, as if she were walking on sand that was shifting beneath her feet. "Louie," she said in her best serious voice, "you do know these cards are a really big secret, don't you?"

Louie nodded. He understood very well that Alex's cards were a huge secret, and he had told no one. Not even Peg, his stuffed elephant. Louie loved secrets. He collected them as other children collected glass pebbles found in the crevices of rocks. Alex's secret was the most exciting one he had ever had, and he thought it was a shame that he now had to share it with Zerra, who he had discovered looking at the cards while Alex was washing her hair just a few days ago. But Zerra had made him promise to keep her secret too, so now he had *two* secrets about the cards. And Louie was determined to keep them both.

Eyes shining with excitement, Louie watched Alex place six of the cards onto the table so they formed a hexagon without a center. His rapt gaze followed the seventh card as Alex carefully laid it into its place in the middle and then fluttered her fingers across the cards like a bird. As soon as she did that it seemed to Louie that the cards came alive. A shimmer of colors ran across the surface like oil on water, and the edges disappeared so the cards now formed one large hexagon.

"Can I stir the colors?" Louie asked.

"Okay," Alex said. Louie stuck out his stubby finger and Alex took hold of his sticky little hand, and then, putting her index finger beside his, she began to make slow rotations above the hexagon.

"We're doing it! We're doing it!" Louie shouted. "Look, look!" Sure enough, a rainbow whirlpool was forming beneath their fingers. "Faster, faster!" said Louie, gasping with excitement. "Make it spin!" With Louie whooping with delight, Alex and Louie whizzed their fingers around the cards until the colors swirled so fast that they coalesced into a brilliant whiteness. Suddenly Louie snatched his hand away. "Hot!" he said. Louie was right, real heat was emanating from the cards.

Alex felt shaken; the cards had never done this before. They lay on Mirram's best table, shimmering so brightly that it hurt to look at them, and Alex prayed they weren't burning the polished rosewood beneath. How would she explain a big hexagonal burn to her foster mother? And then in the glaring whiteness Alex saw an image forming and she knew that a burned table was the least of her worries.

"Look, there's Sentinels," Louie whispered. "It's like a picture, but *moving*."

Alex stared at the image of three Sentinels marching along an alley and stopping at a lamppost with a lizard curling up it. "Stay there, Louie!" Alex said, and she ran to the front door and peered out through the spy hole.

The tiny fish-eye lens showed the narrow, high-walled path stretching out from the front door through the darkness to the pool of light cast by the lamppost at the far end. In the middle of that pool stood three Sentinels, their orange coats shimmering in the glow. They performed a quick turn and in single file began marching briskly down the footpath, their boots keeping in perfect time.

"What is it?" Louie whispered.

Alex wheeled around. "That picture has come true. Those Sentinels are coming for us. We have to hide. Fast!"

Louie's eyes widened with fear. "Are you going to disappear again?" he asked. "Without me?"

Alex was by his side, grabbing his hand. "Whatever do you mean? We'll *both* have to disappear."

"But I don't know how!" Louie wailed.

"Don't be silly, Louie," Alex snapped, frantically trying to think through the options. There weren't many to choose from. "We'll go up to the attic and hide," she said.

Louie pulled back. "No. People always hide in attics. That's the first place they'll go. We have to escape for real."

Alex knew Louie was right, but where could they possibly go? The house was built on the edge of a cliff. "But Louie, where to?"

"Here, Alex. Here!" Louie pulled Alex into the little kitchen, then he clambered up onto a chair and threw open the window that looked out over a drop of three hundred feet down the Luma cliffs to Lemon Valley far below. A gust of cold air blew in.

"No, Louie, not out there! It's a sheer drop."

"It's all right. I've done it before. There's a rope here, Momma's secret rope. She put it here in case *they* came," Louie said, scrambling down from the window.

"She never told *me* about the rope," Alex said.

"She never told me either. The pokkle did," Louie replied, diving beneath the sink.

Alex peered out farther, and sure enough, there was a thick rope hanging from just beneath the windowsill. The feeling of height made her dizzy and she turned away to look back into the cozy kitchen. Alex couldn't believe what was happening. Inside the kitchen everything felt so comforting and familiar—there was the spice dough, now a big round ball beneath the checked cloth, and the bowl with Louie's finger marks all over it. Maybe she'd dreamed up the Sentinels. Maybe the cards had put the whole idea into her head. And then she heard the sound of metal-tipped heels on the outside doorstep and she knew she hadn't. The only people allowed to use metal-tipped heels in Luma were Sentinels.

Louie emerged from under the sink with the pokkle bag. "We have to take the pokkle," he said.

"No way!"

"If we don't take it, it will tell on us," Louie said, slinging the bag over his shoulder.

"It's in its bag, Louie. It won't have heard a thing."

Louie shook his head. "But sometimes it does hear. I *know* it does. It's always telling tales to Momma."

There was a sudden *ratta-tatta-tat* on the door. It sounded oddly apologetic, because Mirram's fairy door knocker was a delicate thing, but it was the most terrifying knock upon a door Alex had ever heard.

The noise sent Louie scrambling out of the window and balancing precariously upon the window ledge, oblivious to the chasm beneath him. Then, in a heart-stopping move, he twisted around and dropped down so that he was resting his elbows upon the window ledge, looking in as casually as if, Alex thought, he had just dropped by for a chat. "Louie, be careful," she hissed.

"It's fine. I've done this hundreds of times instead of going to school."

Alex leaned out of the kitchen window and saw that Louie was balancing perfectly at ease on a broad knot in the rope.

A sudden series of rapid thuds upon the door—the unmistakable sound of a gloved fist upon the wood—pushed all Alex's objections aside. "Okay, Louie, go!" she said.

"You're coming too?" Louie asked.

"You bet," said Alex.

Louie looked relieved. "I'll see you in the cave," he said.

"What cave?" Alex called down, but Louie was already swinging down the rope, disappearing into the night.

"Open up!" came a yell from the other side of the door. "We know you're in there!"

Alex sprang into action. She threw on her wool jacket and then bundled Louie's coat, the honey raisins, a stale loaf of bread and a flask of water into her backpack. Then she swung herself over the windowsill, took hold of the rope and began to gingerly climb down. It was not as difficult as she had feared, for Mirram had put knots in the rope for footholds. As Alex reached the point where the foot of the house met the rock of the cliff, she heard an earsplitting crash followed by the sound of splintering wood. *That,* she thought, *is the front door gone.*

Alex glanced up and saw the open window. Her heart sank. Sentinels were not stupid—they would soon figure out what had happened, and then there would be no escape for her or Louie, just a long fall to the ground once the Sentinels had finished cutting through the rope. Summoning her courage, Alex climbed back up to the window ledge, reached up and pushed the window shut.

And then she began her descent into the unknown.

CHAPTER 5
The Drop

ALEX WAS RELIEVED IT WAS dark—at least she couldn't see the sheer drop beneath her. But the darkness didn't stop her from feeling it. Her bones felt hollowed out with the sensation of the emptiness below, and her hands, despite the chill wind blowing past her, were hot and sticky with fear. But Alex kept on going—if little Louie could do this then she could too.

She climbed slowly and carefully down the rope, glad of the knots tied at intervals for her hands and feet to grip. As she descended Alex could not help but think of Mirram carefully tying the knots, and she wondered why her foster mother had felt the need for an escape route. What was it that Mirram was hiding? Suddenly, Alex knew the answer: Mirram was hiding *her*—or, more precisely, her cards. Alex had not given this a moment's thought before, but now it was obvious. Of course Mirram knew about her cards; Alex could not remember a time without them, and as a tiny child she could not have kept them secret from Mirram. So Mirram must have known the danger the cards posed and yet, despite the risk of being found out, she had let her keep them. Why?

As Alex descended, thuds and bangs drifted down from the house, telling her that the Sentinels were in there, busily searching. She prayed that they would not open the kitchen window and find the rope. Or, if they did, that she and Louie were no longer on it. A sudden gust of wind caught her, setting the rope swinging and her heart racing. *Concentrate*, Alex told herself. *Forget what is above. Forget what is below. Think only about what is here. Now.*

A triumphant shout from above shattered her thoughts. "Rope! There's a rope. Escape! Escape!"

Alex felt an ominous tug from above. "Please, no," she whispered. "Oh, no, no, no."

"Oh yes! Yes, yes, yes!" came a voice as if in reply. "Suspects on the rope."

"Pull it up," came another voice.

"Nah," said a third laconically. "*Cut it*."

Alex froze, listening to the discussion that was deciding her and Louie's fate. But as the vibrations of sawing transmitted themselves to her palms, Alex sprang into action. Throwing all caution aside, she swarmed down the rope like a trapeze artist, moving so fast her hands burned and her feet bounced against the knots in rapid succession. She would catch up with Louie and then she would hold him while they fell and maybe, just maybe, they would land on something soft.

But Alex knew that was not going to happen. Below was nothing but rocks. Jagged, unforgiving rocks. The relentless sawing continued and the rope felt different now, flimsier. Any minute now she would be falling. Falling. Falling. Suddenly the rope gave a lurch and at the same time, something grabbed her ankle. "Psst. Alex. In here." It was Louie. *Louie was in the cliff.*

It all happened so fast. Alex threw herself toward Louie's voice. As she hit a ledge and scrabbled to hold on to it, the rope fell from above. It knocked against her backpack and nearly took her with it, but Louie grabbed her jacket and Alex scrambled into a low-roofed cave, where she lay too shocked to move, listening to voices far above. "Well done, team. A good night's work." Alex heard the bang of the kitchen window being closed, and then there was silence.

Under Louie's instructions, Alex crawled deeper into the cave, which despite its low roof went back a long way. At the far end of the cave Alex found, to her surprise, the softness of a blanket. "It's my den," Louie said proudly.

"Even the pokkle doesn't know."

"It does now," Alex said, laughing with relief.

"Yes. I suppose it does. I suppose it will tell Momma now and then I'll be in big trouble," Louie said sadly.

Alex did not reply. How could she tell Louie that the pokkle telling tales was the least of his problems? If Sentinels were after her—one of them must have seen her in the marketplace after all—then they would be after Mirram too. And possibly even Louie and his sisters. To "Harbor a Beguiler of Prophecy and Enchantment" was a serious offense for which you were automatically found guilty before trial. But Louie, unaware of Alex's thoughts, was prattling happily on. "I love it up here. In the day you can see for miles. And no one knows where you are. I come here when Momma goes out early to market. She has no idea."

"What about your school?" Alex asked. "Don't they tell her you're not there?"

Louie giggled. "They think I'm just a part-time kid."

"Part-time kid, part-time superhero," Alex said, hugging Louie tight. "You saved my life, Louie. You're amazing."

In the darkness Alex could almost hear Louie smiling with pleasure. They sat quietly for a while until Louie said, "I've got a lantern here. Is it safe to light it?"

So Louie does understand the danger, Alex thought. "Maybe not," she said. "Just in case someone sees the light."

It was cold in the cave. Alex gave Louie his jacket and then, to his delight, she opened the bag of honey raisins. They sat together wrapped in the blanket, and Louie insisted on letting the pokkle out of its bag and sharing his raisins with it. "Not too many," Alex said. "They'll upset its tummy."

After a while Louie, his head in Alex's lap, fell asleep, but Alex felt too jangled to sleep. She sat in the darkness, surrounded by the coldness of rock, with one thought whirling around in her mind. *They were halfway up a sheer cliff face. There was no way up and there was no way down. What were they going to do?*

CHAPTER 6
Junior Sentinel

WHILE ALEX LAY WAKEFUL AND worried in the cave, one hundred and fifty feet above her the proud wearer of a new blue-and-orange Junior Sentinel jacket had taken possession of the house from which she and Louie had so recently fled. Zerra D'Arbo was sitting in her mother's armchair with her feet up on her mother's rosewood table—which had a strange hexagonal burn on it. She was eating her way through her mother's secret stock of sugared almonds, while upstairs her sister lay on her bed, crying silently.

Francina did not dare let the Junior Sentinel downstairs know she was upset because it was, as the Junior

Sentinel had informed her, "a reportable offense to be upset at the arrest and incarceration of a Named Harborer of Beguilers." And so Francina lay staring up at the ceiling, her tears running down her neck and soaking into the pillow. Dreadful images kept going around her head: four Vault guards dragging her mother, shrieking, from the marketplace; people laughing and pointing as her sparkly shoes and headband flew off into the crowd and the cords around her dress unwound. And then listening to the piercing screams as her mother was dragged away down Dead End Alley. Then hearing them suddenly silenced by a loud metallic clang, which was, Francina knew, the sound of the nail-studded iron door that led to the Vaults. Images from her compulsory school trip to the Vaults came to her—the horror of all those cages hanging from the ceiling, the sound of dripping water and the soft whimperings in the darkness—and most of all, the smell. And right now, Francina knew, her mother was up there roosting with the other cages, and she couldn't bear it. *She couldn't.*

And what about little Louie? Francina thought about how she had left Zerra and run home to find the door wide open and three Sentinels in the kitchen, laughing about cutting a rope. She'd hidden behind her mother's big chair, and it seemed from what the Sentinels were saying that Louie and Alex were on the rope when they had cut it—they were joking about how high kids could bounce. Francina had very nearly been sick again. The thought of Louie falling down that sheer cliff was unbearable. He was only a little boy. He didn't deserve any of this. Francina hugged Louie's elephant, Peg, tightly to her and gulped back a gasping sob.

And then, suddenly furious, Francina sat up. Zerra had caused all this and she hated her. She was going to go downstairs and tell her what she thought of her and she didn't care what happened. But at the bedroom door Francina's courage failed. She thought of the Junior Sentinel jacket and the power it gave to her sister—because a Junior Sentinel's word was worth twice that of anyone else. And Francina did not doubt that Zerra would Name her too. In fact she was surprised that she hadn't done it before.

Keep calm, Francina told herself. *You don't know for sure what has happened to Louie. All you know is he's escaped. You need to get out of Luma and find out where he is. And you need to try to save Ma, because no one else is going to.* And so, with all her thoughts whirling around her head, Francina crept back into bed and fell into a troubled sleep.

Downstairs, Zerra finished the sugared almonds and sat listening to the unfamiliar quietness of the house. Feeling bored now, she got up from the chair and looked at her reflection in the mirror by the door. She smiled at the neatness of the dark-blue Junior Sentinel jacket, the shine of its gold buttons, and the important-looking single orange stripe on the cuffs. At last, Zerra thought, she looked as important as she knew herself to be. At last people would treat her with the respect she deserved and acknowledge that she was special. That she was way more important than her stupid mother, and her tedious brother and sister, not to mention her annoying foster sister, who kept acting like *she* was the special one. Which she was not. *No way.*

Zerra smiled in the mirror. She would get herself out of this stupid family to which she just knew she did not belong, and then she would fly. She didn't know where and she didn't know how, but she, Zerra D'Arbo, was going places.

CHAPTER 7

The Goat Path

ALEX KNEW SHE MUST HAVE slept because the next thing she noticed was a soft light creeping into the cave. She looked down at Louie, who was still asleep, one arm thrown around the sleeping pokkle, his hair tousled, thumb in his mouth and breathing steadily. She didn't want to wake him. Alex took a small sip of water from the bottle—only one, she mustn't be greedy—and popped a raisin into her mouth. The sweetness swept through her, bringing with it a surge of hope: *It was daylight. She was safe. Louie was safe.* And that, for the moment, Alex decided, was all she was going to think about.

The mouth of the cave was a long, flat semicircle of

brilliant blue, but Alex guessed the cliff was in shadow, because the sun had not reached inside the cave. She remembered that the kitchen was always dark in the mornings, because the sun rose on the other side of the town. Alex's thoughts wandered to the house perched so far above them. She thought of Mirram pottering in the kitchen, having to make her own cup of tea for once, and wondered what she would say about the spicebread dough, which must have collapsed into a soggy heap by now. But then Alex remembered: *Mirram would not be there. Mirram would be in a cage, hanging from the ceiling of the Vaults.*

Louie stirred. "Hey, Louie," Alex whispered, happy to have his company once more.

Louie opened his eyes and looked around in confusion. Then his expression cleared and he smiled. "We slept in the secret cave," he said, excitedly sitting up. "It's true. We really are here!"

"So we are," Alex said, thinking gloomily that they would also be here tomorrow, and the next day and the day after that.

Louie scooped up the pokkle and stood up, his tousled hair brushing the roof. "Shall we go and see the orange trees?" he asked, his eyes shining. "Hey, we can have oranges for breakfast!"

"Louie," Alex said gently, "we're halfway up a cliff. There aren't any orange trees."

"I know that, silly!" Louie laughed. "But there are a *ton* of orange trees at the bottom of the goat path."

Alex felt a flicker of hope. "Goat path?" she asked.

"Come and see." Louie trotted over to the mouth of the cave.

"Okay, Louie. But come away from the edge now."

Looking as though he was humoring an awkward and ancient aunt, Louie stepped back while Alex crawled forward and nervously peered down. She laughed. They were eye-wateringly high, but some ten feet below was a narrow path worn into the soft sides of the sandstone cliff face by goats. And leading to it was a tumble of rocks, easily clambered down. She turned around and hugged her little foster brother. "Louie," she said, "my full-time superhero."

Louie wriggled from her grasp. "Can me and the pokkle have some raisins?" he asked.

"As many as you like," Alex said, laughing.

Fortified by raisins, stale bread and half of the water, Alex and Louie—with the pokkle safely back in its bag—were on the goat path, which was no more than a narrow ledge worn into the soft sandstone cliff face. It was a terrifying height from the ground and made Alex's legs feel hollow. But Louie had not a care. Barefoot, shoes slung carelessly around his neck, he skipped along the path and then stopped and waited patiently for Alex as she edged sideways, her back pressed against the cool sandstone, looking down in case she missed her footing. This didn't help much, because all she could see was the head-spinning drop down to Louie's ton of orange trees, which right now looked like rows of little green puffballs.

Despite the height, Alex could not help but notice how peaceful the wide and verdant valley below looked. The orderly lines of orange and lemon trees, the grazing sheep, the lazily winding river and the little farmhouses dotted here and there were a picture of tranquility. It didn't resemble the fearsome place that she had been told about in school, full of terrible entities that sought out anyone with the slightest whisper of Enchantment about them. Alex was just thinking how much she was looking forward to getting down there when her smooth-soled shoes slipped on the fine sandy surface of the path and, for a heart-stopping moment, she teetered on the edge of the drop before throwing herself back against the cliff.

"Take your shoes off," Louie called back to her. "Like me. Look!" And he lifted up a grubby foot and wiggled his toes.

"Oh Louie, don't *do* that. Not on one leg," Alex pleaded. But she took his advice and very gingerly bent down, pulled off her canvas shoes and slung them around her neck by their laces.

When they were near enough to the ground to see blobs

of orange in the green of the trees Louie stopped and called back, "Alex?" For the first time since their escape, Alex heard fear in Louie's voice. "Alex, I think I can see the Hawke."

Alex's heart missed a beat: the Hawke was the most feared entity of all. A giant bird of prey sent by King Belamus to hunt down the very last of the Enchanters—and particularly their children—who were still in hiding. The Hawke never flew over Luma, for in return for rigorously seeking out and destroying any sign of Enchantment, the city had a no-fly-zone pact with the king. However, Alex had once seen the Hawke from her bedroom window. She had watched it circling, casting a great winged shadow over the brightness of the valley below. It was a frightening sight, but Alex had been most fascinated by its rider, who wore a jacket with a pair of outstretched silver wings emblazoned on the back and sat high up, almost on the head of the Hawke, in a small saddle. She had thought then that to ride the Hawke must be the most exciting thing in the world to do—until you had to kill an Enchanter, of course. Or an Enchanter's child. "Where?" she asked Louie, trying not to sound worried.

Louie pointed to the distant end of the valley, where it rose up toward the foothills of the High Plains. Sure enough, Alex saw a winged shape, dark against the pale early morning sky. She watched it for some seconds and decided that it was cruising on thermals. "It's okay, Louie," Alex said. "It's just gliding."

"I hope so," Louie said.

Alex thought he didn't sound convinced. And she wasn't sure that she was either.

CHAPTER 8
The Hawke

IT WAS DANNY DARK'S FIRST mission as Flyer, and he was loving it. Danny was seated in the tiny Flyer's saddle, which was perched just behind the Hawke's head and formed the back of the half hood that the Hawke wore and was part of its Enchantment. Danny wore his new Flyer's uniform with pride—a short sheepskin jacket emblazoned with outstretched silver wings across its back and a black lambswool headband to hold back his long red hair. Set into the headband were two jet-black beads, signifying that he, Danny Dark, was the eyes of the Hawke. At his waist Danny wore a holster holding the short but deadly Lightning Lance.

As the Hawke flew lazily in circles on the first thermal of the day, Danny sat upright with his feet placed firmly in the stirrups, legs bent with his knees clamped tightly to the Hawke's muscular neck to keep himself steady. He held out his arms like the wings of a bird and felt the rush of the cool morning air against his palms and the wind streaming through his hair. Danny ached to shout with the joy of it, but he was silent. The Hawke did not take well to the shouts of its Flyer, as Danny had found out when, at his very first whoop of delight as they were taking off from Rekadom, the bird had flipped itself almost upside down. Danny had only just saved himself from falling by grabbing hold of the pommel on top of the half hood. That had been an embarrassing start and he had flown away with the laughter of Ratchet, the chief falconer, ringing in his ears.

But now Danny was on his own, and he could do as he pleased. He was fascinated by the lushness spread out before him, which was such a contrast to the bleakness of Rekadom and its surrounding desert of rocks, sand and scrub. Dreamily, he gazed down at the verdant landscape of Lemon Valley far below. It looked jewel-like—the burnished silver of the winding river, the jade-green dots of the neat lines of orange and lemon trees. Over to the southern side he saw white cotton sheep grazing the uplands that sloped gently up to the foothills of the snow-topped Blue Mountains. The landscape was scattered with timber farmhouses, their roofs thatched with reeds from the distant estuary, which he could see on the horizon where the river widened out at and flowed into the sea through a maze of sandbanks.

Suddenly, Danny became aware of a change in the huge raptor beneath him. Its muscles tensed and its head turned toward something in the distance that had taken its attention. Danny felt a shiver of anticipation run through it—the Hawke had seen a Quarry.

As he was trained to do, Danny pushed his feet deep into the stirrups and bent his knees so they were high up, almost by his chin. Then he leaned forward over the smoothness of the half hood and clasped the pommel. He was just in time, for suddenly the Hawke put its head down and took off like a thunderbolt. As the wind whistled past Danny's face, chilling his skin and setting his eyes streaming, he squinted into the distance to check out where the Hawke was heading. It seemed to Danny that the creature was targeting the escarpment that formed the northern side of the valley, above which teetered the pointy-roofed city of Luma and its no-fly zone.

Danny and the Hawke were a team. The Hawke could sense an Enchanter miles away, but Danny had the opposite talent: he was totally impervious to Enchantment. In the Rekadom mews under Ratchet's steely gaze, Danny had triumphantly failed every Beguilement, Fade and Befuddlement test thrown at him, which was why he'd gotten his dream job as Flyer—because no Enchanter could Fade from *him*.

They'd been out on patrol now for five days and so far the Hawke hadn't had a single sighting. Danny was not surprised by this, for everyone knew that, despite what the king thought, there were few, if any, Enchanters—or their poor kids—left. A combination of the wide selection of Enchanter-seeking entities that Haunted the land and the Hawke itself had seen to that. But as the Hawke shot through the air and the cliff face grew ever nearer, Danny began to feel nervous. This was for real. For the first time he was going to have to prove himself.

"Alex, look. It's flying toward us," Louie said anxiously.

Alex shielded her eyes against the sun. "It's probably seen a goat," she said. "It eats goats, you know."

"I don't like it. I think we should hide," Louie said, setting off along the path at a trot.

Alex followed as fast as she dared, but she could see no place to take cover. The rock of the cliff face behind them was so smooth that not even a blade of grass had found a place to root. Louie had stopped to wait for Alex to catch up and was watching the oncoming Hawke and its shadow racing over the farmlands below. "Do you think it knows about your cards?" he whispered.

"I don't see how it can," Alex said, trying to sound reassuring.

"But it can tell Enchanters, can't it?" Louie said. "My teacher said the Hawke can find one from five miles away."

"But I'm not an Enchanter."

"It can tell who's an Enchanter's child too," Louie said, staring up at the sky.

Alex was silent. That was a sore point—she didn't know *whose* child she was. Mirram had refused to tell her, even though Alex was sure she knew. "Well, I'm not one of those either," Alex told him, a little snappily.

Louie turned to look at Alex. His big brown eyes were serious and he seemed so old and wise that Alex suddenly felt as though she were the young one. "But I think you are, Alex. And I think it's coming for you."

Alex looked up at the sky and saw with a shock how near the Hawke was. The yellow glint of its beak tip—which some said was pure gold—shone in the center of a wingspan so wide that it that seemed to cut the sky in half. Its pointed wings beat slowly, but the speed at which the Hawke was approaching was frighteningly fast.

Alex's heart jumped in fear. Suddenly, she knew Louie was right. The Hawke was coming for her.

Danny clung on tight as the Hawke hurtled like a bullet toward the sheer cliff face. He steeled himself for what he had to do for real now. He must take over and direct the Hawke, because—as Ratchet frequently said—Enchanters, being devious creatures, were apt to make themselves disappear when faced with the Hawke. So Danny must see through their Fade, direct the Hawke to its Quarry, take aim and kill the Quarry with his Lightning Lance.

"Alex. I'm scared," Louie whispered, clutching the pokkle bag tight to him.

"It's okay, Louie. It's okay," Alex said, hoping Louie did not hear the fear in her voice. "I'll protect you. Get behind me. Stay back against the cliff."

Louie squeezed behind Alex and she was forced to step even closer to the crumbling edge of the path. She glanced down and saw the soft green tops of a line of orange trees about fifty feet below. Alex wondered if she should take hold of Louie and jump, trusting in a soft landing, but she just couldn't bring herself to do it. The huge winged shadow of the Hawke passed across the treetops and Alex forced herself to look up. It was right above her, hovering. She saw the golden beak: sharp, pointed and cruelly curved. She saw its two shining black eyes locked onto her, and above them she saw the redheaded Flyer pointing his Lightning Lance *straight at her.*

The Hawke was hovering, gauging its dive. This, Danny knew, was where he must take over. He stood up in the stirrups, leaned forward and, using the Hawke's secret name, he spoke the handover phrase so the Hawke understood it was now taking directions from its Flyer. "Dare. I see for you," Danny said as he flipped the front half of the Hawke's hood over its eyes so that the bird was flying blind. Now it would not be confused if its Quarry did a Fade. Then Danny switched his attention to the cliff face and for the first time, he got a close look at the Quarry—a girl and a boy. He gulped. He hadn't expected a couple of kids.

Alex saw the Hawke's golden beak heading toward her. She heard the *swish-ish* of the wings, felt the rush of the downdraft against her face and smelled the dusty tang of feathers. She threw herself back against the softness of little Louie and the hardness of the cliff and closed her eyes. *If only I could blend into this cliff*, Alex thought. *If only I could become the rock behind me.*

The girl was brave, Danny thought. She had thrown herself in front of the little boy and was trying to protect him. But surely the Hawke had made a mistake? These looked no more than normal, terrified kids. Danny pulled the Hawke back up to give himself time to think, but as he did so he saw a telltale flicker run across the girl so that for a moment it looked as though she and the boy were swimming underwater. Danny knew at once that she had done a Fade—and not only that, it seemed she had included the little boy in it. The Hawke was, unfortunately, absolutely right—the girl was clearly an Enchanter, and a powerful one too. He had to do this. *He had to.*

* * *

Surprised to still be alive, Alex opened her eyes and saw the Hawke had flown back up and was hovering once more, its eyes covered by a hood. Puzzled at what had happened, Alex looked up at the Flyer and their eyes met. Refusing to look away, she held his gaze.

Danny looked down at the girl, and as their eyes met, he saw things for what they were: he was about to attack two terrified children stuck halfway up a cliff. It didn't matter who they were or what they were. They were just kids and he was about to kill them. *I can't do this*, he thought. *I just can't.*

CHAPTER 9

I Spy

"I CAN'T BELIEVE IT JUST went away. We were so lucky," Alex said as she and Louie sat contentedly beneath an orange tree.

Louie was cradling the pokkle bag in his arms and poking honey raisins through the flap. "It was because you did that hiding thing again," he said.

"What hiding thing?"

"Oh, you *know* what hiding thing," Louie said, sucking noisily on an orange. "That thing when you disappear into the thing that's behind you."

Alex made a face. "What *thing* behind me?"

Louie sighed at Alex's dim-wittedness. "Anything.

Whatever is behind you, you kind of fade into it. It looks really weird."

"Louie," Alex said, laughing. "You're just making up silly stories."

But Louie stood his ground. "I am *not* making up silly stories," he said. "You remember a few weeks ago when Momma sent me to fetch you and that horrible Sentinel nearly caught you with the magic cards by the sausage stall? Well, I saw you do it then."

Alex stared at Louie. "Do *what* exactly?"

"The Sentinel was walking up to you and you just went fuzzy and *disappeared* so all I could see was the stuff behind you—a pile of cat-meat sausages."

"But how could I do that when I don't even know how?"

Louie shrugged. "I dunno. But I saw you do it. It was really clever."

Alex was quiet for a while. Louie was a truthful boy, so maybe she should pay attention. And what other reason could there be for the Hawke and its Flyer to turn away? It made sense now—it was because *they couldn't see her.* Or Louie either. She had even managed to make him disappear. Alex took out her cards and looked at the neat little pile of seven mother-of-pearl hexagons nestling in the palm of her hand. "It must be the cards," she said. "Because it's not anything that *I* do."

"Well, I think it *is* something you do," Louie told her. "I bet I couldn't disappear even if I had the cards."

"Bet you could," Alex said. "You're my superhero, remember?"

Louie giggled. "But you saved *me* this time. So we're even. Do you want another orange?"

Alex took the small and very juicy orange from Louie. She leaned back against the slender trunk of the orange tree and looked up through the dappled shade of the leaves to the bright blue of the sky above. Right now she didn't care who she was, she was just grateful to be alive and with Louie in such a beautiful place.

"It's not fair, is it?" Louie said suddenly.

"What's not fair?"

"Well, Luma is safe from the Hawke, but it doesn't allow Enchanters to live there. Enchanters are allowed down here, but it's not safe because of the Hawke and all the other weird stuff. So if you're an Enchanter, you're not safe anywhere."

"I think that's the general idea," Alex said.

"Well, I don't think it's a very nice idea," Louie said firmly. "Especially since *you're* an Enchanter."

"I am *not* an Enchanter, Louie. I just have some magic cards, that's all."

"And disappear when you want to."

Alex threw an orange at Louie. "Sometimes, Louie D'Arbo, you are a very annoying little boy."

Louie stuck out his tongue.

There was a sudden explosive gurgle from the pokkle

bag, which was sitting on Louie's lap. "Eurgh!" he yelled, leaping to his feet. "Pokkle poop. It's dripping down my leg." The pokkle had finally succumbed to the effect of a surfeit of honey raisins.

Alex and Louie regarded the soggy bag, which had tumbled to the ground and now lay ominously still. "Do you think the pokkle's all right?" Louie whispered.

Alex looked at the bag doubtfully. "There's only one way to find out," she said.

"You mean open the bag? But if it *is* all right it will fly out," Louie pointed out.

"But we can't leave it in the bag. That would be cruel."

Louie nodded. "Poor pokkle. It must be horrible in there."

Very gingerly, Alex unfastened the bag. "Poo!" said Louie, holding his nose.

Suddenly, the bag gave a convulsive twist and the pokkle shot out. It launched itself into the air, shaking itself like a wet dog. Alex and Louie threw themselves out of the way. "Oh, yuck!" Louie yelled.

The pokkle was a fastidious creature, and had it been on speaking terms with Louie at that moment, it would have agreed that it was indeed yuck. However, highly affronted at being imprisoned in a filthy bag, it was not in a mood for agreeing with anything. Flapping its stumpy, sodden wings, it lurched away at surprising speed.

"Quick, Louie, catch it!" Alex yelled.

"No *way*," Louie said. "You catch it."

They set off through the trees in pursuit. Twice the pokkle was within snatching distance and twice neither Louie nor Alex could bring themselves to try. In this way they arrived at the bank of the river and watched the pokkle dive in.

"No!" Louie cried. "No, pokkle. You'll drown!" He threw himself onto his stomach and leaned into the water, grabbing for the creature, but the depth was deceptive and the pokkle was well out of reach. It sat on the stony riverbed slowly shaking itself and Louie could see an eddying of brown swirls twisting lazily away from it, heading downstream. "Can it breathe underwater?" he asked anxiously.

Alex thought the pokkle looked pretty much at home, sitting on the pebbles preening its feathers beneath the water. "I'm sure it will come up for air if it needs to," she said.

Louie lay watching the pokkle while Alex sat down on the grass and gazed around. She had no memories of living anywhere but the dry and dusty town of Luma, and the soft greenness of the valley was a revelation to her. She took a deep breath and thought how different the air felt here. It was sweeter, cooler and full of scent. And the sounds were gentler too: the plash of the river, the melodic call of birds, and the soporific buzz of the bees. It all felt so peaceful that Alex could not help but wonder if the frightening stories of the entities that Haunted the place could be true. Sure, she'd seen the Hawke, but what about the Grove Garbutts, those poisonous fluffy caterpillars whose nests look just like oranges or lemons, that hung in the tops of citrus trees and dropped on your head and burst all over you? They'd not seen any sign of those at all, and Louie had checked a lot of trees before they had chosen one to sit beneath. And it seemed impossible that such a beautiful, sparkling river could be infested with Stinger Eels.

Stinger Eels!

Alex sprang to her feet. "Louie, take your hands out of the water!"

"Aw, Alex. It's such fun," he protested.

"Not when a Stinger Eel gets you."

Louie snatched his fingers out of the water.

"Didn't they tell you about Stinger Eels at school?" Alex asked.

Louie looked blank. "No."

"I suppose that was one of the days when you were hanging out in your cave," Alex said. "Which just shows why you need to go to school every day. Then you'd know that if you go paddling in the river Stinger Eels creep up on you and leave a thousand little stings embedded in your skin. And when you run away they follow you up onto the bank."

"Gruesome," said Louie and peered into the water.

"Do they sting pokkles?" he asked anxiously.

"Come to think of it, I seem to remember it's just Enchanters—like all the other stuff," Alex admitted.

Louie put his hands back in the water with a grin. "Then that's all right then," he said. "Because it's *you* that can't go in the river, not me and the pokkle. We're just fine in the river. *So there*."

"*So there* to you too," Alex said, watching the brightly colored pokkle lying on the pebbles at the bottom of the river, slowly fanning its stubby wings in the clear, cool water. It looked utterly content, and as a pair of small silvery bubbles of air escaped from its nostrils and drifted lazily up to the surface, Alex felt envious of the pokkle. After living in a dry and dusty city where water had to be laboriously pumped up hundreds of feet and every precious drop of rainwater channeled into underground cisterns, she thought that being immersed in such an abundance of cool running water must feel wonderful. She wriggled down to lie on her front and tentatively put her hands into the river—it was as cool and soft as she had imagined. She let the water trickle through her fingers and watched the pokkle preening itself, its feathers like tiny, sparkling rainbows.

Suddenly, in the weeds a little way out, Alex saw a glint of silver and a long, sinuous creature came flashing out of the depths. She leaped up from the water's edge, pulling Louie with her. A great spume of water rose from the river, and aware that *something* was coming out of the river, Alex set off at a run with Louie. The water arced up above them and something fell down and landed at their feet with a thump. It emitted an indignant squawk.

Alex crouched down and tentatively picked up the pokkle. "You gave us a fright," she told it.

"Fright!" squawked the pokkle. "You! You!"

Alex handed the sodden pokkle to Louie. "Present for you. One clean pokkle."

The pokkle looked extremely displeased. It had been enjoying a little bit of peace and quiet, getting its feathers sorted out away from the silly chatter of young humans. "Pokkle, pokkle, pokkle," it burbled, as it often did when it was annoyed.

Cradling the sulky pokkle, Louie looked up at Alex and smiled. "Shall we go home now?" he said.

Alex was suddenly reminded of how young Louie really was. He had been so confident and brave that she had forgotten he was only seven and had no real understanding of what had happened last night. "Maybe not yet," she said. "The Sentinels might still be looking for us. Let's walk for a while and see what we find."

"Okay." Louie put the pokkle down and it ran ahead, jumping through the scrubby grass looking far more at home than it ever had in Mirram's house, Alex thought. With no idea where to go, Alex decided they may as well follow the pokkle. She and Louie wandered along behind it, threading their way through the orange trees—which Alex was careful not to walk directly beneath—and then into a lemon grove. After a while Louie said, "But we can go home soon, can't we? Because Momma will be wondering where we are, won't she?"

"I expect Zerra will tell her," Alex said somewhat sourly.

"Yes, she will," Louie agreed. "Because Zerra's a know-it-all and she never keeps secrets."

"I don't suppose she does," Alex said, watching the pokkle half jumping, half flying in front of them.

"She saw your magic cards," Louie said. "I was supposed to keep that a secret but I don't want to now, because I think she told on us."

"Zerra saw my cards?" Alex asked, shocked.

"She was looking in your room while you were washing your hair. I told her she was being sneaky, but she didn't care."

Alex was silent, the enormity of the situation dawning on her. Up until now she had cherished a slim hope that maybe the Sentinels had gone to the wrong house; that maybe she had overreacted. But now she knew she hadn't. Zerra had Named her and there was no coming back from that. Ever. So not only could she never go back home, she wasn't at all sure if Louie could either. Alex tried to remember what the Sentinel who had cut the rope had said. "Suspects," he'd said. So there was more than just

Alex. But maybe it was Mirram they had come for? Or Francina? Surely Zerra hadn't Named her little brother? Surely not?

Louie was happily untroubled by any such thoughts. "I wish I'd brought my *I Spy Outside Luma* book with me," he was saying. "I could check one of the boxes in the Enchanter-hunting section, because I've seen the Hawke now."

Alex let Louie chatter on about his book while she looked up at the top of the escarpment to the silver-topped points of the roofs of Luma, which were glowing in the bright morning sun. Too late, she realized just how safe she'd been up there. *If only I had known,* she thought, *I would never have risked it all just for the sake of fooling around with some cards.*

"Guess!" Louie was saying. "Go on, Alex, guess!"

"Guess what?" asked Alex, still distracted.

"You're sounding just like Momma now. She doesn't listen either," Louie complained. "Guess what is the most *dangerous* and *scariest* of the Twilight Hauntings?"

"The Gray Walker," Alex said.

"Oh." Louie sounded deflated. "You know."

"Yes, Louie. I know," Alex said. Everyone knew about the Gray Walker. Alex had even seen it once. She had been leaning out of her window one particularly hot night, and in the light of the full moon she had watched its gray luminescence drift across the valley floor far below. It

made her shiver just to think about it. You didn't forget
something like that. She and Louie were going to have to
find shelter before sundown.

"I'm hungry," Louie announced.

Alex was hungry too. There were only so many oranges
you could eat at once.

They had reached a dusty track running along the edge
of an orange grove. "Okay," said Alex, scooping up the
pokkle, "let's go find some breakfast."

But as they followed the dusty track, Alex could not
help but wonder how you found breakfast when you had
no money, knew no one and had nowhere to go.

CHAPTER 10

Hagos RavenStarr

HAGOS RAVENSTARR WAS TAKING HIS usual early morning dip in a small lake in the middle of the Seven Snake Forest on the northern edge of the kingdom. He was as far away from Rekadom as it was possible to get without venturing across the snow-topped Blue Mountains, which Hagos had no wish to do. He refused to be hounded from his own land by a deranged monarch. The now very skinny and somewhat wrinkled Enchanter floated on his back in the deep green water feeling the warmth of the sun and gazing up at the clear blue sky, taking care to keep near to the edge of the lake, with its reed bed and the protection of the dense trees beyond.

Every morning, Hagos allowed himself an hour's respite from the tyranny of trees. Over the years spent hiding in the forest he had grown to dislike trees intensely. They gave a chill to the air even in the height of summer, and the deep unending gloom of the winters made Hagos miserable. But the forest was safe. Its dense trees protected him from the Hawke, and he had managed to get rid of its only Haunting—Sigbin, an enormous snake—by feeding it a large rock.

Now, with his wife long dead of dungeon lung and his little daughter gone to who knew where, Hagos had no desire for anything but to feel the comfort of warmth and the lightness of floating. Which was exactly what he was doing this morning, and so he was content. Wasn't he?

Hagos closed his eyes and allowed the feeling of peace to soak into him. Some minutes later he felt the chill that came from a cloud drifting across the sun. Which was odd, Hagos thought dreamily, because when he'd last looked the sky had been beautifully clear.

Danny was some hundred feet above a skinny old man floating in a lake and the Hawke was hovering, its golden beak pointing down to the figure below. Danny felt relieved—he hadn't expected to have another Quarry so soon. It meant he could forget about those kids now and actually get something. And at least, he thought, the old guy in the water did actually look like an Enchanter. He unsheathed his Lightning Lance and primed it, feeling a buzz of charge through the grip, and then he leaned forward to get a better look.

Hagos opened his eyes to look at the cloud—and very nearly inhaled half the lake in shock. There, hovering above him, was not only the Hawke but also the brilliant blue eye of a primed Lightning Lance pointing right at him.

Instinctively, Hagos did a Fade.

Danny saw the old man growing fuzzy around the edges—the telltale signs of a Fade—and he felt a thrill of excitement. This was the real deal. With the words, "Dare, I see for you," Danny flipped down the half hood and sent the image of the Enchanter into the Hawke's mind. The raptor dropped toward the Quarry at an exhilarating speed. And then the old guy sank. Just like that. Danny saw him, frog-like in the green water, dropping into the darkness of the bottom of the lake. He yelled in frustration as the Hawke's talons slammed into the surface of the lake, sending a plume of water up over its Flyer and soaking its underbelly feathers. With a frantic beating of wings the Hawke rose up into the air, and under Danny's direction it resumed its hover—but much lower. They would wait. The Enchanter couldn't hold his breath forever.

* * *

Hagos sank down, down through the cold green water until he reached the lake bed, thick with rotted leaves and pine needles. Suspending his breathing, he considered what to do. Should he stay here and wait it out? He thought not. He'd not done a Suspend-of-Breath-Underwater for years and he didn't know how long he could last—not half as long as the Hawke could hover, that was for sure. Hagos knew exactly what the Hawke was capable of, for it was he who had Engendered the creature from a fledgling hawk, and he who had advised the irascible Ratchet in its training. Yet again one of his own creatures was being used against him. It was infuriating. Air bubbles of indignation escaped from his mouth and Hagos forced himself to calm down—getting angry would not help him hold his breath. *You always knew that one day the Hawke would come for you*, he told himself. *And now it has. So deal with it.*

Hagos made a decision. Swimming beneath the water, he headed over to the reeds at the side of the lake and wriggled his skinny body through their close-knit stems. Not bothering to glance up—there was no point, either the Flyer would shoot him or not—Hagos hauled himself out of the reeds and fled, dripping, into the forest.

Danny saw a scrawny figure in soggy underpants hurtle out of the reeds in a panicked scramble—the sight would have been funny if it weren't so serious. Quickly, Danny aimed his Lightning Lance and squeezed the grip. The figure made a sudden swerve at the same time that a sizzling blue bolt of charge shot from the tip of the lance and slammed into a tree. The tree exploded into flames. Danny swore.

Danny took the Hawke down onto the well-worn grass beside the lake where a tattered tunic and threadbare coat lay. They made a wretched pile of clothes, Danny thought as he flipped up the Hawke's half hood and let the creature see daylight once again. The Hawke looked around in sharp, jerky movements. Danny knew the creature could sense its Quarry, he could tell it was itching to be off in pursuit. "Quarry gone to ground," Danny told the Hawke. "I will pursue. You will wait here." Aware that every second the Enchanter was getting farther away, Danny instructed the Hawke, "Dismount," and the creature lowered its head. Keeping hold of the jesses—two long, thin strips of leather fixed to the bridle above the Hawke's beak—Danny slipped down from the saddle and looped the jesses through the stirrups, neatly tying them up as Ratchet had shown him.

The Hawke, free of its Flyer, stood up to its full height and looked down at Danny with a bright, suspicious stare. Danny saw the nictitating membrane move slowly across the surface of its eyes, clearing away the film of dirty lake water. Goose bumps ran down Danny's neck—he had the distinct feeling that the Hawke was considering whether to make *him* the Quarry and be done with it.

Danny knew he must reassert his authority fast. He raised the small silver whistle that hung on a lanyard around his neck to his lips. This was the Harken, the sound of which the Hawke was trained to obey. He gave two sharp shrills upon the Harken—which he knew was far too close for the Hawke's delicate hearing—and to his relief the Hawke obediently rose into the air and hovered just above the treetops, waiting for the single shrill that would bring it back to its Flyer.

Two piercing shrills echoing through the trees stopped Hagos in his tracks. "My Harken," he whispered. The Harken had once been one of Hagos's most treasured possessions, but in order to try to save his dear Pearl when she was dying from dungeon lung deep beneath Rekadom, he had subverted the Harken's delicate Enchantment to create an instrument of command for the Hawke. Hagos had always feared that one day he would hear it used in pursuit of himself. Now that fear had come true.

At the edge of Seven Snake Forest, Danny paused for a moment. He had a deep fear of snakes and could not shake off the thought of the forest floor seething with snakes. But he was well aware of the suspicious eyes of the Hawke upon him as it hovered above the lake. *Snakes or Hawke food*, Danny told himself. *You choose.*

Danny chose snakes. He set off at a run into the darkness of the forest, the flickering shimmer of the lance lighting his way. Danny kept his eyes fixed upon the floor of the forest, ready to leap out of the way at any suspicion of a slither. Out of the corner of his eye he caught glimpses of movement, but it was always going away from him. It seemed that snakes liked him as little as he liked them, which suited Danny very well. It also meant he could concentrate on tracking the Quarry, and for this the forest floor was perfect. It was bare of any vegetation; its dry and dusty needles easily showed the disturbance caused by his Quarry's feet. All he had to do was follow the dark trail of damp needles and earth revealed by the frantic, skittering run of the scrawny old Enchanter.

Zigzagging one way and then another like a snake himself, never able to run in a straight line, Danny very soon decided that he hated trees. He hated the way they crowded in on him, he hated how tall they were, how superior they acted, how they took away the light and made him dodge around them. Danny knew he was being unreasonable, but what he hated most of all was how *they would not get out of the way*. It was just so inconsiderate. The whole snaky, nasty forest gave him the creeps. Danny loved wide-open spaces; he loved to breathe fresh air and feel wind upon his face, but with every step he took the light grew dimmer, the sounds more muffled and the trees closer. And then he saw his

Quarry—a flash of movement in a fuzzy beam of sunlight. Danny raised the Lightning Lance and fired.

Hagos hurled himself to the ground and the lightning bolt whizzed over him and slammed into a young oak a few feet ahead. The terrible sound of splintering and cracking overwhelmed Hagos as the tree's trunk twisted itself apart in agony, its sapwood unfurling from its heartwood in long, curling ribbons. A deep bass groan traveled out from the shattered oak, as it understood it would never reach its maturity, and sent a wave of sympathetic rustling spreading out through the forest.

Danny dared not move. He felt surrounded by anger and overwhelmed by a sense of hostility, but he had no idea where it was coming from—all around was nothing but trees. And then Danny understood. The feeling came from the trees themselves. Every trunk, every bough, every leaf, wished him ill. He was a murderer, a destroyer of life, and he was not welcome here. Danny strengthened his grip on the Lighting Lance and looked anxiously around. He suppressed a longing to run screaming from the forest and forced himself to continue onward. The Quarry had gone, but his tracks had not. He would get him eventually. Whatever it took.

* * *

Wheezing, with his legs beginning to give way under him, Hagos at last reached the edge of the dip in which lay the strange contraption he called home. He hurtled down the steep slope, ran straight past a ramshackle arrangement of branches and leaves built out from a hollow tree, and scooted around a stand of giant ferns. Here he fell to his knees and scrabbled at the dusty layers of pine needles until his fingers scratched upon the rough wood of a trapdoor. Hurriedly, Hagos pulled it up and threw himself into the hole in the ground beneath, and then he stuck his head back up like a meerkat, scooped earth and leaves upon the top of the door and pulled the trapdoor into place above his head.

Then he sat in his tiny earthen burrow and waited.

CHAPTER 11

Gone to Ground

HE MUST THINK I'M REALLY *stupid*, Danny thought as he brushed away the freshly turned leaves that had been scattered in a pathetic attempt to hide a wooden hatch in the forest floor.

The Flyer's brushing away the leaves, Hagos thought in a panic. *What shall I do?*

Grasping his Lightning Lance in one hand, Danny considered what to do next. The Enchanter was in there for sure: he could hear his breath, a soft, rapid rasp like the rustle of dried leaves. Danny raised the lance and pointed it at the trapdoor.

Suddenly—from where, he did not know—a wave of anger washed over Hagos. *What are you doing cowering in a hole in the ground, scared at the sound of someone brushing away leaves?* he asked himself. *How come you, Hagos RavenStarr, once the most powerful Enchanter in the land, second in power only to the king, are now communing with the worms, no higher than a creature that crawls upon its belly? Enough is enough. It is time to fight back.*

Danny's hand tightened slowly upon the grip of the Lightning Lance and he readied himself to fry the Enchanter alive. *What a horrible thing to do to an old man*, he thought. *To anyone, in fact. Even a tree*. But do it he must.

Hagos stood up, the top of his head brushing the underside of the trapdoor. And then, with the pent-up power of rage at what had befallen him over the last terrible ten years, Hagos mustered his every last vestige of Enchantment and let loose a blast with the focused power of a tornado. The trapdoor flew open and Hagos came hurtling out from his burrow.

Danny went flying. Spinning upward through the trees,

crashing into leaves, twigs, branches, and then falling, falling, falling . . . everything grabbing at him, scratching and pulling as he plummeted back down and smashed onto a wide bough, where he lay bruised and winded. As Danny fought for breath, he saw some twenty feet below a man apparently made of mud whirling around searching, Danny guessed, for him. With a cold feeling in the pit of his stomach, Danny saw that his Lightning Lance was lying at the Enchanter's feet. He watched the man bend to pick it up, and then, slowly and deliberately, raise the lance and point its brilliant blue eye straight at him.

"No!" Danny yelled out. "Don't fire. Please!"

It was the first voice Hagos had heard for eight years. The husky voice of a boy of thirteen or fourteen, it reminded Hagos of another boy—a charming rogue who had been just that age when he'd arrived at his door and begged to become his apprentice. Hagos had taken him on, but it had not ended well. They were reckless at that age, Hagos thought, and much too young to die. Slowly, he lowered the lance. "Come down, you idiot," he yelled. "I won't shoot!"

Danny stayed where he was. He suspected a trap.

"Scared, are you?" Hagos called up.

This stung. "I am *not* scared," Danny said sulkily.

"Do I have the pleasure of conversing with a Mr. Dark, perchance?" Hagos asked.

"How do you know my name?" Danny called down suspiciously.

"You're all called Dark, aren't you?" Hagos said. "All Flyers are. New name, new life, isn't that what they say?"

"Who told you that?"

"No one needed to tell me," Hagos said irritably. "Seeing as it was my idea in the first place. To give you crazy kids a new start."

"So who are *you* then, Mr. Know-It-All?" Danny called down.

"If you want to find out, I suggest you descend from your perch and join me. I don't talk to things in trees."

Danny stared down at the wild-looking man below. He guessed he wasn't as old as he looked. He was just very skinny and caked in mud, which had wrinkled. And he didn't seem particularly angry either. And, most important, he had lowered the Lightning Lance. Danny decided to take a chance—he couldn't stay up in the tree forever and he had the distinct feeling the tree wanted him gone. Danny clambered down its deliberately unhelpful branches and jumped lightly onto the forest floor. He stood eyeing his lance, which lay loosely in the mud man's hand. He wondered if he could make a grab for it.

"Don't even think about it," Hagos warned him.

Danny sighed. "But it's my job. It's what I'm supposed to do."

"Do you always do what you are supposed to?" Hagos inquired.

Danny thought of the kids on the cliff face that morning.

"No," he said. He scuffed the ground with his foot, suddenly angry with himself. "Basically, I just mess up."

Hagos grimaced. "Well, that makes two of us, then."

Danny regarded Hagos with some confusion. The man seemed just about the most reasonable person he had spoken to ever. All the things he had been told about Enchanters—which he clearly was—just didn't make sense. "Who *are* you?" he asked.

"I, Mr. Dark, am Hagos RavenStarr."

"No!" Danny exclaimed. "Not the king's Enchanter?"

"I think you will find I am the king's *ex*-Enchanter," Hagos corrected dryly.

Danny laughed. "Wow. I hit the jackpot with you. Well, I would have if I'd managed to . . ."

"Kill me? Yes indeed, so you would."

Danny shook his head in amazement. Of all the things he'd ever messed up, this was the biggest by far. He could never go back to Rekadom now.

"But of course you haven't killed me, have you?" Hagos observed. "Not only am I still alive, I now have possession of my Lightning Lance—"

"*My* Lightning Lance," Danny corrected him.

Hagos smiled. "I think you will find it is mine. *My* lance, created with *my* Enchantment. And just so you know, the Harken, which you wear so casually around your neck like a cheap tin whistle, was once *my* tool of Enchantment. Indeed, your Hawke is *my* Engenderment.

You, Mr. Dark, fly courtesy of *my* Enchantment."

Danny watched the still-primed blue tip of the Lightning Lance, which Hagos, in his excitement, was waving around uncomfortably close to him. "Okay," he said. "*Your* Lightning Lance. *Your* Harken. *Your* Hawke."

"And *you're* Quarry too now," Hagos told him.

"Me?"

"You're out of sight and you have not blown the Harken for more than thirteen minutes now. I've been counting."

Danny frowned. "They never told me that."

"Well, they wouldn't, would they? It's a test of loyalty. Too easy to fake if you know about it."

"Are you sure?"

Hagos laughed. "You're talking to the very person who made that rule, Mr. Dark. Belamus was afraid of being double-crossed by the Flyer. So I suggested this little, er, modification. My apologies. But like I said, my Hawke, my Harken, my Enchantment."

Danny was beginning to realize how powerful this man had once been, and was feeling a little in awe of him. However, he had no intention of letting it show. "Is *everything* yours?" he asked sarcastically.

Hagos smiled ruefully. "Nothing is mine now. But once everything was. A lesson you'd do well to learn, Mr. Dark. If you go back to Rekadom now, you will discover that you too have lost everything. We're both Quarry now." He looked up at the ominous shadow of the Hawke hovering above the trees. "But we have the advantage, believe it or not."

"Doesn't seem like much of an advantage to me, being Quarry," Danny said.

"We have strategy. The Hawke merely has rules. There are two of us, and only one of the Hawke. We're in this together now, Mr. Dark. And on that basis, I have a proposal to put to you. A quest in which I would value your assistance."

Danny felt as though his world was being turned upside down. "You and me? On a *quest*?"

"Perhaps we could discuss this over a bite to eat?" Hagos suggested. "You do, if I may say so, look a little faint. Extremely faint, actually."

Was it Hagos's power of suggestion or would it have happened anyway? Danny was never quite sure. But whatever the reason, his ears began to ring, stars danced in his eyes and the ground came up to meet him with a thud.

Lightning Lance in his hand, still primed, Hagos looked down at the boy lying at his feet in a dead faint. He could finish him now or he could go and find some dried snake. Hagos smiled: it was the first real choice he had had in ten long years.

CHAPTER 12

Snake on the Rocks

DRIED SNAKE, FOREST BERRIES AND distilled water—
a feast of which Hagos felt proud as he meticulously laid
a small square of worn grayish cloth upon the flat rock in
the middle of the clearing. Upon the cloth he placed a roll
of leaves, which he unwound to reveal thin brown strips
that looked like tree bark. He laid the strips out in careful lines and then, from a small box at his feet, he took a
handful of yellow berries, three of which he placed neatly
between each strip. Two cups made of hollowed-out wood
and carved with magical symbols held clear water; these
he put side by side at the foot of the cloth.

Danny, still feeling a little woozy, watched quietly. He

was impressed. Hagos lived a very basic life, but he lived it in style. Danny liked that.

Hagos joined him, sitting cross-legged on the ground beside the rock. "Dried snake and forest berries. Do please help yourself," he told Danny.

Danny was not entirely happy with the idea of eating snake, but his stomach was rumbling with hunger and he convinced himself that the long brown strips looked more like toffee than snake—apart from the odd glint of skin, which he tried to ignore. Tentatively he reached out and took a strip. It was surprisingly good—slightly salty, with a chewy texture.

"So, Mr. Dark," said Hagos. "Do you have another name by which I may address you? Something less formal perhaps?"

Danny nodded. His mouth was too full of snake to speak.

"You may call me Hagos. There's no need for any of the fancy formal Rekadom stuff here. I do not expect you to call me 'Your Eminence' or even 'Your Most Excellent Eminent Enchanter,' as some did." Hagos sighed. "Those days are gone."

Danny suppressed a shudder. He had managed to swallow the snake, but sharp little rib bones grazed the back of his throat as it went down.

"Mind you," Hagos continued, enjoying the novelty of hearing his own voice talking to another person, "I wasn't called anything like that after that idiotic prophecy the stupid Oracle gave the king."

"I thought the Oracle was infallible, not stupid," Danny said, trying to pull an irritating strip of snakeskin that was stuck between his front teeth.

"Ha!" Hagos snorted bitterly. "Never trust the Oracle, Danny. I thought we were friends and she betrayed me. What a fool I was to trust her."

Danny looked shocked. "You were friends with the Oracle? You mean it is an actual, real-life person?"

"Deela Ming is her name. Wretched woman. What got into her, I do not know. Deela and I had a perfectly good arrangement. I'd tell her what to say to the king and she'd say it. It kept everything in Rekadom running smoothly. Kept old Belamus happy too. Until that terrible day . . ." Hagos shook his head in dismay.

"When the Oracle told him he'd die," Danny finished for Hagos, triumphantly pulling the snakeskin out from his teeth and flicking it onto the ground.

"The dying bit wasn't the problem," Hagos said. "It was how it was going to happen that ruined all of us in the Enchanting business. The Oracle took it into her head to tell the king that he 'would die at the hand of an Enchanter's child.'" Hagos shook his head. "I still don't understand what got into her. She even sent me a long rambling letter begging my forgiveness, actually blaming someone else for doing it, but of course I never replied."

"Well, maybe someone else did act as the Oracle that day." Danny laughed. "Maybe it was someone who really did know the future, huh? Wouldn't it be weird if that really did happen one day? If an Enchanter's child actually did kill the king?"

Hagos shook the thought from his head. He never allowed himself to think about children—especially those belonging to Enchanters.

"I remember those other names we used to call you," Danny said. "We chanted them at school."

"What fun," Hagos said dryly.

"Yeah. It was fun. I never realized they were talking about *you* though."

"Sham Sorcerer?" Hagos murmured. "I remember people shouting that at me."

"Evil Enchanter," countered Danny.

"Beastly Beguiler," said Hagos, smiling.

"Oh, I've got a much better one than that," Danny chuckled. "Rattlesnake of Rekadom!"

Hagos laughed for the very first time in years. It was raspy and a little flat, but it was a laugh even so. "Ha ha. I've not heard that one before. That's good. You will no doubt observe that old Belamus has a thing for alliteration."

"A thing for what?" Danny asked.

"He likes his insults to begin with the same letters. No

doubt he would call you the Devious Mr. Dark. Or the Deceiving Mr. Dark, or the Dastardly Mr. Dark or the Daft—"

"Okay, okay, I get it," Danny interrupted. "All beginning with *D*. He'd be right too. About my first name, I mean. It really does begin with a *D*. It's Danny."

"Such serendipity," Hagos said, picking up another strip of snake.

"Uh?" asked Danny, feeling woozy with words.

"A happy chance. Which I find your presence to be. Now, try a forest berry. It goes well with snake. Helps the digestion. Neutralizes any venom."

Danny spluttered. "*Venom?*" he said.

Hagos smiled. "Sometimes these forest snakes leak venom into the tissues when they're stressed," he said. "But I dry the flesh in the sun, which denatures most of it."

"*Most* of it?" Danny asked.

"The berry juice does the rest. Here, take one. Chew it thoroughly, mind."

Danny took the small red berry and inspected it warily. "Why?" he asked.

"To crunch up the spider eggs you often find in them. That way they don't hatch in your stomach."

Danny laid the berry down. "You know, I'm not really hungry right now," he said.

"Funnily enough, I find that I am," Hagos said, and he reached over, delicately took the berry and dropped it into his mouth.

Watching Hagos happily eating his venom and spider eggs, Danny sat in silence thinking how yet again his life had taken a sudden change of direction. Ever since his parents had disappeared into the dungeons beneath Rekadom, Danny had understood he had to pay his way. He had cleaned his uncle's house, he had swept the streets, and most recently he had been recruited to be a Flyer. Danny had never had a choice; he had merely done what he had to do. But now he couldn't do it anymore. He could not kill—not kids and not even a weird old Enchanter. So where did that leave him?

Hagos passed him a cup of distilled water. It tasted woody, yet clean and cool, and slowly Danny's thoughts became clearer.

"So, Mr. Dark, will you throw your lot in with me? Do I have a partner on my quest?" Hagos inquired, idly picking up the Lightning Lance and fondly polishing its silver pommel, clearly pleased to have an old friend back.

Warily, Danny eyed the Lightning Lance. He wondered if this was yet another no-choice moment. To his surprise, Hagos threw the lance to the ground, where it landed at Danny's feet. "Choose freely," he said. "I want a partner, not a prisoner."

Danny stared at the fat silver tube with its thick gold

guard and ebony grip with its concealed trigger. Aware that Hagos was watching his every move, Danny reached down for the lance and picked it up, closing his hand around its heavy smoothness. He could so easily send a lethal bolt of blue charge into the scrawny man in front of him, and his job would be done. "You take it," Danny said. "Like you said, it's your creation." He held the lance out to Hagos and smiled. "You have a partner on your quest."

Hagos took the lance. "Thank you, Danny," he murmured. "Now, I'd like to do a few tests, if you don't mind, to assess your suitability."

"Okay . . . ," Danny said warily.

"Close your eyes," Hagos instructed.

No way, Danny thought. He lowered his eyelids and peered out beneath the cover of his thick, dark eyelashes.

"Close your eyes, Danny," Hagos told him. "I trusted you with the lance. Now you must trust me."

Reluctantly, Danny closed his eyes and heard the rustle of leaves as the Enchanter crept stealthily away.

"You can open them now," came Hagos's voice.

Danny looked to where the voice had come from and saw nothing. For a moment he thought that Hagos had succeeded in doing a Fade that he could not see through. But, remembering the direction the footsteps had taken, he swung around and saw Hagos standing bizarrely on one leg with his index fingers in his ears. Danny grinned.

"Where am I?" Hagos threw his voice up into the tree above Danny.

Danny looked directly at the Enchanter, whose edges were shimmering. "You're there," he said, pointing at Hagos.

"Wrong, wrong, wrong," Hagos's voice mocked him from the tree.

"No. I'm right, right, *right*," Danny said.

"So what am I doing?" Hagos asked Danny.

Danny laughed. "Standing on one leg with your fingers stuck in your ears."

Hagos removed his right index finger from his ear. "Both ears?" he inquired.

"Only one now," Danny said. "Left hand. It makes you look a bit crazy, if you don't mind me saying so."

The shimmer around Hagos—which was making Danny feel queasy—disappeared. "I don't mind you saying so at all. I appreciate honesty. So what do you see now?" There was a flash of light and suddenly Hagos was there, right in front of him, holding out his hand. Danny reached out and shook it.

"Danny Dark," Hagos said, "I am honored to make your acquaintance. I hope you will forgive the little subterfuge in the test."

"Subterfuge?" asked Danny.

"My little deceit when I told you I wasn't where I actually was. I needed to check how steadfast you are. I am glad to see you are not prey to self-doubt, and are indeed a true Dark. I tried the most powerful Fade Enchantment on you and you were completely unaffected. Very impressive."

"You did look at bit hazy around the edges," Danny admitted.

Hagos laughed. "I should hope so. I'd hate to think that none of my power showed up."

"So I'm suitable, huh?" Danny asked with a grin. "For this quest of yours. Whatever it is."

Hagos picked up the last piece of dried snake and offered it to Danny, who shook his head. His throat was still sore from the little bones. "Well, Danny, you and your Hawke did me a favor; you made me see how bad things had gotten. So, I'm not going to hide anymore. I want my power back—all of it. And every last thing that Belamus stole from me, I want back too: my Hex cards, my codex, my Tau, my best velvet cloak with the ruby clasp, my little gold astrolabe, my Manifest, my star charts, my log tables, my silver measuring spoons—*everything*."

"A bit light-fingered, that king," Danny observed.

"Nothing more than a lowlife thief," Hagos said indignantly. "Although in truth I think it was probably my assistant who took my codex. And it was I who gave away the Hex cards."

"Who to?" Danny asked.

Hagos paused for a moment. He'd not said this word for a very long time. "My daughter."

Danny was surprised. Hagos didn't seem like a family man. "You have a *daughter*?"

"Not anymore. I gave her away too."

Danny was shocked into silence.

"But I'd like her back now," Hagos said. "And my Hex cards."

CHAPTER 13
Santa Pesca

ALEX AND LOUIE WERE WALKING slowly along a dusty, seemingly endless track. The sun was high in the sky and it felt as hot as any street in Luma. They were heading toward a narrow bridge over the river that led into a village strung out along the opposite bank. Louie was tired and fretful; he trailed behind Alex, scuffing his shoes along in the dust.

"Don't do that, Louie," Alex said irritably. "You'll make a hole in your shoes and you haven't got another pair."

"I've got more at home," Louie said sulkily.

"Well, we're not at home, are we?" Alex snapped.

"Because you're making us walk the wrong way," Louie said, suddenly sitting down in the dust. "I want to go home. I want to see Momma." A big, fat tear made a clean track down Louie's dusty cheek.

Feeling guilty for snapping at him, Alex squatted beside Louie and wiped away the tear with her thumb. "Louie, you know the bad people we ran away from?"

Louie nodded.

"Well, they are still looking for us. So we can't go home just yet."

"But Momma will be worried," Louie said.

"She'll understand," Alex told him.

Louie did not look convinced. His lower lip wobbled uncertainly. "I'm hungry," he said. "And I don't want another orange. *Ever.*"

"Neither do I. So let's go see what we can find in the village, shall we?" Alex said, trying to stay upbeat.

Louie looked up at Alex. "Don't you mean steal?" he said. "Because we don't have any money, do we?"

"No, we don't," Alex admitted. "But that doesn't mean we have to steal. We can sell the pokkle." This seemed like a good solution to Alex. A talking pokkle could get good money—enough to get them a bed for the night for sure.

Louie stared at Alex, aghast. "We can't sell the pokkle. Momma *loves* the pokkle."

"We are going to have to do *something* to get some money," Alex told him.

"You can do your magic cards," Louie said.

Alex shook her head. There was no way she was going to risk showing those cards in public ever again. Suppose there were spies from Luma down here, looking for her. "No more cards, Louie," she said. "How about you sing a song?"

"You know I can't sing," Louie said sulkily. "And neither can you."

"Exactly," Alex agreed. "So we shall just have to sell the pokkle. Come on, Louie, get up now. *Please.*"

Louie did not move, but an unexpected smile lit up his dusty face. "The pokkle can talk! Momma says it's the only one in the whole world that can do that. Why don't we charge people to ask it a question and the pokkle can answer?"

Alex frowned. "Because the pokkle never answers questions," she said.

"It will for me. I have a secret method," Louie said mysteriously.

"Oh, Louie, you're just saying that. Now please, *will you get up?*" Alex could hear the impatience in her voice, but she was too tired and hungry to pretend anymore.

"Oh please, Alex. Let me try," Louie begged. "Momma will be so sad if we sell her pokkle."

Alex sighed. She couldn't face telling Louie that his momma had far bigger problems than the pokkle being sold. By now Mirram would be in a cage waiting for her show trial for Harboring a Beguiler. And it was all, Alex thought guiltily, because of her. None of this would have happened if she hadn't been so reckless with her cards. Her hand slipped into her pocket and closed around their soft leather wallet. The trouble was, the cards needed to be out in the light, to be talked to, asked questions, to be part of life. Alex could no more keep them hidden away in darkness than she could a living, breathing creature. But she had learned her lesson—she'd not use them in public again. And so, with no alternative to offer, Alex agreed to let Louie have his way. "Okay, Louie," she said. "The pokkle can answer questions."

The pokkle, which had been dozing in the crook of Alex's arm, opened one eye and looked down at Louie lugubriously. "Pokkle questions," it said. "Pokkle pokkle questions."

Louie laughed and jumped up. "Hey, pokkle! You understand don't you?"

"Don't you?" the pokkle echoed. "Don't you, don't you?"

"You're so clever, pokkle," Louie said, gently smoothing the pokkle's feathers. "This is going to be such fun!"

"Fun," the pokkle squawked. "Clever pokkle."

Louie skipped ahead across the bridge and Alex followed, carrying the pokkle. "Fun. Clever fun," it said.

Alex caught up with Louie, who was slowly reading a beautifully painted sign bidding them "Welcome to Santa

Pesca. Where all deeds are in Her Gracious Honor."

"Who is Gracious Honor?" Louie wanted to know.

"Santa Pesca, I suppose," Alex said.

"But *who* is Santa Pesca?" Louie persisted.

Alex felt too weary to answer any more questions. "I don't know, Louie. I guess we'll find out. Come on, the sooner we get this pokkle working for a living, the sooner we get to eat."

They walked through a low archway into a shady street bordered by timbered houses colored in faded pinks and purples. The shadows were cool and the street deserted, but at the far end Alex saw the brightness of a village square in sunlight and heard the purposeful babble of voices—the familiar sounds of a market in progress. Alex began to feel hopeful; there would be plenty of people here to pay to watch the pokkle perform.

They headed into the square, in the middle of which a few canopied stalls were set out in the bright sunlight selling vegetables, bread, cheese, hams and an array of buckets, pans, brooms and cheap teddy bears. The far side of the square was covered by a colonnade in the shade of which children were playing while people sat and talked or rocked babies in little wheeled carts, and a group of old men silently knit long colorful scarves. Over to the right of the square was a café where Alex and Louie could see people drinking mouth-wateringly cool drinks from tall glasses and dipping long-handled spoons into deep bowls.

What was in the bowls they had no idea, but it smelled unbearably delicious.

"I am *so* hungry," Louie moaned.

"Me too," Alex said. "So let's get this pokkle working. Now where would be best to go?"

"There!" Louie pointed to a large semicircular fountain set into a wall. It consisted of a huge, very impressive bronze fish with lacy silver wings, which was balancing upon its tail, arching gracefully forward, its pursed mouth spouting a clear, cool stream of water into the pool below. Louie set off toward the fountain and Alex followed.

"See, it's perfect," Louie said. "This ledge here can be the stage and the pokkle can sit on it and everyone can see it. And we can have a drink too." Louie put the pokkle on the wide, smooth marble ledge that surrounded the pool and leaned over to hold his hands in the stream flowing from the fish's mouth. He drank three handfuls of delicious coolness, rubbed his wet hand over his dusty face, then offered a cupped hand of water to the pokkle. As if it were doing Louie a great favor the pokkle leaned forward and, pursing its lips, sucked up the offering with a noise like water going down a drain. Then it ruffled its stubbly wings to shake the dust out and sat back on its hind legs in the manner of a small dog, staring at Louie as if to say, *What now?*

The pokkle was not a sentimental creature, but despite its newfound freedom—which it was greatly enjoying—it missed Mirram's soothing stream of endearments she would croon to it whenever they were alone in the house (Mirram's robust attitude to her children did not extend to her pet). Had the pokkle been able to understand the meaning of words as well as speak them it would have said it was sad because it was pining for Mirram, but its feathers spoke for it: they were now an unprepossessing shade of gray.

"I wish it would go a nicer color," Louie said to Alex. He tickled the pokkle under its chin. "Hey, pokkle-pokkle. Make your feathers happy again."

The pokkle flicked its fat little black tongue out at Louie grumpily, then stood up on its stumpy, scaly legs and looked lugubriously around, its bulging, lidded eyes slowly blinking. The pokkle did not like what it saw. A small group of bossy-looking people had gathered in the middle of the square and were muttering among themselves and pointing at it. The pokkle did not like being pointed at. In its experience being pointed at led to unpleasant things happening to it. It raised its stumpy wings, spread out its feathers so that it looked twice its size and hissed a spray of pokkle spit into the air.

"Don't do that, pokkle," Louie chided. "You have to be nice and talk. Look, there are people coming over to see you."

"They don't look very happy," Alex murmured. A somewhat menacing group of people—men in somber gray jackets buttoned up to their throats and women in long black dresses with starched white collars—had gathered about twenty feet away and were talking among themselves, throwing hostile glances across to Alex and Louie. Alex smiled at them but got no response. Her instinct was to get up and leave, but where would they go? What would they do? This *had* to work. Mustering her courage, she stood up and called across to the growing crowd, "Ladies and gentlemen! We present the only talking pokkle in the world. For a silver penny the pokkle will answer any question you ask it!"

With relief Alex saw that her speech seemed to have worked—a tall woman with a dark-blue sash wound around her waist had detached herself from the group and was coming over. "Get the pokkle ready, Louie," Alex whispered. "We've got our first customer."

Louie shoved his hand into his pocket and took out what looked like a dusty stone, which he held beneath the sparkling stream pouring from the fish's mouth. The cool water trickled through his fingers, washing off the dust and revealing a gleaming honey raisin. The pokkle lunged for the raisin, but Louie snatched it away. The pokkle swished its tail back and forth, and as Louie had hoped, a blush of pink irritation began to appear on the ends of the feathers, which spread rapidly until the pokkle was growing a brilliant, angry red. Louie was pleased. This was looking good.

The woman, however, did not seem to be of the same opinion. She stood in front of Alex, arms folded. "Girl," she inquired icily, "what do you think you are doing?"

Thinking that she would never have dreamed of saying to the woman who stood so aggressively in front of her, *Woman, what do you think you are doing?* Alex bit back her annoyance at the rudeness and forced herself to smile. This was their first customer and they needed the money. "Today we have brought to Santa Pesca the only talking pokkle in the land. For one silver penny you can ask it any question and it will answer."

The woman looked down at Alex. "I have only one question," she said. "And that is for you, girl, not this . . . this blasphemous pile of feathers."

Despite her distinct feeling this was not going well, Alex was determined to do the best she could. Trying to stay upbeat, she smiled and said, "But asking the pokkle is much more fun."

"Fun!" The woman spit out the word as though it disgusted her. "Do you think it is fun to defile the sacred fountain of Santa Pesca by not only sitting upon the Altar of Intention as though it is no more than a common public bench but, even worse, by placing a feathered monstrosity upon it? You think that is *fun*, do you?"

Aghast, Alex stared at the woman as she ranted on, but Louie—convinced that if only he could get the pokkle to say something all would be well—decided to take action.

"Do you want a raisin, pokkle?" he whispered, holding out his palm with the very last honey raisin nestling on it.

The woman finished her tirade and not only she but the entire marketplace fell silent. Alex was aware there was a communal glare directed at her, Louie and the pokkle, but she dared not look up. Instead, she found herself following the woman's piercing stare and they both watched as the pokkle dipped its head over Louie's hand and very delicately sucked up the offered raisin. The result was instantaneous. The pokkle's gut heaved in protest at the intake of yet another honey raisin and a large squirt of liquid pokkle poop arched into the clear blue waters of the fountain.

The woman shrieked out in fury. "Filth! Filth!" She stooped to snatch up the pokkle, but Louie got there first—he grabbed it and ran. The woman lunged at Alex, catching the collar of her jacket, but Alex wriggled free and raced off.

"Defilers! Defilers!" the woman shrieked. "Catch the defilers!"

The whole marketplace erupted. Like a tidal wave it thundered toward Alex as she hurtled after Louie, scooting into the shadows of an alley. They raced along, pursued by the pounding of running feet, amplified into a rhythmic roar, and when Alex glanced back she saw a sea of people closing in on them. Fast. They shot around a blind corner and then dived into an even narrower alley, which ran between the backyards of some large houses. Ahead Alex saw to her dismay that the alley ended at the sparkly waters of the river—they were trapped.

Suddenly a door in a garden wall swung open and completely blocked their path. Louie skidded into it and the pokkle flew from his hands. Desperately Alex pulled Louie up, and it was only when he was on his feet that she realized that another pair of hands had helped her. She looked up and saw a smile she recognized. "Benn!" she gasped.

"Alex! What are you doing here?"

"Being chased. Can you hide us?"

Benn heard the pounding of approaching feet. Quickly he shoved Louie and Alex into an overgrown garden, closed the door and threw a large bolt across it.

"Pokkle!" Louie wailed.

Alex pushed her hand over his mouth. "*Shh*," she hissed. "They'll hear you."

Crouching silently in the long grass, they heard the sharp voice of the woman yelling, "Justice for Santa Pesca! Justice!" This was echoed, pokkle-like, by the crowd, "Justice! Justice!" They listened to the angry feet of the mob pounding by on the other side of the wall; the noise seemed to go on forever. Alex shuddered to think what a narrow escape they had had.

"Stay down," Benn whispered. He pointed to the substantial stone house that rose up some distance away at the far end of the long, untidy yard, half hidden by the tall grass and rampaging brambles. "We don't want my father to see us."

"Your *father*?" Alex asked, surprised.

"He's the mayor here," Benn explained. "I don't know what you've done to upset his deputy, but you can be sure whatever has got her goat will get his too."

"I can't see a goat," Louie said, half standing up to get a better look.

"Get down, Louie," Alex hissed, giving a sharp yank on his jacket.

Benn grinned. "It's a village saying," he explained to Louie. "It means to annoy someone." He turned to Alex, grinning. "So what exactly *did* you do? Sounds like you've provoked the entire village."

Alex sighed, and as she told Benn the unfortunate turn of events, his eyes widened and he had to stuff his hands over his mouth to stop spluttering with laughter. "You're telling me that your pokkle . . . ," he said, gasping for breath, *"pooped in the sacred fountain?"*

Alex nodded miserably. "We had no idea it was a sacred fountain," she said. "It just looked like a big, shiny fish and somewhere nice to sit. It wasn't like there was a sign or anything. And I didn't know Louie was going to give the pokkle another raisin either," she said, glaring at Louie.

Benn shook his head. "They're going to be talking

about this for years," he said. "My father will hit the roof. Oh, it's so *perfect*."

"You're not upset?" Alex asked, feeling very relieved.

"*Shh*," Benn hissed. "Listen. They're coming back from the river."

"Suppose they come in here looking for us?" Louie whispered, eyes wide with fear.

"They won't. The Honorable Ty Markham would never Harbor a Defiler, would he?"

Alex sighed inwardly. She seemed to keep acquiring labels. Yesterday she had become a Beguiler and now she was a Defiler. What would she find herself being labeled tomorrow, she wondered? Nothing good, that was for sure.

They sat in the tall grass, leaning against the warm brick of the garden wall, until all footsteps had long gone. "Okay," Benn whispered. "Let's go."

"But where?" Alex asked. "We don't have anywhere to go to."

"To Gramma Nella," Benn said. "Where I live."

"But don't you live here?" Alex asked. "With your father?"

Benn shook his head. "Oh, he doesn't want the bother of looking after me," he said. "I've lived with Gramma ever since Mom died. Since I was six. But I have to visit my father every week. We have lunch and he tests me on math or history or whatever. And I can never get anything right and he looks grumpy and tells me I'm holding my fork wrong and then he gives me a silver dollar for Gramma for my keep and I go home." Benn grinned. "Unless I bump into two kids who've defiled the sacred fountain."

"*We* didn't defile it," Louie objected. "The pokkle did."

"So where is this pokkle?" Benn asked.

Louie sighed. "I expect they caught it. Poor pokkle. Poor Momma. She'll be so sad."

Benn looked puzzled. "Is your mom here too?" he asked.

Alex shook her head. "It's a long story," she said.

"Then you can tell me on the way to Gramma's," Benn said. "Let's get going."

CHAPTER 14
Merry the Wherry

MERRY, BENN'S SAILBOAT, WAS TIED up to the walkway that ran for a few yards along the river's edge. She was an elegant little boat shaped like a leaf and she sat lightly upon the water. Her mast was down and lay along the length of the boat, with its red sail wrapped around it, and a long pair of finely crafted oars made from maple and walnut were neatly placed beside the mast.

"The river's for rowing, really," Benn said as he helped Alex and Louie step into the unfamiliar territory of something that floated upon water. "But sometimes, if the wind is right, I put the sail up. She doesn't get the chance very often though. Poor Merry. She loves to sail."

"Is Merry real?" Louie wanted to know as Benn untied the boat.

"She feels real to me. Like she's my friend," Benn said as he skillfully slipped the oars into the oarlocks and took them out into the middle of the river. Alex was pleased that he rowed fast and seemed just as keen as she was to put some distance between them and Santa Pesca.

"Why is Merry a girl?" Louie persisted.

Benn grinned. "I don't know. All boats are called *she*. That's just how it is."

Benn's answer seemed to satisfy Louie. It was the kind of response he would have gotten from his mother, although *Don't ask me, Louie. That's just how it is* was more Mirram's style. Louie snuggled up next to Alex and, lulled by the rhythmic motion of the boat, he fell asleep.

Benn rounded the first long bend in the river and Santa Pesca disappeared from view. "They won't come after us now," he said. "You were lucky. It's a nasty place. Almost as bad as Luma."

"Do you go to the market in Santa Pesca too?" Alex asked.

Ben laughed. "No way. My father won't allow his son to be seen selling lemons on his doorstep. Which is why I have to walk Howard—he's the donkey—up the worst hill in the world three times a week."

"I guess it must be pretty steep," Alex said.

Benn looked puzzled. "Well, you came down it this morning, right?"

Alex shook her head. "Nope. Down a rope. Down the cliff. Last night."

Benn very nearly dropped the oars in shock. He inhaled a long, low whistle of breath and shook his head in amazement. "Wow. That is . . . scary stuff."

As Benn rowed steadily on, Alex told him all that had happened since she had done the cards for him in the marketplace. And as she talked, the enormity of her situation began to dawn on her. When she reached the end of her story, Benn looked shocked. Even his short spiky hair seemed to be standing on end with surprise. "You can't ever go back there," he said.

"I know."

A pensive silence fell, broken after some minutes by Benn. "Gramma will know what to do. My cousin, Sol. He was an Enchanter too. Well, sort of."

"But I'm *not* an Enchanter," Alex said.

"Enchanter's child then. You must be."

"How would I know?" Alex said sharply. She hated not knowing where she was from.

"Oh." Benn sounded surprised. "Don't you know who your parents are?"

"No," said Alex. "But Mirram, my foster mother, she knows."

"So why doesn't she tell you?"

"I dunno." Alex thought it was the meanest thing Mirram had ever done, refusing to tell her who her parents were. She was sure that Mirram knew. Mirram was not a good liar—she always went pink when Alex asked her.

"That is *so* nasty," Benn said. "Gramma is always talking about my mom to me. And at least I get to see my father, even though he's kind of mean too."

"Mine's probably just as bad," Alex said. "Mirram said he didn't want me because he gave me away. And that he wasn't worth knowing anyway."

"Sheesh," Benn said. "That's such a horrible thing to say."

"Yes. It is." Alex had never talked to anyone about Mirram or her parents—whoever they were. It felt good to have someone on her side.

"You okay?" Benn asked.

Alex smiled. No one had ever asked her that before either. She supposed it was because no one had ever really wanted to know. "Yes," she said, "I am. Thanks."

She leaned back against the warm wood of the transom, cuddled Louie tightly and decided to enjoy their good fortune at finding Benn and the novelty of being in a boat. Alex loved the way the riverbank slipped slowly by, and she felt lulled by Merry's purposeful rocking as Benn took them down the river. She gazed out at the lush lemon and orange groves and the occasional field of corn as the little boat followed the long, lazy loops of the river as it swung down the valley, and once or twice she was sure she caught sight of a flash of brightly colored feathers leaping along the riverbank. She was tempted to wake Louie and see if he could see them—Louie was very good at spotting the pokkle—but he was sleeping so peacefully, his head resting in her lap, that Alex didn't have the heart to wake him. And so she sat quietly, trailing her fingers in the coolness of the water until Benn said, "Uh. Maybe safer to keep your hand out of the water. Just in case." And Alex snatched her hand back into the boat.

"Stingers," Benn said apologetically.

It was so easy to forget about the Hauntings, Alex thought, so easy to forget that even something as peaceful as rowing along a quiet river was not safe—at least, not for her if she was indeed what Louie said she was: an Enchanter's child. But how would she ever find out now? The one person who knew wasn't there anymore to ask.

A change in the movement of the boat made Alex look up to see that Benn was heading into a narrow channel that ran through the middle of a vineyard. "This cuts off the big bend and saves us at least a mile," he explained. "We're nearly home now."

A small wiggle of nervousness twisted in Alex's stomach. *Home for Benn*, she thought, *but not for us. We don't actually have a home anymore.*

The cut was only just wide enough for Merry's oar span and they progressed slowly along, with Benn taking care not to hit the banks. A band of people picking grapes waved and he called out a cheery "Hello!" while ahead Alex watched the broad sweep of the river grow ever closer. Soon they were edging out into the current and Benn was rowing across the flow to the bank on the far side, where a squat round tower surrounded by a high wall sat about fifty yards back from the water. It did not, Alex thought, look particularly welcoming.

Benn took Merry alongside a small jetty and tied up to a post. He stowed the oars and jumped out. "Here we are," he said, somewhat unnecessarily.

"Wake up, Louie," Alex said, nudging the little boy.

Louie stirred and opened his eyes. "Where are we?" he mumbled.

"Home," Benn said.

Louie brightened. "Is Momma here?"

"No, Louie, I'm afraid she's not," Alex said, and waited for an outburst.

But Louie said nothing. He got quietly out of the boat with Alex and stood, gazing solemnly around. Alex could see that Louie was beginning to understand that life was different now. She offered him her hand and he took it without a word. Alex smiled. His hand was sticky, as ever. Some things never changed.

A well-trodden footpath led to an archway through the high wall that surrounded the roundhouse, which sat squat and stolid behind it like a pile of thick coins. It was a strange place to live, Alex thought.

"It was a fort guarding the river in the old days," Benn explained as he led the way up the path. "When the pirates raided the valley, Gramma's great-grandmother used to fire cannonballs at them. Look, you can see the little round holes where the cannon poked out—they're called 'cannon-shots.' That's my bedroom now," he said proudly, pointing up to the top of the roundhouse. Alex saw a vertical slit in the stonework at the foot of which was a fat, round opening. She could easily imagine the dark nose of a cannon poking out of it. "The slit is for arrows," Benn said. "It was wild then."

They walked along the path between neat ranks of tiny trees with paper wrapped around their slim trunks. "The lemon nursery," Benn explained. "They're Gramma's babies and she likes to keep them close to home. But they're getting big now and she'll be digging them up soon and putting them in a field of their own. And then she'll plant some more."

Alex noticed how proud Benn was of his grandmother and how at ease he was with his home. She'd never felt like that in her home in Luma. In fact, she'd not really thought of Mirram's house as her home at all, even though she could not remember living anywhere else. She had always felt like a guest who had long outstayed her welcome.

They walked through the arch into a cobbled court-yard and approached the heavy oak front door, which was covered with an impressive array of metal studs. Alex looked up at the heavyset walls of the little fortress and a shiver ran through her—the great bulk of stone reminded her of the Vaults beneath Luma. Like all Luma schoolchildren, Alex had been taken there as a warning to behave.

But Benn seemed quite at ease with the fortress in which he lived. He gave the studded door a hefty shove and it swung slowly open. Beyond was a cool dimness of a kitchen into which Benn happily hurried, calling out, "Hey, Gramma, I'm home!"

Alex hovered on the threshold, unsure what to do. "It's dark in there," Louie whispered. "There might be wolves."

"Wolves?" Alex said, surprised.

"With teeth," Louie clarified.

Benn came to the door. "Hey, come on in," he said. "Gramma says so."

"Is Gramma a wolf?" Louie asked anxiously.

"Don't be silly, Louie," Alex told him.

Benn grinned. "She's not a wolf. She's my grandmother."

Louie did not look convinced. "Sometimes wolves dress up as grandmothers," he said.

"Come on, Louie," Alex said, and she swept him up in her arms and carried him into the soft dimness of the roundhouse kitchen.

CHAPTER 15
In the Roundhouse

ALEX AND LOUIE FOUND THEMSELVES in a large, circular room, which smelled of fresh bread. Alex stood uncertainly while her eyes adjusted to the gloom, and soon she could see a curved flight of steps running up the far wall, a low stone sink and a big cast iron stove with a thick black pipe snaking up through the ceiling. Standing at the stove was a woman in a flowery frock, with an untidy pile of white hair knotted on top of her head with long tendrils escaping and cascading down to her shoulders and smudges of flour on her face. "Come in, come in," the woman said. "Sit yourself down. Make yourself at home." She waved her hand at the round table in the middle of the room around which was ranged an assortment of chairs.

"This is Alex and Louie, Gramma," Benn said. "They need to stay with us tonight. That's okay, isn't it?"

"Of course it is. It will be lovely to have company." Benn's grandmother came over to the table, ruffled Louie's hair and held out her hand to Alex. "I'm Nella Lau," she said. "Any friend of Benn's is welcome here."

A little self-consciously, Alex shook Nella's hand. "I'm Alex," she said. "And thank you very much."

Louie had brightened up considerably since smelling the bread and finding no wolves whatsoever in the kitchen. "My name is Louie D'Arbo," he said, "and I am honored to make your acquaintance, Mistress Nella."

"And I too am honored, Master D'Arbo," Nella Lau replied. "Would you like some cake?"

"Ooh, yes please," Louie said. "We haven't had *anything* to eat all day except for raisins and oranges." ·

"In that case you need some bread and soup first to settle your stomach. Then cake," Nella told Louie. "So, Benn, while I fix the soup why don't you show Louie and Alex the house? They can sleep in your room on the big cushions."

They climbed the stairs that hugged the curving wall and Alex discovered that the roundhouse was simply three rooms stacked one on top of the other. The middle room was Nella's and the top was Benn's. The striking thing in

Benn's room was the cannon. It wasn't so much that the cannon was under Benn's bed, it was that Benn's bed was over the cannon. The narrow bed with its patchwork quilt was perched on long, spindly legs like a stork. Below it sat a small, efficient-looking tube of cast iron mounted on a wheeled wooden trolley. Louie squealed with excitement when he saw it.

While Benn showed Louie the cannon, Alex peered out through the cannon-shot, feeling the soft evening air scented with lemons blow onto her face. She gazed down on the peaceful scene below. The high walls swept around the roundhouse, enclosing the courtyard, which was paved with cobbles laid in concentric circles in a variety of hues—reds, whites, grays, yellows and blacks—making the roundhouse, Alex thought uneasily, into the bull's-eye at the center of the target.

Beyond the high courtyard wall, Alex saw lemon and orange groves planted in perfect lines like rigidly drilled soldiers, forming a multitude of patterns invisible from the ground. Whichever way she looked they formed geometric shapes—diamonds, squares, even triangles, but positively no circles. Alex understood why someone had built the roundhouse and all its circles—it was surely a rebellion against those ranks of trees.

The sky was turning red with the setting sun and shadows were deepening. Just on the other side of the courtyard wall was an enclosure with a few ancient olive trees—one of which had a swing hanging from it—and a large duck pond with a collection of ducks standing around the edge peering into the dark water like reluctant swimmers. Set back from the pond was a duck house with some bad-tempered hustling going on around the top of the ramp. It seemed the duck house was not quite big enough for all who suddenly wished to be inside. The sound of indignant quacking drifted up in the still air.

"What's up with the ducks?" Benn asked, leaving Louie peering down the bore of the cannon.

"They're fighting to get into the duck house," Alex said, moving aside to let Benn look out through the cannon-shot.

"Weird," Benn said. "Never seen them do that before."

"Soup!" A shout came from below.

Louie's eyes lit up. "I am *so* hungry," he said, and he ran off down the stairs as happily as if he had lived in the roundhouse all his life. Alex wished she felt the same, but she could not shake off a growing sensation of unease.

They sat around the kitchen table eating thick vegetable soup that had a distinct tang of lemon and fresh bread with crispy orange-peel crust while Benn, with enthusiastic prompting from Louie, told Nella of their escape down the cliff face and their night in the cave. Alex noticed that Benn left out how he had first met her in Luma, and she guessed that, just like everyone else, Nella disapproved of Prophecy. When Louie took over the story of the attack by the Hawke, standing on tiptoe and pointing at the ceiling to show how big the Hawke was, Alex noticed Nella's deep blue eyes were fixed not upon Louie but upon her with an unsettlingly scrutinizing gaze. Nella did not approve of her, of that Alex was sure.

Somewhat sharply, Alex thought, Nella said, "So, Alex. Why *exactly* were the Sentinels after you?" Alex felt very flustered. *Was Nella Lau an informer for Luma? Had Benn tricked her and brought her to a prison?* The roundhouse, with its high perimeter wall and tiny windows, did look remarkably like a prison. And what about that heavy front door with all the studs in it? That was definitely a door to a dungeon. A sudden rush of fear came over Alex and she leaped to her feet.

Nella did not move. She continued to hold Alex in her steady, cool gaze and Alex felt as if she were already Nella's prisoner. She glanced around at the door and saw that now a massive bolt was drawn across at the top. They were trapped. *What a fool she had been.*

As if from a great distance, Alex heard Nella's voice, calm and cool: "Sit down, child." Out of the corner of her eye she saw Louie staring up at her, suddenly scared. She must act before it was too late. She must get out of here with Louie. *Right now.*

Alex reached down and grabbed Louie's hand. She pulled him up from his seat and, ignoring his protests, dragged him over to the door. Then she had to drop Louie's hand to jump up and shoot back the bolt. As she yanked the door open Alex was aware that Louie was no longer at her side. She wheeled around and saw him standing by Nella, who had her arm around him. *So Louie is against me too*, Alex thought.

"Alex!" Louie cried out. "What are you doing? What's wrong?"

"You betrayed me, Louie!" Alex yelled, and she turned and raced out of the door.

Behind her came Louie's shout: "Alex! Alex, come back! *Alex!*"

Panic upon her now, Alex hurtled across the rings of cobbles, through the arch in the wall and down the path to the river. She would take Merry and then she'd be safe. They'd not be able to catch her. But she could hear feet pounding after her, closing in on her. Suddenly a hand grabbed her jacket and Alex swung around. It was Benn.

"Let go!" she yelled, shaking him off.

Benn let his arm drop, but as she ran off she found Benn sprinting beside her. "Alex. What's wrong? *What is it?*"

Alex stopped and faced Benn angrily. "Your grand-mother. She's a Sentinel. You're all in it. I know that now. You set a trap."

"Gramma—a *Sentinel?*" Benn was incredulous. "We set a *trap?* Are you crazy—*oh sheesh.*" Benn grabbed hold of Alex's wrist.

"Let go of me!"

But this time Benn would not be shaken off. "Alex," he said in a half whisper. "Behind you. Coming toward us through the trees. There's a shadow. Like fog. I think it's the Gray Walker." Alex caught the fear in Benn's voice. She knew it was real and it cut through the craziness of her terror. "If we run now, *fast*, I think we can get home okay," Benn whispered. "Will you do that?"

Alex looked into Benn's eyes, trying to catch the reflection of what he was staring at over her shoulder, but all she saw was his complete honesty. "Yes," she whispered. "Yes. I'll do that."

Together, they fled back up the path. And behind them flowed the clutching tendrils of Hagos RavenStarr's most dangerous Haunting.

CHAPTER 16

The Gray Walker

BENN AND ALEX HURTLED IN through the door and Nella sprang into action. She threw the well-oiled bolt across the top and then, in a sweeping motion, she ran a thick, fuzzy-looking cloth around the tiny gap between the door and its frame and Alex saw a glimmer of light follow the cloth and fall into the crevice. Benn let go of her wrist and they looked at each other awkwardly while Alex rubbed the circulation back into her hand. Louie ran to her, wrapped his arms around her waist and looked up at her with wide, shining eyes. He looked, Alex thought, as though he had been crying. "Why did you run away?"

he asked, pulling her away from the door as if he was afraid she might try to go again.

"I . . . I don't know," Alex admitted as she sat back down in her place and stared at the remains of her soup. She didn't understand what had just happened. She watched Nella moving quietly but rapidly around the kitchen, running the cloth over the gaps between the shutters, filling the spaces with a shimmer of light, which glowed bright for a few seconds and then turned into a thick darkness. Soon the kitchen was deep in shadow and a heavy hush hung over it. Benn lit a lantern and placed it on the table and Nella ran upstairs with the cloth. They sat in silence as they listened to the creak of her footsteps above as she moved purposefully around.

A few minutes later, Nella returned. She carefully folded the cloth, which sparkled in the lantern light, and put it into a blue lacquer box with silver symbols painted around the sides. "I never thought to be using this again," she said sadly. She sat down next to Alex. "Now, dear," she said, her voice calm and slow, as if soothing a frightened animal. "What has happened is that sundown has brought a Twilight Haunting to our door—the Night Wraith that people call the Gray Walker. Have you heard of it?"

Alex nodded.

"The Gray Walker only Haunts Enchanters and those

who carry Enchantment within them. I feel strongly that you have some Enchantment about you. Do *you* think you do?"

Alex thought of her cards nestling deep in her pocket. She thought of the eyes of the Hawke fixed upon her. And most of all she remembered what Louie had told her: *You just disappeared, Alex. You just faded away.* In a voice barely above a whisper, Alex admitted for the first time, "Yes. I think I do."

"So do I. This is why you are feeling so very afraid. It's the Twilight Terrors. It used to happen to my nephew. Poor Sol. He wasn't the greatest of Enchanters, but he did bring home quite a few useful bits and pieces." She lifted the sparkly cloth from its box. "This is one of them—a Sealing Cloth. And unlike many things Sol had, it does seem to work."

"Will Alex be safe, Gramma?" Benn asked anxiously.

As if in answer came a noise at the door: *tappa-tippa-tap.*

The room fell silent and all eyes turned fearfully to the door. Nella reached for Alex's hand. "You are more powerful than you know, my dear," she said in a low voice. "The Gray Walker is manifesting sound."

"You mean that's it *knocking*?" Alex whispered.

"Yes. It is knocking."

"Why?" Louie wanted to know.

"Why does anything knock upon a door?" Nella said.

"Because it wishes to come in." She stood up purposefully and picked up the blue box with the Sealing Cloth. "We'll go upstairs to your room, Benn. I've Sealed all the windows, but yours are the smallest and the highest up too."

Louie got up; he put his hand in Alex's and led her over to the stairs. "Come on, Alex," he said. "We can shoot it with the cannon."

They walked up the winding stairs and waited on the landing while Nella went into her room and returned with an armful of quilts and pillows. Alex noticed how she locked her door behind her and ran the Sealing Cloth around it. "We will all stay in Benn's room tonight," Nella said. "And in the morning it will be gone."

"So will it be outside all night?" Louie asked.

Nella did not answer directly. "Come on now, Louie. You've had a very tiring day."

Up in Benn's room, Alex wrapped Louie in a quilt and within a few seconds of his head hitting the pillow, he was asleep. She made her bed up next to him and curled up beside him, feeling the soft rise and fall of his breath. In no more than a few minutes, Alex too was asleep, exhausted by the strangest twenty-four hours she could remember.

But Benn and his grandmother sat watchful and alert. It was not the first night Nella had kept vigil with the Gray Walker outside, but she was determined it must be the last. "Tomorrow, Benn," she said in a low voice, "you must take Alex to the cavern. Jay can take her through the old tunnel to the other side of the mountains, where there are no Hauntings."

"But what will she do there?" asked Benn.

"There's a little town in the foothills on the far side. I wanted Sol to go there, but he wouldn't. They have an orphanage there, not a bad place by all—well, most—accounts. They'll take her in with no questions asked."

"That's so horrible," Benn said.

"Not as horrible as being caught by the Gray Walker," Nella said.

"What about Louie?"

"Well, Louie can stay here if he wants. He's a lovely little boy, don't you think?"

"He's nice, Gramma. But then Alex will be all alone. With no one. It's so unfair."

"I know, it's terrible for her. But she has to leave. What happened to Sol will happen to Alex too. For sure."

Silence fell for a while as Benn and his grandmother listened to the quietness of the house and the eerie rustlings outside. Benn thought the noises sounded like a dog sniffing out a bone, or a rat trying to find its way up inside a wall. They were the creepiest sounds he had ever heard. "Gramma," he whispered, "what did happen to Sol?"

Nella sighed. "I suppose it is time you knew."

Benn was surprised. Usually when he asked Gramma questions she would tell him to wait until he was older. But tonight she seemed different. "You know Sol was your cousin, my brother's son?" she asked.

Benn nodded. That was just about all he knew. He hoped Gramma would tell him a bit more than that.

"Sol had a small amount of Enchantment about him, not much. We've had much more than that in our family in the past, but it has faded to nothing now. For which I am very thankful. But poor Sol was proud of his 'little bit of sparkle,' as he called it when he was tiny, and he was determined to do what he could with it. Your uncle Tobias forbade him to 'meddle,' but Sol was headstrong. One night when he was, oh, about fourteen I think, Sol sneaked out and took the midnight train to Rekadom."

Hearing his grandmother talk about the midnight train to Rekadom gave Benn a buzz of excitement. "It must have been amazing to just get on the train and go anywhere you wanted."

"Not quite anywhere, dear. They did run on rails, you know. You had to go where the rails went."

"I *know* that, Gramma," Benn said a little grumpily. "You can still trace the track in some places. The rails are not far beneath the sand."

Nella pursed her mouth disapprovingly. She did not approve of the train.

"But, Gramma," said Benn, "to see the train . . . the engine . . . the steam . . . all working and just knowing you could travel across the whole, huge desert all the way to the other side. What an amazing thing!"

"A *bad* thing," Nella told him. "And a dangerous thing to be connected to that evil place, Rekadom."

Benn would not be put off. "But think of all the places in between. There were stops along the track, weren't there?"

"Halts. That's what they were called. And yes, you would ring the bell, which would sound in the driver's cab, and they'd stop the train at the next one. There was one on the cliff above Oracle Rock. I went to see a friend there once. Dear Deela." Nella smiled. "My dead cousin's child lives with her now. Terrible story, the poor girl— Palla she was called—was sent to the Luma Orphanage. As soon as I heard that she'd ended up in that awful place, I wrote offering her a home with me, but they'd already sold her off to be ship's drudge in some rotten hulk. Can you imagine? She was only nine. Anyway, the ship sank in a storm and Deela rescued her. Goodness, she must be all grown up by now."

Benn listened, enthralled. His grandmother was talking to him as though he were a man now, no longer a boy. "You have such a big family, Gramma," he said, a little wistfully.

"They're your family too, Benn. You'll meet them one day. I'm sure."

"But not Sol?"

Nella's eyes filled with tears. "No, dear. Not Sol."

"What did Sol do in Rekadom, Gramma?"

Nella smiled. "He did surprisingly well. He became assistant to the king's Enchanter, would you believe? Mind you, Sol could talk his way into anything. He came back home a few times, always bringing little trinkets with him. I think he was trying to win his father over, but he never did. And then one day—this was after Tobias had died—Sol came back for good. He'd left the king's Enchanter, but he wouldn't say why. And then two years later, the Gray Walker came Haunting. And Sol got the Twilight Terrors."

"What happened then, Gramma?"

"We kept it out for two nights by using Sol's Sealing Cloth, but on the third night Sol forgot to Seal the drain in the kitchen sink and the Gray Walker came up through it." Nella shuddered. "I saw it coming out. It filled the kitchen and went screaming through the house and . . . and then . . . then it found him." Nella lapsed into silence and in it Benn caught a faint whisper from outside the shutters like wind blowing dry leaves. "And before you ask me, yes, I have indeed Sealed the sink tonight. And the bathroom. We are as secure as we can be."

Benn wanted to know what the Gray Walker had actually done to Sol. But he knew he could never ask that, so he said, "Gramma. Why doesn't the Gray Walker ever go up to Luma?"

Nella made an effort to rid herself of her sad thoughts. "Luma signed an anti-Beguilement treaty with King

Belamus, so he leaves them in peace. Luma Sentinels swore never to allow Enchanters or their kin to set foot in their town. And they stick to their word. I dread to think what would have happened to Alex if they had caught her. And to anyone who had had anything to do with her up there."

Nella saw that Benn was twisting the long tassels of her shawl into a tight spiral. "Benn, what's wrong?" she asked.

"In Luma I bought a Prophecy from Alex."

Nella stared in shock at her grandson, normally so cautious and law-abiding. "Do you realize the danger you put yourself in, Benn Markham?"

"But I wanted to know about Jay and the engine, because I'm *never* allowed to go there. I wanted to *see* it. And I wanted to know when it will be ready."

Nella tutted. "Never, I hope. So, what kind of prophecy did Alex actually do?"

"She had these amazing cards, Gramma. Little hexagons that joined together and made big swirling patterns, which *moved*."

"She had *Hex cards* in *Luma*? Is the girl crazy?" Nella gave a rueful chuckle. "Sol would have been so jealous, he longed for a pack of Hex cards. How on earth did Alex get those?"

Benn shook his head. "I dunno. I think she kept them secret."

"She must have, if she lived in Luma. She'd not be

around to Beguile my grandson if she hadn't.'"

"Grandma, I've put us in danger, haven't I?" Benn whispered.

"Nothing we can't deal with," Nella said briskly. "But I don't want you taking risks like that ever again. Understand?"

Benn nodded.

"And I am sorry if I have been too hard on you, making you trek up to Luma three times a week to sell the lemons when I know you want to help Jay with the engine. But times are hard, Benn. The Hauntings have driven so many good people away."

"I know, Gramma. It's okay."

"You're a good boy, Benn. When you take Alex tomorrow you can stay over in the cave with Jay if you like. And if he wants you to help him with the engine, then you go ahead. I mustn't stop you."

Benn's face lit up. "Thank you, Gramma. And then, when the engine is working and they take it out to the far side of the mountains, can I go along with them? Because then I can go and see Alex in the orphanage and—"

Nella interrupted him sharply. "Benn, please. One step at a time."

"But Jay said I could help him drive it."

"Jay says a lot of things he shouldn't," Nella told Benn. "Which is why it is you selling lemons up in Luma and not him."

Maybe, Benn thought, *I should be a bit more like Jay. Then I'd get to do what I want just like he does.*

A soft rattle upon the window shutters sent Nella rushing to them with the Sealing Cloth. Benn watched the Seals glow and then fade to darkness once more while a whispering hiss outside sent goose bumps running down his spine. He allowed Nella to wrap his quilt around him and then they sat together, watching the shutters and listening anxiously to the rustlings outside.

Benn thought of Alex and how sad she would be tomorrow when she would have to leave Louie behind. And how horrible it would be when he would have to say goodbye to her and let Jay take her through the tunnel under the mountain to the orphanage on the other side. He thought how lonely Alex would be in the orphanage, which was not, despite what Gramma said, a nice place. He thought how much he wanted Alex to stay and be his friend, and help out on the farm, and sail Merry with him, but she couldn't. And all because Alex had the amazing gift of Enchantment. It was so unfair.

Benn sighed. *Why was it such a bad thing to be an Enchanter? Why couldn't it be a good thing?*

CHAPTER 17
Broom and Bucket

EARLY THE NEXT MORNING, AS the sun rose over the mist that hung low over the river, the Gray Walker unwrapped itself from the roundhouse. Slowly it pulled out its tendrils from all the crevices it had been exploring, then it laid itself down in the courtyard like a soft blanket of fine gray wool and began to fade.

Nella woke with the sun, as she always did. She crept downstairs, found her yard broom, and then she summoned the courage to open the shutter on the kitchen window and peer out. The early morning sun sent long slanting shadows across the courtyard, which was, Nella was relieved to see, empty of any gray wisps of Wraith.

A few minutes later she was outside, sweeping the court-yard with short, angry strokes, sending dust flying out of the gate and into the duck pond in the old lemon grove beyond. The ducks saw her coming. Quacking their dis-approval, they scattered to the other side of the pond and watched in a huddle while Nella dumped a cloud of dusty dirt into their home.

Nella stood leaning on the broom watching—she hoped—the invisible remnants of the Gray Walker sink-ing into the pond along with the dirt. "Try getting out of *there*, you nasty old fog," she muttered.

A small brown duck left the huddle, waddled up to Nella and pecked indignantly at the broom. Nella went inside to find some oats as a peace offering, which the ducks ate in sulky silence. They were not won over, Nella could tell.

Nella walked across the courtyard and went to the stable to check on Howard, the donkey. Nella thought he looked relieved to see her. "Go on, Howard," she said, opening his stable door. "Kick off the dust from last night." Howard shot past Nella and she watched him hur-tle by the ducks and take refuge in the most distant corner of the old olive grove.

Nella returned to the dimness of the kitchen to make a jug of hot, sweet lemon tea. As she put a pinch of tea into a jug, then squeezed the lemons and waited for the water to boil, she thought about the long journey down the river that her grandson and Alex would be making that morning. She thought about the Hawke and prayed it would not be patrolling today. And then her thoughts turned to their destination, where her other grandson, Jay, had marooned himself deep in the damp and gloom, refusing to come out, working on his crazy scheme to get the old train running to "get out of this dump," as he referred to their beautiful valley. Jay had never been the same since Sol had died. He was angry and wanted out, and in her heart, Nella did not blame him. She took her lemon tea outside and went to sit among the ducks, which quacked and fussed at the intrusion. Nella settled down beside the pond and watched the sun climb slowly into the sky. It was going to be a beautiful day.

"It's going to be a beautiful day," Hagos told the bleary-eyed Danny.

"Oh, *really*?" Danny said, pulling the threadbare blanket over his head.

"Oh, really, Mr. Dark. And the sooner we are out in it the better."

Danny sat up, trying to remember where he was. Wherever it was, the beds were terrible. He gazed around at the ramshackle shelter festooned with tattered cloth and at the mass of tree trunks beyond, and then he turned his gaze to the skinny, barefoot man in a faded tunic who was looking down at him with an amused expression. Danny didn't like being found amusing, particularly so early in the morning.

"Breakfast?" the man asked.

"Uh?" said Danny.

"I have a little hoard of dried bark beetle that I have been saving for a special occasion. I think the embarkation morning of our quest merits such a designation, does it not, Mr. Dark?" Hagos said.

"What?" Danny mumbled.

"Breakfast. Bark beetle. Want some?" Hagos was already learning Danny-speak.

"No. Push off." Danny lay back down with the blanket over his head. Hagos sighed and went to fetch a bucket of water.

"Hey! What'd you do that for?" Danny sprang to his feet, dripping wet.

"You agreed to accompany me on my quest. And now it is time to go. Get up."

"I *am* up, thanks to you. And your stupid bucket."

Hagos allowed himself a smile. "I do not think it is the *bucket* that is stupid, Mr. Dark. The bucket was performing its job. You, however, were not." Hagos picked up his traveling pack—like an excited child, he had already been up for hours getting ready—strapped the Lightning Lance holster around his waist, and said, "As you do not require breakfast, Mr. Dark, we will be on our way at once."

Danny spluttered with indignation—this Enchanter

was even worse than the Chief Falconer. He had jumped out of the frying pan and into the fire. He was such a loser.

Hagos left Danny in the shelter and set off through the forest with his traveling pack. He had no idea if Danny would follow or not, but he wanted him to come of his own free will. An unwilling companion always led to trouble, and he needed to be able to trust Danny completely. At the edge of the trees Hagos halted and looked warily up at the sky. After the loss of a Flyer, the Hawke was trained to return to Rekadom, but Hagos was concerned. The Hawke clearly knew where Danny was, as it had been hovering above the tree canopy, watching. So would it have returned to Rekadom or not? Hagos was not sure. He waited for some minutes in the shelter of the trees, watching the empty circle of blue sky high above the lake. It looked promising, he thought.

Hagos scooped up his tattered clothes from the previous day and folded them neatly into his traveling pack. Then he walked quietly out from the cover of the trees and sat down on his favorite rock beside the deep-green waters of the lake to think. Danny had not followed him, so what was he to do? Hagos stared glumly at his reflection. It had all felt so promising the evening before. And he liked Danny. He had thought they could be a good team—friends even. *Wrong again, you old fool,* he thought. *Whatever made you think you might find a friend who didn't let you down?*

Hagos was so caught up in his misery that he did not notice soft footsteps behind him. "Bark beetle?" came a voice. Startled, Hagos twisted around and saw Danny waving the jar of bark beetles at him. "Want one?" Danny inquired.

"Yes, please," Hagos replied, the exuberance of relief sweeping over him.

Danny sat down beside Hagos, unscrewed the top of the jar and offered it to him. A sweet, citrus scent wafted out. Hagos took a dried beetle and crunched it in his back teeth, enjoying the tang that fizzed into his mouth like a rocket.

"Sorry I was a grump," Danny said. "I'm not a morning person. But I keep my word. I said I'd go on your quest and I will, too."

"Thank you," Hagos said. "I appreciate that. Would *you* like a bark beetle?"

"Maybe later."

His energy and feeling of hope restored, Hagos got to his feet. "I suggest we get on our way. I want to be under cover by nightfall."

Danny glanced up at the sky a little anxiously. "The Flyer before me," he said slowly. "She's the reason I got the job so suddenly. The Hawke came back with her jacket, but not with her. So will it come back for my jacket too?"

"Ah. Well, yes, I suppose that is a possibility," Hagos admitted. "They call it proof of dispatch. Belamus likes proof. And he doesn't like buying new jackets. You'll find all Flyers are much the same size—medium height with broad shoulders."

Danny looked aghast. *"You mean I'm wearing her jacket?"* He shrugged it off and threw it onto the ground. It lay facedown, the outstretched silver wings and the chunky gold triangle of the beak glinting in the sunlight.

"Of course you are," Hagos told him. "There is only one Flyer jacket. Silver leaf is not cheap. And neither is gold."

"Real gold?" Danny picked up the jacket and ran his finger over the beaky gold stud. He laughed. "I've never had anything gold before. I'm keeping this."

"Run!" Hagos yelled.

Danny did not need to be told twice. The sudden appearance of a dark winged shape in the circle of blue above the lake was impossible to miss. Safe in the cover of the trees, Danny whispered, "What do we do?"

"I shall use what little Enchantment I have left," Hagos said. He rooted in his traveling pack and took a small square of red cloth out from a pouch. "I've been keeping this for emergencies," he said. "I think this situation qualifies for that appellation, don't you?"

Danny at least understood "situation" and "emergencies." "Yes," he said. He watched Hagos shake the square out to reveal a cloak of impossibly delicate fabric, shot through with threads of gold and silver. The cloak settled onto Hagos's shoulders like an old friend and Danny felt the same sense of awe as he had the evening before, but this time he did not try to hide it. He shook his head in wonder at the cloak. The fine fabric fell like a soft shower of rain, and within its brilliance Danny saw swirls of embroidered symbols that seemed to pulse with energy. Hagos stood taller, he held his head higher, and he had an air of authority about him. Danny recognized the confidence a uniform could give you. He'd felt that way when he had first put on the Flyer's jacket.

From behind a tree—Hagos had insisted he stay safe—Danny watched the Enchanter walk out into the open space by the lake. And then it all happened very fast. The Hawke set its wings back flat against its body and dropped like a stone, heading straight for Hagos. Danny saw the Enchanter stand his ground, his arms raised, the cloak sweeping down like the wings of a yet another great bird. At the moment the Hawke leveled out, dropping its feet so that the talons were head height to Hagos, Danny saw the Hawke pull up as if someone had thrown a rope around it from behind. It reared up backward, wings flapping. There was a blinding flash of white, an enormous splash, and the next moment Danny saw a disheveled, angry-looking swan sitting in the lake, its eyes blazing with fury, its wings up in the attack position. The swan saw Hagos and set off toward him, head down and hissing loudly. Hagos turned and ran to join Danny behind his tree.

"You changed it into a swan." Danny sounded disappointed. "I thought you were going to kill it."

Hagos shook his head. "I don't kill. I've seen enough of that. The creature will do no damage as a swan."

"So it's a swan forever now?" Danny asked.

"Unless someone addresses it by its secret name, which I think is highly unlikely," Hagos said with a smile. "To be on the safe side, Mr. Dark, I suggest we avoid that word in its hearing. Just in case. Substitute it with . . . er . . ."

"Marshmallow?" Danny suggested, grinning.

Hagos laughed. "Very comical. Oh, talk of the devil, here it is."

The swan had come waddling into the trees, where it now stopped and eyeballed Hagos. It hissed and aimed a peck at his legs, which he easily sidestepped. "Shoo, Marshmallow!" said Hagos, laughing. "Shoo!" The swan, as if aware of this ignominious turn of events, hung its head and did as it was told.

"I feel kind of sorry for it," Danny said, as he watched the swan despondently waddle away.

"Don't," Hagos replied, curtly. "It was a killer."

Danny reflected that he was supposed to be a killer too. He said nothing, but Hagos caught his expression.

"And what about you?" Hagos asked. "Are you a killer too?"

"I killed two trees yesterday," Danny said quietly. "And I should have killed a child. But . . ."

"You didn't?"

"No. I couldn't do it."

"We are of one mind then," Hagos said. "This bodes well for our partnership, do you not agree?"

Danny did not reply. He was thinking of the terror in the girl's eyes and how brave she had been to shield the boy. He hoped they had gotten down from the cliff okay. He wondered what they were doing now.

CHAPTER 18

Francina

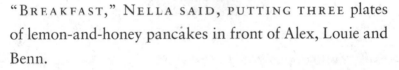

"Breakfast," Nella said, putting three plates of lemon-and-honey pancakes in front of Alex, Louie and Benn.

While they ate quietly, still bleary with sleep, Nella went up to her room and from a locked drawer in the back of her little desk she took a small, almost square book bound in blue leather. Nella stood cradling the book in her hands for a few minutes, gazing out of the window at the peaceful scene beyond. The quietness of the court-yard betrayed no sign of its vile inhabitant from the night before, the ducks were gliding lazily across the pond, and at the end of the old olive grove Howard was tackling his favorite patch of thistles. Nella sighed. She felt so sad that Alex had to leave. The girl looked like she could do with a settled home and some affection, both of which Nella longed to give her. It would have been company for Benn too, who Nella knew was often lonely. But it could not be—Alex was in great danger here and she must leave as soon as possible. Nella tucked the book into her apron pocket and went downstairs to the kitchen to face the day.

It was a subdued group around the table. Alex hated the thought of leaving. All she wanted to do was to stay here with Benn, Nella and Louie. It was so unfair that she couldn't. *So unfair.* She watched Nella top off her glass with hot sugared lemon tea and thought how much more caring Nella was compared with Mirram. Back in Luma it would have been *her* topping off Mirram's glass. *And* making the pancakes. And clearing up, all without a word of affection or even thanks. "Thank you," Alex said, smiling up at Nella.

Nella returned the smile and sat down opposite Alex. "Alex, dear," she said, "about these cards that you read Benn's fortune with . . ."

Alex glared at Benn. *So he was a tattletale, was he?* Benn, who was busy eating his pancakes, did not notice. "What cards?" Alex asked, after just a little too long.

"I don't want to pry," said Nella, "but you do know that your Hex cards are very rare and precious? And extremely powerful too."

"*Hex* cards?" asked Alex.

"That's what they're called. For their shape and their power. My dear nephew Sol, who was an assistant to the king's Enchanter, no less, told me all about them. He longed for a set. Do you know how you got your cards, Alex?" Nella asked gently.

Alex shook her head. "I always had them," she said.

"From your parents maybe?"

Alex shrugged.

"Forgive me for asking, but your parents—do you know who they are?"

Alex wished people would stop asking her about her parents. "I told Benn already. I don't know and I don't care *who* they are. They gave me away to Mirram. They didn't want me."

"Of course they wanted you," Nella said gently.

"No they didn't. Mirram said my mother *made* her take me, even though Mirram didn't want me either."

Nella reached out and took Alex's hand "Well, I want you, Alex. And so does Benn. We would love you to stay here with us, but . . ."

"But I can't. Because of the Gray Walker."

"Yes. And the other Hauntings. And the Hawke will be back for sure. You would be in constant danger here."

"I could throw away the cards," Alex offered. "Then I would be just like everyone else, wouldn't I?"

Nella shook her head. "I believe the Enchantment is

within you too, Alex. Do you not feel that?"

Alex didn't know what she felt—apart from totally miserable. She had always known she didn't belong with Mirram in Luma, but yesterday evening around the kitchen table she had allowed herself to think she might at last have found somewhere she truly did belong. But the truth was she belonged *nowhere*.

Her thoughts were cut short by a sudden frantic knocking on the kitchen door. For a moment, everyone stared at the door in silence, and then Nella got up slowly. "It's all right," she said, "the sun's up. It can't be the Gray Walker. That murky piece of malice is lying at the bottom of the duck pond."

Benn, Louie and Alex watched warily as Nella pulled open the heavy door. There was a sudden shriek and something multicolored, small and feathery came scuttling in. "Pokkle!" Louie yelled as he threw himself off his chair and scooted after it.

From outside the door Alex heard a familiar voice. "Alex! I need Alex! The pokkle said she was here. Is she? Oh, *please*."

"Franny, Franny, Franny!" Louie yelled, hurling himself at his sister while the pokkle scuttled beneath Nella's long skirts. Nella was not a fan of feathered reptiles, especially those trying to bite her ankles. She gave a high-pitched scream and the pokkle shot out again and went scuttling across the kitchen floor. Louie raced after it, leaving Alex and Francina staring at one another.

"What do you want?" Alex asked Francina angrily.

Francina burst into tears.

"Oh dear," said Nella. "You'd better come in."

Ten minutes and two cups of hot, sweet lemon tea later Francina was in a fit state to speak. "It's Ma," she said. "They're putting her on trial today. For Harboring." Francina looked accusingly at Alex. "That's Harboring *you*, Alex, with those stupid cards. It's all your fault."

"It is not!" Alex flared angrily. "You can blame the lowdown sneak who told on me."

"Well, it wasn't *me*," Francina protested.

"Liar," Alex retorted.

"Now, now," Nella said, "let's sort this out calmly, shall we?"

"I bet it was Zerra who sneaked," Louie said.

Francina stared at her little brother. "How do you know?"

"I bet it was Francina too," Alex told Louie as if Francina was not there. "Because Francina always does what Zerra tells her."

It was Francina's turn to be angry now. "I do not!" she declared. "I tried to stop her, I really did. But she marched straight up to the Sentinel Gate and pressed the informer bell. It was horrible. I thought she was going to

Name me, but she Named Ma and you, Alex, and then *Louie.* Because she said he knew about the cards and kept it secret."

"I always keep secrets," Louie said proudly. "Because if you don't, they're not secrets anymore, are they?"

At last Nella managed to get a word in. "Francina, dear. I'm very sorry to hear about your mother, but what happened to her is not Alex's fault."

Alex looked gratefully at Nella. It was wonderful to have someone to take her side, rather than blame her.

"But Alex could save her. I *know* she could." Francina said.

"*Me?* How can I possibly save Mirram?" Alex asked incredulously.

"You could come back to Luma and tell them that it's all a mistake and your cards are just toys—"

"*Toys?*" Alex said indignantly. "They are *not* toys."

Francina looked at her foster sister, pleading. "But couldn't you say that? Please? To save Ma's life? *Please, Alex.*"

"No *way*," Alex said.

Francina put her head in her hands and began to sob.

Louie wriggled off his chair and went to comfort his sister. "Don't make Franny cry," he told Alex severely.

"It's not *my* fault she's crying," Alex said angrily.

Benn, who had kept quiet up until then, felt that Alex had already been blamed for far too much. "Exactly. You can't blame Alex for Luma being full of nasty people."

Louie burst into tears in sympathy with his sister. "It's *not* full of nasty people," he said.

"Yes, it is," Alex snapped back at him. "There's Zerra for one."

"But *Momma's* there and she's not nasty. I miss Momma. I want to go *hoooooome*," Louie wailed.

Nella, who had become accustomed to a quiet life with her easygoing grandson, felt as though a storm had blown into her kitchen. "Now, now, everyone, calm down," she said. "I'm sure we can sort something out. But first, Benn and Alex, it's time to get going. You've got a long journey ahead of you."

Alex felt a stone drop into her stomach. She looked around the kitchen and saw Francina sitting in *her* chair with Louie on her lap. She saw Benn, who was *her* friend, sitting next to Francina in that casual comfortable way he had about him and Nella pouring Francina another cup of lemon tea. Alex felt sick—Francina had taken her place and everyone was waiting for her to just *go away*.

"So I'm leaving here *forever*," Alex said quietly, "but Francina and Louie get to stay here for as long as they want?"

Nella sighed. "I wish it weren't so, Alex. But we talked about this already. You need to go to the other side of the mountains where there are no Hauntings. There's a nice orphanage there that will take you in and give you a good start in life. Where else can you go?"

Alex knew where. "Luma," she said. "I'll go back, I'll tell them the cards are toys and that Zerra lied, just like Francina asked me to. Then everyone can go home again and it will all be okay."

"I don't think it will be quite that simple, Alex," said Nella.

"I don't care," Alex said. "I'm not going to live in some horrible orphanage. I'm going to Luma."

CHAPTER 19

Hauntings

"I'm going to Luma. That's the only place she could have survived," Hagos was saying as he and Danny sat resting and eating bark beetles. They had followed the stream that led from the lake and had reached the edge of Seven Snake Forest. They were now looking out over the High Plains, the great expanse of barren moorland sprinkled with purple heathers and yellow gorse, which would take them to the upper reaches of Lemon Valley. After so many long years in the confines of the forest, Hagos was feeling quite overwhelmed by the vast emptiness of the space before him. "Look at all that sky," he murmured.

"And look at all those Air-Weavers," Danny replied.

"Thousands of them." Some distance away, out on the plain, Danny could see what looked like big and rather beautiful multicolored butterflies drifting aimlessly in the breeze. Air-Weavers had once been part of the Anti-Enchanter Hauntings, but they had since mutated and were now a deadly, invisible hazard to anyone—unless, like Danny, you were impervious to Enchantment and so could actually see them. Consequently, no one—not even sheep—set foot on the High Plains now. Or if they did they certainly never returned.

"*Thousands?*" Hagos was shocked. "But I only Engendered four. Wish I'd not made them self-replicating."

"Wish you'd not made them at all," Danny said. "Whatever were you thinking of?"

"I was trying to save my wife. My lovely Pearl," Hagos said quietly. "But it didn't work."

"Oh. I'm sorry." Danny felt embarrassed. He kept forgetting that Hagos had once had a family.

"Not your fault, Danny," said Hagos gruffly. "You see, Belamus held Pearl hostage in the dungeons to force me to Engender the Anti-Enchanter Hauntings. He kept promising he'd free her if I made just one more Haunting. And every time he went back on his word. I remember after I Engendered the Giant Skorpas—they were lethal—he let Pearl out for a day and then he sent her back. So then I did Rekadom Rocadites, and after that the Grove Garbutts. I'm not looking forward to those."

"The Garbutts have pretty much all gone," Danny said. "Eaten by feral cats, so they say."

"Good. Well, Pearl never got out after I did them either. So then, in desperation, I did a series of Xin."

"Xin?" asked Danny.

"Nasty little sharp points like glass. They make themselves into a net and have a vicious sting. Oh, and they push people off cliff edges. Quite charming, don't you think? They sing too—a horrible teeth-on-edge noise that disorients people wonderfully. I put some particularly vicious ones on the Titan cliffs and then some smaller ones along the coast right up to the walls of Rekadom. They were, even if I say so myself, masterful. But Belamus *still* didn't let my Pearl go."

"Why did you keep on believing he would?"

Hagos brushed his hand across his eyes. "What was the alternative, Danny? I would have done anything to save my precious Pearl. Anything."

Danny understood. He too would have done anything to save his mum and dad from the dungeons. But no one had ever asked him to.

They headed cautiously out onto the springy turf of the moorland. Danny kept a wary eye on the nearest group of Air-Weavers, which were floating lazily toward them, looking like little strips of shimmering gauze. They were beautiful, and yet Danny knew that if you touched one, you were finished. It would stick to your skin and act as a magnet for others to join it. Soon your arms and legs would be stuck together with hundreds of Air-Weavers until, unable to move, you fell over. And there you would stay, stuck to the ground like a fly to flypaper.

"Can you see any Air-Weavers nearby?" Hagos asked anxiously.

"Yep. And they're coming this way. Just hold my hand, we'll walk slowly and try not to create any air currents. We don't want to draw them toward us."

And so, hand in hand, Danny and Hagos walked carefully across the High Plains following the stream as it wound down to Lemon Valley. Hagos had never put total trust in anyone—not even Pearl—before. But as Danny led him on a meandering path through the drifting shoals of Air-Weavers, accompanied by occasional barked instructions to "Duck!" Hagos found it felt good to trust someone so completely. He allowed himself to be led like a little child through the danger and never once objected. And Danny, pleased at the confidence Hagos clearly had in him, began to feel more confident in himself. *Maybe*, he thought, *I'm not such a loser after all.*

CHAPTER 20

The Luma Twist

HOWARD WAS NOT HAPPY. THE donkey was in the courtyard of the roundhouse, harnessed to a cart piled high with lemons, and Howard knew that meant he was going to be pulling it all up the steepest, nastiest road in the world. And when he got to the top the drinking trough would very likely be empty.

The truth was that no one in that courtyard was happy. Despite her bravado Alex was frightened at the prospect of going back to Luma. Benn felt scared and Nella was terrified—she did not expect to see Alex again. Francina was convinced that everyone hated her and Louie felt that his whole world was upside down. He didn't want Alex to go. And yet he did, because Francina said that was the only chance to get Momma back. He clung on tight to the only certainty in his life—the pokkle.

While Benn checked Alex's hiding place—the long box on which the cart driver sat—Alex handed Nella her precious wallet containing the Hex cards. "It's not safe for me to take these to Luma," she said. "Can you look after them for me until . . . until I see you again?"

Nella gave Alex a strained smile and looked at the soft blue wallet in her hand, feeling a little in awe of it. Even she could feel the buzz of Enchantment emanating from it—there was something very special about Alex, and no mistake.

"Of course I can, Alex. I won't let them out of my sight. I promise. They will be here waiting for you. Always." Nella put the wallet into her apron pocket, where it sat comfortably next to the heavy little book she had been going to give Alex before Francina's arrival threw everything into disarray. And then, as if in return for the cards, she thrust a small cloth bag into Alex's hand. "Alex, dear, take these."

Alex tipped out a pack of seven hexagonal cards shaped exactly like her Hex cards. They were made of wood and each one was painted a different color of the rainbow. They looked like a child's toy. "They belonged to Sol,"

Nella explained. "He had them when he was a little boy. Show them to a Sentinel and say that these toys are what Zerra was talking about. Tell them she was playing a silly trick."

"Will Zerra be in trouble?" Louie asked, anxiously.

"Zerra started this, so she must take the consequences," Nella said sternly. "We can't make it right for everyone."

Louie nodded solemnly. That seemed fair to him. He would far rather have his mother and his two best sisters back than spiky, pinching Zerra anyway.

"Now, Alex," Nella said, "remember, if they ask where you've been, don't tell them you left Luma, because that will make you appear guilty. Think of somewhere you could have been in Luma where they wouldn't have found you." Nella enveloped Alex in a hug. "I will miss you, child. I will keep your beautiful Hex cards safe with me until we see you again . . . I pray all will be well with you." And then she broke away and ran back into the roundhouse.

Francina, following Nella's example, attempted an awkward hug. "Thank you, Alex," she said. "I know I've not been very nice to you sometimes. I . . . I'm sorry."

Alex shrugged Francina off. "Gotta go," she said. "Bye, Louie. See you soon, hey?"

Louie threw his arms around Alex. "Thank you for going to rescue Momma," he said, and thrust the pokkle into Alex's hands. "The pokkle wants to help."

"No, Louie, not the pokkle."

Louie's face crumpled and Alex relented. "Okay. It can go in the box that Benn sits on." The pokkle was not too pleased with the arrangement, but it did not resist when Alex placed it into what would soon be her hiding place too. The pokkle knew when not to push its luck.

Howard clattered out of the courtyard with Alex and Benn walking on either side of him. The donkey plodded miserably along the track through the lemon groves. "Do you think you'll get them to free your foster mother?" Benn said anxiously as soon as they were out of earshot.

"I don't know. But I'm going to try," Alex said.

"It's so dangerous. You're a Named person, remember? They'll arrest you as soon as they see you."

Alex grinned. "Well, I guess I'll just have to make sure they don't see me, won't I?"

Benn shook his head. "Can you really disappear?" he asked. "I mean, do a Fade like Gramma said Sol was always trying to do and never could?"

"Louie says I can, and I believe him. I think that's why the Hawke went away."

"But it's such a risk," Benn said. "Are you totally sure?"

Alex felt it was time for some straight talking. "Look, Benn, you're lucky. You know who you are, who your family is and where you belong. I don't know anything like that and I want to find out. Okay?"

"Okay, but why do you have to go to Luma for that?" Benn asked.

In the safety of the roundhouse, Alex had done some thinking. Mirram may have refused to tell her who her parents were, but even so she had carefully preserved the only connection Alex had with her past—her cards. Not only that, Mirram had clearly known how dangerous her cards were—why else would she have an escape rope—and yet even so, she had let Alex keep them. Mirram, Alex was beginning to realize, was not all bad. It seemed to Alex that Mirram might actually have a good reason for not telling her who her parents were—and the only reason was that one of Alex's parents was an Enchanter. Alex felt sure now that if she asked Mirram that question, Mirram would answer. "Mirram knows about my family. I know she does. And I want to ask her one last time," she told Benn. "So first I have to save her, because I won't be able to ask her anything if she's hanging up in a cage in the Vaults, will I?"

Benn sighed. "But she never told you before. Why would she now?"

"Because I'm different now. I'm stronger than Mirram. And I know the questions to ask."

They had now reached the scrubby, dry area beyond the irrigation system. Benn looked up to the city, with its pointed roofs tipped with silver and its high walls that teetered so precariously upon the top of the cliff. It looked like a giant prison to him. "Aren't you scared going back up there?" he asked.

"Of course I'm scared," Alex said. "I'd be crazy not to be."

They walked on in silence and soon reached the cold shadows that the Luma cliffs cast across the edge of the valley. They followed the well-worn track and some minutes later came to a long platform made of blocks of stone where a makeshift market was set up selling cheap clothes, food and drinks. Set back from the platform was a tall, redbrick building with lines of tiny windows and a faded sign above its door proclaiming it to be "Station Inn. Cheap Rooms. Vermin-Control Approved. Vacancies."

They stopped at the platform. Benn gave Howard his last handful of grass and filled up his bucket with water from a nearby tap. Alex sat on the edge, drinking from the flask of honey water Nella had given her for the journey. "I remember that place," she said, pointing to Station Inn.

"You've stayed there?" Benn asked.

"No. I don't think so. I just remember seeing it—so big, so busy, so strange." Alex shivered. A jumble of memories was flooding into her mind: steam, hissing, shouting, people pushing and shoving past her, feeling lost but trapped, and all the while wanting something so badly . . . but what? What *was* it she had wanted? She couldn't remember. All she could recall was the empty hollowness of *wanting*.

Benn took away Howard's water bucket and hung it on its hook at the back of the cart. "This is the old railway station for Luma," he said. "You must have been really little, because they stopped the train ten years ago now." Scuffing up the sandy ground with the heel of his boot, Benn uncovered a long piece of metal. The steel was surprisingly shiny and he knelt down and ran his hand over it. "So *smooth*," he murmured. He looked up at Alex. "This is the track that your train arrived on. There used to be a line from Rekadom that went all through the land, right across the desert to Seven Snake Forest, then out across the High Plains and along Lemon Valley. From here it went along the river, over the bridge to Lemon Dock out at the estuary." Benn glanced around and lowered his voice. "That's where the engine is now. Big Puffer, they used to call it. They were supposed to break it up, but no one could be bothered. So they left it to rot in a cave under the hills."

"That's sad," Alex said.

"I know, but not anymore. Jay and his girlfriend, Bella, are getting it going again."

"I'd love to see it," Alex said wistfully.

Benn grinned. "You already have. That was the monster you saw in your cards. Eating fire."

Alex stared at Benn in surprise. "Oh, I see! The monster in the cave." She shivered. "It felt so cold. And sad."

"I hope it won't be for much longer," Benn said. "Jay thinks he might get it going soon. I'd love to ride the Big Puffer one day. Gramma's been on it to Rekadom six times, she says. But of course there's no way anyone can get there now. Not that they would want to."

Alex knew all about Rekadom from school; she had even drawn pictures of its three towers perched above the ocean, guarding the land from marauders and keeping everyone safe. "Maybe I'd belong there," she said wistfully.

"No way," said Benn. "Gramma says it's a hundred times worse than up there." He jabbed his finger up toward Luma. "Alex, are you sure you want to go back there?"

Alex nodded. "As sure as I'll ever be."

"Okay. Come on then, Howard," said Benn. "Time for your favorite walk."

Howard, who had no appreciation of irony, eyed the track ahead with a dismal expression. Howard hated everything about the Luma Twist: its tight hairpin bends, the steep drop from the edges—Howard had a mortal fear of heights—and most of all its sandy surface that made his hooves skid and slide backward. It took a whole bunch of carrots to get the donkey moving, but slowly the lemon cart moved off and they all began the long, steep plod up the Luma Twist. The higher they climbed the more butterflies of anxiety Alex felt fluttering in her stomach. She could not help glancing up at the squat, square gatehouse of Sentinel Gate, with its massive iron sliding doors drawn open to show the dark, round shape of the archway into the town beyond. It looked—and felt—like a trap waiting to be sprung.

They stopped at a drinking trough one bend away from Sentinel Gate. Finding the trough empty, Benn poured the last of his own water into Howard's bucket and gave it to the donkey. "Last chance to turn around," he said to Alex.

"I know. But I'm going in there. You don't have to come if you don't want to."

"If you're going in, then I'm going in," Benn told her.

Five minutes later Alex was curled up inside the box beneath the driver's seat with the pokkle for company and Howard was trotting toward Sentinel Gate. As they approached, Benn read the sign over the gatehouse with more interest than usual. It said:

WELCOME TO LUMA

NO ENTRY TO BEGUILERS, ENCHANTERS,

CONJURORS AND CHILDREN THEREOF

PENALTY FOR ILLEGAL ENTRY: CAGED FOR LIFE

And as Howard clattered over the cobbles into the gloom of the Sentinel Gate, all Benn could think about were the words *Caged for Life*.

Was that what was going to happen to Alex?

CHAPTER 21

Lemons

THE LEMON CART CLATTERED INTO the shadows beneath the gatehouse, its wooden wheels bumping across the cobbles. Benn stared resolutely ahead at Howard's long ears—which had perked up considerably now that he was at the top of the hill—while a Sentinel checked his trader's pass, commented that he was "going to be popular with all them lemons," and then scooped up a handful for himself. Benn bit back a protest—he dared not get on the wrong side of a Sentinel today—and smiled through gritted teeth. To his relief the Sentinel waved him through and Ben drove the cart into the sunlight of the market-place. The place was unusually busy and there seemed to be an atmosphere of expectation in the air. Benn slipped down from the driving seat so he could lead Howard to his usual pitch on the far side of the square, and as he clattered along—hoping that Alex wasn't getting too bumped around—Benn saw a large poster in big red letters pasted on the wall. It read:

TRIAL
PRISONER MIRRAM D'ARBO, HARBORER OF
BEGUILERS AND PROMOTER OF ENCHANTMENT,
WILL BE TRIED TODAY AT 3 P.M. IN THE MARKETPLACE.
THE PRISONER'S PARADE BEGINS AT THE
VAULTS AT 2 P.M. PRECISELY.
NB: NO EGGS TO BE THROWN DUE TO SHORTAGE.

Benn checked the clock on the gatehouse tower behind him—it was a quarter to three.

"Gee-up, Howard!" He urged the donkey forward until they reached a quiet spot by a patch of dusty rosemary bushes. He looped Howard's reins around a bush, ran around to the back of the cart, pushed the lemons to one side and opened the lid to the driver's seat. A pungent smell wafted out, quickly followed by Alex, who leaped up, scrambled over the side and stood away from the cart fanning herself and taking deep breaths of fresh air. "That pokkle has a massive problem with gas. What is *wrong* with it?"

Benn had no time to discuss the finer details of the pokkle's digestive system. "Your foster mother is Mirram D'Arbo, right?" he asked.

"Yes. Why, what's happened?" Alex said, suddenly anxious.

"It's more what's *going* to happen," Benn said. "Her trial starts in"—he glanced back at the clock—"five minutes."

"Five *minutes*?"

"Yep. You got the fake cards?"

Alex nodded, trying not to panic. It was all happening so fast.

"Do you want the pokkle?"

"No, I do *not* want the pokkle, Benn. Thank you," Alex snapped back, irritable with nerves.

"Okay. Just asking." Benn closed the side of the box, leaving the pokkle alone with its noxious fumes.

Alex could see that everyone was gathering around the stage used two nights ago for the drummers. "I need to get over there right now," she said.

"I'll wait here, shall I?" Benn asked. "Just in case?"

Alex looked at Benn in panic. "In case of what?"

"I . . . I dunno. Good luck."

"Thanks," said Alex, and without a backward glance she slipped into the crowd. As she vanished from view it crossed Benn's mind that he might never see Alex again. He was about to take Howard along to their usual place when he found himself besieged with eager lemon buyers.

Two food crazes were doing the rounds of Luma: one for pancakes dripping with lemon juice and sugar and the other for lemon meringue pie—hence the egg shortage. Until Benn and his lemon cart had arrived unexpectedly that afternoon, there was not a lemon to be had in the town.

Benn wanted to keep a good supply of lemons in the cart in case he had to hide either Alex or her foster mother beneath them—there was not room for both in the box— and this did not go down well with his buyers. But he was determined to ration the lemons to "no more than four per person please . . . no sir, I cannot make an exception for people named Lemony . . . Hey, you've had four already, give those back!" But quite a few determined customers took more than their ration, for Benn kept glancing over the sea of heads to the stage over by the far wall.

Alex wriggled and pushed her way to the front of the crowd and was soon beside the stage, her hands resting on the rich red carpet that now covered it. To the left was a ramp, up which the prisoner's cage would be pushed once it had done its tour of shame through the town. Alex knew that would be happening to Mirram right now and she tried not to think of the filthy mess that was surely being thrown at her and the names she was being called. Instead, Alex concentrated on where she was right then. She was eye level with the ornate, bandy legs of three gold-painted chairs set along the back of the platform, which were, for now, empty. At the back of the stage where it met the wall, a long black curtain was draped, hiding the door that led directly to the judges' chambers, and to her right, at the edge of the stage, was a small gilt chair where Mirram's accuser would sit. Alex glared at it as fiercely as if Zerra were already sitting there.

A soft hissing from the crowd began and grew ever louder. Alex heard the words *shame . . . shame . . . shame . . . shame . . .* then the clatter of wheels upon cobbles and harsh shouts of "Make way for the prisoner! Make way!" Guards with batons pushed people away from the ramp and Alex heard a rumble and then what looked like a giant parrot's cage—complete with a large ring at the top where the bars met at a point—on four sturdy wheels came rattling up the ramp, with four guards pushing it. The cage came to rest so close to Alex that she could have reached out and touched it. Alex's heart did a flip of pity. Inside was Mirram cowering with her hands over her head, her once vibrant silks now spattered with rotten tomatoes and all kinds of dirt.

"Filthy cow, what a stink," someone behind Alex said loudly. It was true: the fastidious Mirram did not smell good. But Mirram did not react. She crouched against the bars, lost in her own world of terror.

A drum roll from an invisible drummer somewhere behind the black curtains at the back of the stage began and the crowd fell silent with expectation. Slowly, the curtains were drawn back to reveal an orange-painted doorway in the wall. The crowd watched as this swung open and three judges sashayed through, heads held high, staring straight ahead to keep their tall brushlike wigs of upswept white horsehair from tipping forward. Their orange silk robes, held fast with blue sashes, swished across the carpet as they glided toward their seats. But it was not the judges that took Alex's attention—it was her foster sister who followed them. *Like a little pet*, Alex thought. As the judges settled themselves on their seats like a trio of self-satisfied hens, Alex watched Zerra walk across to the little gilt chair on the edge of the stage and nervously sit down so that she was facing her mother in her cage on the opposite corner of the stage. Alex noticed that despite Zerra's new Junior Sentinel jacket—dark blue silk with orange flashes and sprinkled with some very fancy gold buttons—her foster sister looked very ill at ease and kept her eyes firmly cast down, not once daring to look up at her mother or, indeed, at anyone.

The drum roll morphed into a menacingly slow beat and Alex began to feel very nervous. She looked at the judges, trying to work out what mood they were in, but their stern, chiseled features gave nothing away. Alex thought she had never seen such a coldhearted bunch of people in her life. She took the fake cards from her pocket and stared at them in dismay. What chance did these pathetic pieces of painted wood have of convincing those hard-faced officials of Mirram's—and therefore of her own—innocence? None, Alex thought.

Another drum roll took Alex by surprise. "Prisoner will stand!" the guards shouted in unison. Mirram did not move and one of the guards pushed his baton into the cage and jabbed at her. She staggered to her feet and clung to the bars for support. Alex felt she could not bear it a moment longer.

The judge in the middle began to read out the charges in a bored drone. "Prisoner Mirram D'Arbo . . . Harboring a Beguiler . . . knowingly importing Cards of Prophecy . . . Corruption of the Minds of the Young . . . Assisting Escape of Wanted Persons . . ." The voice continued relentlessly and Alex clutched the cards so hard that their points stuck into her palm.

At last the judge reached the end of her drone and the shorter one to her right stepped forward. He looked down at the audience with distaste—as though, Alex thought, he had opened the door to his cellar and found a crowd of rats having a party. "All charges have been proven," he boomed. "However, we in Luma believe in a fair trial, and so now call upon all present to show any evidence to support the prisoner's plea of 'not guilty.'"

Alex took a deep breath and yelled out, "I have evidence!"

There was a collective gasp and those next to her moved away in case anyone might think it was they who had shouted. Alex saw Zerra staring down at her in shock, which was, to Alex's satisfaction, quickly replaced by terror. Mirram too was staring at Alex in confusion, and then, as she recognized who had spoken, her eyes opened wide in amazement and Alex saw real concern flood into them. It was then that Alex understood that Mirram really did care for her, and it gave her courage. The crowd stepped back from Alex as she made her way to the steps at the side of the stage and climbed up onto the stage. She paused for a moment to control her nerves, walked past Zerra without a glance and stopped in front of the middle judge.

The judge stared at her, dumbfounded.

Trying—but not succeeding—to stop her hand from trembling, Alex held out Sol's toy cards. "Your Honor," she said. "This is my evidence to show that Mirram D'Arbo is not guilty. I am Alex, foster daughter of Mirram D'Arbo. My foster sister, Zerra D'Arbo Named me for possessing Cards of Prophecy. But these cards are nothing but a toy to teach the colors of the rainbow. Your Honor, Mirram D'Arbo is innocent. She was Harboring no one. And I am no Beguiler." Alex swung around and pointed at her foster sister, whose mouth hung open in astonishment. "Zerra D'Arbo is a liar!"

The crowd below gasped and Zerra leaped to her feet, yelling, "No I'm not. Those aren't your cards, Alex. I know what I saw. *You're* the liar!"

Alex quailed. The problem was, Zerra was right—she was indeed a liar.

"Give me those cards," the judge demanded. Trembling, Alex handed them over. The judge flipped through them, clattering them like castanets, and then looked up with an expression of distaste. "You are Alex D'Arbo?"

"Yes. I am," Alex answered, even though she never thought of herself as a D'Arbo.

"Alex D'Arbo. Your name is known to us. You are on our Watch Register due to suspicious behavior in the marketplace. Your foster sister, however, is a Junior Sentinel and has no suspicious behavior to cloud her name. We therefore find her statement to be true and yours to be false. Guards, arrest this Beguiler!"

Alex saw Zerra's smug little smile, she saw Mirram's horror, and in slow motion, it seemed to her, she saw the four guards advancing on her from all corners of the stage. It was now, Alex thought, that she would truly discover whether it was her Enchantment that produced a Fade or her Hex cards. Alex focused on the judge, channeling her fear, and as she began to feel her boundaries shifting she plunged into the sensation of losing herself and becoming part of the world around her. When the crowd erupted in screams Alex knew she had done it. She dodged an oncoming guard and brushed against his sleeve. "She's here!" he yelled. "Here!" The crowd began to surge forward, those in the front clambering onto the

stage, screaming, "Get her! Get her! Get the Beguiler!"
Deciding to let the oncoming horde do their work for
them, the judges hurried away through the curtain and
locked the door behind them.

Alex watched the murderous throng with horror. In a
crowd her Fade would be useless—an invisible girl still
takes up space. She retreated to the back of the stage,
looking desperately for a clear path out. Suddenly, she
saw Benn and the lemon cart just beyond the ramp—he
was yelling, "Alex! Alex! Where are you?" Twisting and
turning like a snake, slipping by people who jumped at
her touch and shouted, "Here! She's here!" and then set
their arms flailing like windmills grabbing at thin air,
Alex leaped down from the stage and raced over to the
lemon cart.

Alex grabbed Benn's sleeve. "Benn," she whispered,
"I'm here!"

Benn grinned with relief. "Great!" he said. "Get in the
cart. Let's go."

But Alex knew she could not leave Mirram to her fate.
"Mirram," she said. "We have to take Mirram."

Benn looked up at the stage, which was milling with
people, hands outstretched, searching for the invisible
Alex. It looked like a weird game of blindman's buff without the blindfolds. "That's crazy," he said. "There's no
way we can—"

Alex stopped him. "Yes there is. The rope. You tie one

end to the cart and give me the other end. And the pok-kle." She flipped open the top of the driver's seat.

The pokkle leaped out, pleased to be free at last, but it was grabbed by an invisible hand. The pokkle decided it had had enough. It arched back and aimed a bite at the invisible thing, only to hear a familiar laugh. "Hey, pok-kle, it's me. Now, I'm going to hold you and you can bite whoever you want to."

Alex moved quickly up the ramp holding the pokkle, which gave the impression of flying, right down to flut-tering its stubby wings in excitement. Clearing a path for Alex, it took its first nip of a fat red forearm. It was rewarded with a shriek and immediately snapped at a different arm, which was a little scrawny but just as satis-fying. And so Alex and the pokkle progressed until they reached the cage in which dwelt the pokkle's former pro-vider of honey raisins. Alex put the pokkle on top of the cage, where it amused itself by biting anyone who came near. Meanwhile, no one noticed a rope apparently tying itself to one of the bars of the cage.

Leaving the pokkle to fend people off Mirram, Alex raced back to Benn. "All done," she said, breathlessly. "Let's go!"

Benn grinned with relief at the sound of Alex's voice right beside him. He swung himself up onto the driver's seat and leaned down toward the voice. An invisible hand took his and Benn felt Alex jump up beside him. He flicked the reins over Howard's dusty back, calling out, "Home, Howard, home! Fast as you can!"

Howard set off like a rocket. The rope between the lemon cart and Mirram's cage jerked tight and shot forward. A shriek came from the occupant of the cage as she was thrown back against the bars and the pokkle was catapulted unceremoniously into the air. The wheeled cage hurtled down the ramp, sending people leaping out of its way. Mirram clung to the bars, eyes wide with shock, watching her tormentors scattering. "Ai-yai-yai!" she yelled as the cage bumped over the cobbles, her head hitting its pointy top with each bump and with every lemon that tumbled down and rolled beneath the wheels.

Still deep in her Fade, Alex looked back at the cage lurching along behind them, afraid that it might topple at any moment. But Mirram was instinctively doing the right thing—she was crouched on the floor, keeping the center of gravity low as four pairs of wooden wheels clattered across the marketplace and Howard galloped for freedom.

They had a clear run to the Sentinel gatehouse, but to Benn's dismay he saw the three judges walking briskly toward it. Alex saw them too, and as Howard hurtled past, the judges were caught in a hail of well-aimed lemons, which seemed to be hurling themselves through the air of their own accord. Alex burst out laughing as they went running for cover. She sent two wigs tumbling to the ground and scored a direct hit on a posterior as the smallest judge bent to retrieve his wig.

Benn, however, wasn't laughing at all. Two strong-looking guards were pulling at the massive town gates and they were closing fast.

"Alex!" Benn yelled above the clatter. "They're closing the gates!"

Alex wheeled around and the lemons began to fly forward now, landing in a yellow barrage upon the guards. As the lemons unerringly found their mark, the gates lost their momentum and Howard cantered full tilt into the archway, his hooves echoing tinnily against the brick walls. Another fusillade of lemons found their target and the closing gates ground to a halt, leaving only a narrow gap that Alex feared was not wide enough for the cart. But Benn knew better. With unerring accuracy he sent the cart hammering through with no more than a hair's breadth to spare on either side. At the last moment a quick-thinking guard with a knife leaped forward to try to cut the rope between the cart and the cage, but a well-aimed lemon sent the knife flying from his hand. With a shout of triumph from Alex, they were free—for it was forbidden for any Sentinel to venture outside the gates of Luma.

Howard took a sharp turn to the left and they were off, racing down the hill with Benn pulling hard on the brake to stop the cart from overtaking Howard, the clattering cage bouncing along behind the lemon cart like a small dog trying to keep up. As the cavalcade rattled around the bends, Benn became aware of people lining the walls above, staring down at them. "They're watching us," he told Alex.

Alex glanced up and saw the angry face of a Sentinel staring down. "They can watch all they like, but they won't see me," she said, laughing.

Mirram's cage bounced behind the cart, clattering and bumping into the back. With every bump Mirram let out a loud shriek. Benn looked back at it anxiously, afraid that the weight of the cage would smash the back of the cart to pieces. But he was pulling on the wheel brake with one hand and had Howard's reins in the other and there was nothing he could do about it. "Can you hang on to the cage?" he asked Alex. "Stop it from bumping?"

"Okay!" Alex scrambled over the few remaining lemons that were rolling around the floor of the cart, and the next time the cage banged up again the cart, accompanied by a wild scream from Mirram, she grabbed one of the thick iron bars with both hands and held it tight. The cage's wild push-pull motion stopped at once and it settled down to follow the cart. "Are you all right?" Alex called down to Mirram, forgetting about her Fade. Mirram stared up at the space that Alex inhabited and gave a low moan.

It was now that Alex realized they were missing a

small, feathered member of the rescue team, and she felt sad to think of the pokkle left behind, alone in Luma. However, up in the marketplace the pokkle gave Alex not a moment's thought—it had found the honey-raisin stall, upended a jar and gulped down as many as it could before the stallholder noticed and sent it flying on its way. It was now lying beneath a rosemary bush feeling somewhat unwell.

The pokkle was not, however, the only member of the family left in Luma. From the top of the wall, anxiously biting her lip, Zerra watched her mother clatter her way to freedom. Suddenly there came a peremptory tap upon her shoulder and she spun around to see the stony faces of three Sentinels regarding her.

It was the middle one who spoke. "Zerra D'Arbo. Come with us."

CHAPTER 22
Parrot's Cage

"PARROT'S CAGE," SAID DANNY.

"Where?" asked Hagos, surveying the disparate group of stalls on the platform of the old Luma Station.

"Here," said Danny, pointing to his mouth. "The bottom of a parrot's cage, to be precise. A parrot's cage that has not been cleaned out for weeks, if you must know. And my tongue is stuck to it."

"All right, all right. I'll get us a drink," Hagos said. "But we must be up in Luma before they close the gates. I don't want to be down here in the Hauntings tonight."

Danny threw himself down onto the dusty platform and lay like a starfish, his eyes closed, savoring the wonderful sensation of not walking. Once the last of the Air-Weavers was safely behind them, Hagos had set such a fast pace through Lemon Valley that Danny had had to trot to keep up. Hagos had refused to stop for even a second and had walked barefoot with an ease that had made Danny, in his boots, feel clumsy.

"Orange water," came Hagos's voice from above, as he handed Danny a cool stone bottle and sat down beside him on the edge of the platform. Danny drank the contents down in one long gulp. He thought that he had never tasted anything quite as good.

"For the hill up to Luma," Hagos said, handing over a waxed-paper package. "Duck and orange pie. We're going to have to move fast. They close the gates at sunset."

Danny looked gloomily at the hairpin bends that wound up the almost vertical face of the cliff. "We've got time to eat the pies first," he said.

"You can eat your pie on the way," Hagos told him.

Danny clarified the matter. "*You* can eat your pie on the way. *I'm* eating mine here."

"I am leaving now for Luma," Hagos said frostily.

"Okeydokey," said Danny, taking a large bite of his pie.

Spluttering with annoyance, Hagos jumped down from the platform and strode away. Danny, equally annoyed, watched him go. He'd give him a few minutes, then he'd catch up with the old grump, he thought. But as Hagos reached the foot of Luma Twist, he performed a remarkably athletic leap backward, and a second later Danny saw a donkey cart emerge from the foot of the Twist at breakneck speed. It narrowly avoided Hagos and careered across the wide, dusty expanse that lay in front of the platform. But it was not the speed of the cart that took Danny's attention, it was what followed the cart: an iron contraption about five feet high shaped like a parrot's cage, which clattered along on four battered wheels. In the cage crouched a woman in rags, clinging to the bars, staring ahead with an expression of utter shock. In the back of the cart Danny saw a wild-eyed girl, clinging onto the cage, holding the whole bizarre train together.

"Hey!" someone on the platform yelled. "That's cruel. Let her go!"

"Cut the rope! Poor creature!"

But another demurred. "That's a prison cage. Looks like he's rescuing her. Brave lad."

The cart swung onto the dirt track and clattered toward the watchers. A few raised a cheer, which the boy driving acknowledged with a wave.

Danny stared at the girl in the back. There was something odd about her—a certain fuzziness around the edges. As the cart hurtled by, the girl caught his eye and Danny coolly returned her gaze. The girl looked shocked and turned away, but not before Danny had felt goose bumps running down his spine. He'd seen that gaze before—staring up at him from the face of a cliff.

"Sheesh," Danny muttered to himself as he watched the cart heading away along the wide track toward the distant orange groves. "She can't be his daughter, can she?" But Danny already knew the answer. Suddenly back on duty, he slipped down from the platform and ran across to Hagos, who waited for him.

"I see you've come to your senses," Hagos said somewhat ungraciously.

"You mean I've *used* my senses," Danny shot back. "How many people did you see in that cart?"

"Why?" asked Hagos, still irritable.

"Look, Mr. RavenStarr. Just remember why you asked me to come with you. How many did you see?"

"Well, there was a boy driving the cart and that poor woman in the cage."

"That was all?"

"Of course. Now let's get up to Luma before it's too late."

"I think it already is too late," Danny said.

"What on earth do you mean?" asked Hagos.

"What I mean is it's too late to go to Luma to find your daughter. Because she has already left Luma. In that cart."

Hagos stared at Danny. "Are you serious?"

"Never more so," Danny said. "There was a girl in the back of the cart hanging on to the cage, and *you* couldn't see her. She had fuzzy edges typical of a very powerful

Fade, just like the one you did to test me. And she knew she was doing it, too, because it freaked her out when she realized I'd seen her."

Hagos looked stunned. "No. It can't be."

"Whyever not?"

"What did she look like?"

"I told you. A bit fuzzy around the edges."

"No, I mean her *features*. What color hair? Eyes? What was she *like*?"

"Dark hair, curly, with a thick green headband. Quite small and skinny. But strong. She seemed kind of lively. You know, lots of energy."

Hagos nodded. "Yes, yes. She was always a little bundle of energy. And dark hair. A mass of curls."

Danny was surprised at the sudden tenderness in Hagos's voice.

"So perhaps we—I mean, you—could follow the cart tracks?" Hagos asked tentatively. "We could see where . . . where she lives?"

Danny cast a longing glance at the Station Inn and its faded sign proclaiming "Vacancies." "It will be dark soon. It's hard to follow tracks in the dark. Best wait till morning."

"I don't want to wait," said Hagos. "I want to go now. *Right now.*"

CHAPTER 23
Tracks

"THAT BOY ON THE PLATFORM eating a pie," Alex was saying as Howard plodded wearily on, "he saw through the Fade."

Benn looked surprised. "How do you know?"

"He was staring at me. So I stared back. And our eyes met."

Benn laughed. "Romantic, huh?"

"Benn!" Alex protested. "That is not what I meant and you know it."

"Sorry." Benn grinned. "So you think he saw through your Fade?"

"I know he did. And more than that—I think he was the boy on the Hawke."

Benn looked puzzled. "But . . . but he can't be. Why isn't he on the Hawke?"

"It *was* him, I know it. He had the same long red hair. And you don't forget someone who's tried to kill you, do you?"

"I guess not," Benn said.

Howard dawdled on along the sandy tracks, and as the shadows grew ever longer, Benn began to be afraid they might not make it home by dark. At the turnoff from the Santa Pesca road he said, "Let's get off and walk. It will be less weight for Howard."

Benn walked beside the weary donkey, urging him on with bunches of fresh grass snatched from the side of the track. Alex went back to talk to her foster mother, but with little success. Mirram just clung to the bars, staring ahead as if in a trance. It was at the mention of Louie that she first reacted. Desperately searching for something to say, Alex said, "Louie will be so happy to see you."

Mirram looked agitated. "No! Not like this."

"He won't mind," Alex reassured Mirram.

"*I* mind," Mirram retorted, glaring at Alex.

Alex grinned. The spiky old Mirram was still there.

At last the perimeter wall of the roundhouse came into view and Alex ran ahead to warn Nella to keep Louie out of the way. At the sight of Alex coming into the kitchen,

Nella gave a delighted squeal, swept her up into a hug and spun her around in delight. Alex had never had such a welcome in all her life. "Oh, sweetheart," Nella said, "I was so worried. But you're safe. So tell me, how was it? Did they let your foster mother go free?"

"We're fine," said Alex, trying to get a word in. "Benn's on his way with Mirram."

"Oh, you brought her back with you? Well, that's lovely. I sent Francina and Louie over to Jay's girlfriend, Bella. She lives on the farm just down the road. I thought it best, just in case things didn't go so well. I'll run and tell them."

"Best not," Alex said. "Mirram doesn't want Louie to see her in, um, in the cage."

"Cage?" asked Nella. The clattering of wheels coming into the courtyard sent Nella to the door. She gave a gasp of shock and her hand flew to her mouth in dismay. "You *towed* her? Like *that*? All the way? I know you don't like your foster mother very much, but that wasn't very nice, was it? Oh, that poor woman." Nella ran out to the cart, leaving Alex fuming. Why did anything to do with Mirram always seem to be her fault?

Ten minutes later Alex received the first apology of her life. "I'm so sorry, Alex. I had no idea she was trapped in that awful cage," Nella said, unable to take her eyes off what she considered to be an abomination parked in the middle of her kitchen.

Inside the warm, domestic space the cage looked even more brutal. Nella thought it looked like a massive parrot cage, which she had always considered a cruelty to parrots. To put a human being inside such a thing was barbarous. Nella looked down at the human, crouched and clinging to the bars as if she expected the cage to take off on yet another headlong flight behind yet another reckless donkey. "I don't understand why it doesn't have a door," Nella said, shaking her head. "How did she get in?"

Benn felt uncomfortable talking about Mirram as though she wasn't there, but Mirram had so far refused to even look at them. "They put her—I mean, Mrs. D'Arbo—in the cage and then welded the last bar in place," he whispered. "That's what they do. The sausage stall person told me."

"They told us at school that if they put you in a cage you never got out," Alex said quietly. "But I never believed it. Until now."

Nella was aghast. "That's *awful*. You mean she has to do . . . well . . . *everything* in there? In public? In that tiny space? You wouldn't treat an animal like that. There's hardly room to turn around." Nella knelt down beside the bars and reached in to take Mirram's hand. It lay unresponsive in hers. "Mrs. D'Arbo, may I call you Mirram?" she asked.

Mirram looked up and nodded slowly.

"Mirram, I am so sorry for what has happened to you.

But you are safe here. We will get you out of this . . . this *monstrosity* as soon as we can."

Very slowly two big tears ran down Mirram's grubby face. "There, there now," Nella said, patting Mirram's hand. "There, there."

Alex knew she ought to comfort Mirram, but she wasn't sure how. She decided on the well-tried tactic she used whenever Mirram came home in a bad mood—which had been most days. "Would you like a cup of tea?" she asked.

"Yes, please," Mirram said, her voice no more than a thin whisper.

Alex was so astounded at the pathetic "please"— Mirram never said "please"—that tears sprang to her eyes in sympathy.

Nella felt as tearful as Alex. "Let's get that kettle going, shall we?" she said briskly, and hurried away to busy herself with the stove, the teapot, a couple of lemons and a huge stone jar of honey, chopping at the lemons as if they were the bars of the cage, affronted by the inhumanity that had been brought to her kitchen.

They sat around the cage with Mirram, trying to act as though they drank tea with a person in a giant parrot cage every day. Mirram gulped hers down fast and Nella refilled her mug twice. "I don't suppose they gave you anything to drink in there?" Nella asked. Mirram shook her head. She was looking, Nella thought, a little uncomfortable.

"Benn, dear," Nella said, "I think Mirram would like to be alone for a while."

"Oh. Why's that?" Benn asked.

Alex knew why—Mirram needed to pee. She linked her arm through Benn's and said, "Let's go find a saw, shall we?"

Nella prided herself on her well-equipped and tidy shed. "The saws are on the back wall." She looked out of the window. "Don't be too long. The sun will be going down soon."

"The sun will be going down soon," Hagos said a little anxiously. He and Danny were at a small turnoff with a signpost on which pieces of wood bearing various names of farms and families had been nailed in a haphazard fashion. Danny was crouched on the ground inspecting some scuffmarks in the dirt. "This way," Danny said. He looked up and grinned. "It's easy now, it's only the one cart along here."

Hagos looked dubiously down at the tracks. "Are you sure?"

"Mr. RavenStarr, I do know what I'm doing. Okay?"

"Okay," Hagos said meekly.

Mollified, Danny explained, "You see, the tracks are unmistakable. Here are the narrower wheels of the cage in between the wider, heavier ones of the cart. And here, look, the boy is walking beside the donkey and the girl beside the cage."

"Where?" Hagos asked.

"Where what?"

"Where is the girl walking? Show me the prints. Please."

Danny pointed to some light scuff marks in the dust. "These must be hers. I noticed the boy was barefoot, but here, you see, is a shoe—a small foot. The girl was in the cart holding on to the cage when I saw her and of course the boy was in the cart too. So it looks like they both got off at the same time. Perhaps the donkey was tired."

Hagos stared at the footprints, now quite clear to him in the sand. "I can't believe that is *her*," he said in a half whisper. "She's so big. Not a baby anymore."

"I should hope not," Danny said. "It would be very weird if she still was."

"She'd be eleven and a half now," Hagos murmured.

"Yes. That would be about right," Danny said. He could not get the image of the girl staring up at him from the cliff out of his mind. *He had nearly killed Hagos's daughter.*

Hagos looked at Danny sharply. "There's something else. What is it?"

Danny's mouth went dry. He swallowed hard. "It was her. Your daughter. On the cliff. She was the one I was meant to . . . *you know*."

"Kill?" said Hagos.

Danny nodded.

"But you didn't. And because you didn't she is still walking this earth." Hagos looked down at the precious tracks in the dust. "Thank you," he murmured.

They set off a few minutes later, Danny noticing how Hagos carefully walked next to his daughter's footprints. "What's your daughter's name?" he asked.

"I wonder. I would love to know."

Danny was confused. "But you must know her name."

"We Enchanters don't name our children. They choose their own name on their seventh birthday. It is such an imposition to name someone without their consent, do you not think?"

Danny thought that made a lot of sense. He liked his name, but his mother had once confided that she had wished to call him Cedric. So much more refined, she had said. Danny was very relieved his father had refused to consider it. "But you must have called her something?" he asked.

"Oh yes. Everyone did that. You used a baby name until they were seven." Hagos sighed. "I do wish Pearl had been able to go with the child. Such a cruel parting."

"So who *did* your wife give her to?"

"If I knew that, I'd know where to find her, wouldn't I?" Hagos said sharply.

Danny let the riposte pass; he could see that Hagos was

upset. "Well, I guess you'll find out soon enough," he said soothingly. "Come on, the sun will be setting soon."

Danny set a brisk pace, following the track as it skirted the edges of innumerable lemon and orange groves until at last the wheel marks and footprints turned off down an even narrower track that followed the riverbank and sported just the one sign: "Lau: The Roundhouse Groves."

CHAPTER 24
Twilight Terrors

MIRRAM—CLEAN AND SWEET-SMELLING AFTER Nella's ministrations and immersed in one of her large, floral lemon-picking dresses—was sitting hunched up in the cage while Benn sawed energetically at one of the bars. He had barely scratched the surface. "I don't know what's wrong with this stupid saw," he said to Nella as she came downstairs from Sealing the shutters.

"That, Benn Markham, is my best pruning saw," Nella said, quietly locking the front door and dropping its big key deep into her pocket. She inspected the saw's now blunt teeth. "It won't work on metal; it's a soft, gentle saw, this one. You need a hacksaw—the D-shaped ones with the little blades—from the rack above."

Benn felt annoyed. If Gramma would let him help Jay sometimes, then he would have known he'd needed a hacksaw—and what one looked like. "I'll go get one," he said.

"It's too late now," said Nella. "I've locked and Sealed the door, and the sun is setting. It will have to be tomorrow." She went and knelt down beside the cage. "I'm so sorry, Mirram. We can't get you out tonight, but we'll do it first thing tomorrow. I promise."

Reunited with her Hex cards, Alex was sitting silently at the table, clicking them into a pile, feeling their comforting warmth in her hands. The excitement and sheer terror of the day had evaporated, leaving her feeling empty and sad. Nothing had changed. Tomorrow she would still be leaving Nella and Benn for some lonely orphanage in a strange land. She would be replaced by Francina and Louie and they could all play happy families with Nella and Benn and forget about her. Alex stared at Mirram angrily, wondering why she had gone to all the trouble of rescuing her. Mirram had never wanted her, her real parents hadn't wanted her and now Nella and Benn didn't want her either. Everything was awful—*totally and utterly awful*. Alex made a decision—if she wasn't wanted here she would go now, when *she* chose, not when it was convenient for everyone else. She scraped her chair back and got to her feet.

Nella eyed her warily. "Alex? Are you all right?"

Alex spun around, sending her chair clattering to the floor. "What do you care whether I'm all right or not?" she demanded. She ran to the door and pulled at it. It would not budge. "Let me out!" she yelled. "Let me out!"

Nella hurried over to her. "Alex, the Twilight Terrors have come over you. This is how you felt last night, remember?"

Alex stared at Nella. "No! I want to go. Right now. You can't keep me here. I'm not a prisoner. I'm not!"

Nella put her arms around Alex and, despite her struggling, held her tight. "There, there," she said, stroking Alex's dusty curls. "There, there now. It's all right, Alex. You are safe here. We all love you, Alex. We really do." Nella looked over to Mirram, hoping she would add a few soothing words. But Mirram stared stonily ahead as if embarrassed by her foster daughter's outburst.

Nella's calmness seeped into Alex's consciousness, dampening down the fear and anger that had overwhelmed her. Alex allowed herself to be led away from the door and sat down at the table with Nella's shawl wrapped around her. Nella stayed with Alex holding her hand, murmuring, "You're not alone, Alex. We're here with you. We're here."

"We're here!" Danny said, stopping outside the archway into the courtyard.

Hagos looked doubtfully up at the dark and solid

cylinder of the roundhouse. "It looks deserted," he said. "All the shutters are closed."

"Well, it's getting dark now. And there's the cart—look. They must be here," Danny said, pointing to Howard's cart, which was standing outside a line of outbuildings on the far side of the courtyard.

Hagos looked around the courtyard uneasily. "You know, I never imagined her living in a place like this. I always thought of her being up in Luma. I suppose that means it's safe down here after all."

"Let's hope so," Danny said. "Are you going to knock on the door or am I?"

Hagos seemed nervous. "I did a Twilight Manifestation for this valley," he said in a low voice. "Pearl was dead by then. Belamus made it a condition of my own release. I Engendered a Night Wraith. Nasty thing, it was. Drawn to anyone with even the smallest whisper of Enchantment about them. It was a nightmare making it, and the vile thing nearly got me a couple of times. But I managed to coax it into a flask and handed it over to Belamus. To my amazement, he actually kept his word and let me go."

"First time for everything," Danny said dryly.

"Belamus was no fool. He knew that Engendering the Night Wraith used up most of my powers. I did wonder if that was the real reason he asked me to do it, and that he never actually intended to use the Wraith. So if she . . . my daughter . . . lives here, then I'm right. The Night Wraith is still stuck in its flask in Rekadom. Although there's a very odd atmosphere here . . ."

Danny was losing patience with Hagos's dithering. It had been an exhausting day and all he wanted now was to be invited into a warm kitchen and sat down to a farmhouse supper while Hagos had a happy reunion with his daughter. He figured he'd earned it. And so Danny strode across the colored bands of cobbles to the studded front door. "Are you going to knock or am I?" he demanded.

Hagos hung back, uncertain.

Danny lost patience. He picked up a loose cobble and with it he gave three loud knocks upon the door.

Knock, knock, knock.

Everyone in the kitchen jumped. "Quick, Alex, let's get you upstairs," said Nella. Alex, still shaky from the Twilight Terrors, allowed herself to be hurried up the stairs.

"What about *me*?" came a petulant wail from the cage.

"Me, me, me," Nella muttered under her breath. "That's all that matters, isn't it?"

Alex smiled. She was pleased to see that Nella was getting the hang of Mirram. Nella threw open the door to Benn's room and Alex slipped gratefully inside.

Nella put her hand into her apron pocket and brought out the little blue book she had taken from her desk that morning. "I was going to give this to you this morning but then Francina came and it went right out of my mind," she said, pressing it into her hand. "This is Sol's little book. He called it a codex, I think. Whatever that is. He brought it with him when he fled Rekadom. I would like you to have it, Alex."

Alex looked down at the book in wonder. It was tiny, no bigger than her hand, and the soft leather that bound it showed some of the symbols that would occasionally flash across her cards when she first laid them out. And stamped across the front were three big faded gold letters: *HEX*. Tears sprang into her eyes—no one had ever given her such a thoughtful gift before. "Oh, Nella. Thank you. But I can't take this. It belonged to your Sol."

"I have a feeling that it belongs to you far more than it ever belonged to Sol," Nella said. "And it goes with your cards. I think they work together in some way. I've no idea how, but I'm sure you will understand it, Alex."

Alex gazed at the little book nestling in her palm. "It is so beautiful," she breathed.

"And heavy too for such a tiny thing," Nella said. "I like to think that's because of all the knowledge stored inside it."

Another loud bang came from the kitchen below, followed by a wail of fear from Mirram. "Oh dear," Nella said, "I suppose I can't leave our guest all alone. I'd better go down. Are you all right, Alex?"

Alex realized she was. Nella had hugged the Twilight

Terrors away and the thick shutters on the tiny windows made her feel safe and secure. But most of all, the little book in her hand felt like a friend. She was alone no more.

Alex settled down on her cushions. With a strange sense of something significant about to happen, she tentatively opened the codex. A subtle scent drifted out, dusty and musty with a hint of sandalwood and she felt a pang of wistfulness. It reminded her of something, but she could not think what. She sat for some seconds, breathing in the scent, trying to catch hold of an elusive memory, but the more she tried, the further it seemed to slip away. Slowly, she leafed through the tissue-thin pages, but to her disappointment she found that the tiny, spidery writing that filled them made no sense at all: it was no more than an unintelligible series of spiky zigzags. At the back of the book matters were even worse—a clump of pages was actually stuck together, sealed with a blue wax that shimmered like a butterfly wing. On the front of these pages was an empty T-shaped pocket with yet more indecipherable writing around it. Alex picked at the edge of the wax to see if she could loosen the pages, but they seemed to shrink away beneath her finger. "Sorry," she whispered.

Alex turned again to the front of the codex and on the inside of the cover she now saw an empty pocket, four-sided and exactly the same size as her Hex cards. Alex smiled—she knew what this pocket was for. She slipped her cards out of their wallet and dropped them into the pocket. At once they burst into a brilliant blue so bright that she gasped in surprise.

Fearful that the light might attract attention from outside, Alex pulled the quilt over her head. In the softness of her quilt-cavern she found herself surrounded by the buzz of Enchantment and the brilliance of a deep blue light. Slowly she turned the tissue-thin pages of the book, and this time she found that the spiky words all made sense.

Entranced, Alex read about one wonder after another. There were her own Hex cards and their mysterious companion, something called the Tau. Then there was something called a Manifest, and complex instructions on how to navigate using it. As the book progressed, darker things appeared upon its pages: *the Harken and the Hawke, the Mind of the Jackal* and *the Zinging of the Xin.* At last Alex reached the sealed pages and found she could now read the words written around the empty T-shaped pocket: "One is One, Two is One, and Tau is Three." And below: "One to make it. Three to break it."

Alex looked at this for a long time, feeling as though she was on the brink of understanding something very important, although she was not sure what. But one thing she was sure of—here was a whole new world, and it was one to which she truly did belong.

CHAPTER 25
Wraith Attack

"ANYONE THERE?" DANNY SHOUTED.

"It's speaking!" said Nella. "Oh. I feel quite strange. That sounds like Sol."

"Oh, Gramma . . . it can't be Sol. Can it?"

"No. No, it can't be," Nella said.

Benn thought she didn't sound too sure.

"I know you're in there!" Danny yelled, losing patience.

"Ooooh!" wailed Mirram. "They've come for me. They've come to take me back to Luma."

"Nonsense," said Nella briskly. "No Sentinel ever sets foot out of Luma."

Another yell sent Mirram wailing in fear. "Hide me! You have to hide me!"

Nella felt exasperated. How did Mirram expect her to hide a giant parrot cage sitting in the middle of her kitchen?

"I'll do it, Gramma," Benn said, and with a flourish he pulled the tablecloth up into the air and threw it over the cage. "There," he said, grinning. "Hidden."

Nella suppressed a giggle. "Silly boy," she whispered. But then a great thud upon the door took her smile away.

"It's no good," Hagos said. "The place is clearly deserted."

"It can't be," Danny insisted. "The cart's here. Where else would they be? And I'm sure there's someone in there. I heard a voice."

"So why isn't anyone answering?" Hagos demanded.

"How would I know?" Danny said snappily.

"I am beginning to think, Mr. Dark, that you don't know much at all," Hagos retorted. "I don't know why I let myself believe you and your so-called tracking skills. Indeed, it is my opinion that this had been a wild goose chase."

Danny had had enough. He was footsore, tired and as disappointed as Hagos was that no one would answer the door. Cobble still in his hand, Danny rounded angrily on

Hagos. "I don't give a monkey's nose for your opinion, you old fool. I'm off." With that Danny hurled the cobble to the ground and sent it bouncing across the yard.

"It's throwing cobbles," Nella whispered. "I don't like this. It's even worse than when it came for Sol."

"It's not getting Alex," Benn said fiercely. "I won't let it."

"Neither will I, sweetheart . . . shh . . ." Nella put her finger to her lips. "More shouting. Perhaps we can hear what it's saying this time." Nella got up, tiptoed to the door. She came right back and thrust her hands over her grandson's ears. "I won't have you hearing those kinds of words," she said. "What a foulmouthed thing it is, to be sure. Disgraceful."

"Don't you swear at me, Dark," Hagos was telling Danny, who was in the archway delivering his parting tirade. Danny made a rude sign with his fingers and strode out into the rapidly darkening lemon grove beyond, but as he reached the first tree he heard a wild ululating scream of fear. He stopped dead and the hairs on the back of his neck rose. Danny had heard a scream like that only once before—in his final live practice session with the Hawke when he had been forced to dive the raptor onto a prisoner.

Danny turned and ran back through the arch.

* * *

Inside the kitchen, Benn whispered, "It sounds terrified. I feel almost sorry for it. And that we should go and rescue it."

"Trickery. Evil trickery," Nella muttered grimly. "It's trying anything it can to get us outside."

"But we won't go outside, will we, Gramma?" Benn whispered.

Nella held her grandson tight to her. "Benn, you and I are staying right here. I promise."

"I'm scared, Gramma," Benn whispered. "Are you?"

"Yes, Benn. I am."

Danny was disgusted—once again the old Enchanter had fooled him. There was Hagos in the middle of the courtyard twirling around, waving his arms in some kind of mock fight with thin air. It was ridiculous the lengths to which the man would go in order to get his attention. This time Danny was having none of it. But as he turned to go, Hagos let out a half-strangled shout: "Night . . . Wraith . . . ," then collapsed onto the cobbles and lay gasping, pulling at his clothes as though trying desperately to breathe.

Now Danny was confused—either Hagos was a better actor than he gave him credit for or something really was attacking him. Danny walked uncertainly toward

Hagos, half expecting him to jump up and say, "Fooled you, Mr. Dark." But Hagos did no such thing, and as Danny approached he felt the air grow cold around his feet as though he were walking through a cloud of ice. Suddenly Danny felt very scared indeed. He ran to Hagos and dropped to his knees beside him.

"It's quiet now, Gramma," Benn whispered.

Nella hugged Benn close. "What a relief."

"I think it was pretending it had caught someone so that we would go and rescue them," Benn whispered. "It's clever, isn't it?"

"Not as clever as us, Benn," Nella said fiercely.

Hagos stared up at Danny. His eyes were bulging, his face purple and his hands grabbing at his neck as if trying to loosen a noose.

"Sheesh," Danny muttered, trying to haul Hagos up by his shoulders so that he could breathe more easily. It was like lifting a lead weight. *How come such a scrawny guy weighs so much*, Danny wondered. *It feels as though someone is sitting right on top of him.*

And then Danny understood. Something *was* sitting right on top of Hagos—some kind of entity that he, being a Dark, could not see. Hagos looked up at him, gasping for breath. "Don't . . . leave . . . me."

"I won't leave you, Mr. RavenStarr." Gently, Danny

laid Hagos back down on the cobbles. He tried to remember what he'd been told in his Enchantment Awareness course. He knew that this must be a Wraith because he could not see it, because it had no substance to see. A Wraith was pure Enchantment. He remembered that a Wraith killed by fear, relying on its victims being so terrified that they would lose the strength to fight back and so allow themselves to be smothered to death. But Hagos was still fighting—he had now begun to roll across the cobbles like a crocodile trying to drown its prey. So maybe, Danny thought, with two of them fighting together, they had a chance. Especially as the Wraith was clearly not at all interested in him. *Like is drawn to like*, he remembered now, and the Wraith was after the Enchanter. And maybe, Danny suddenly thought, it was after the girl inside the roundhouse too. Maybe that was why the shutters were up, and why no one answered the door even though they clearly were in there.

"We're fighting this," Danny told Hagos. "You and me both."

Hagos was struggling to speak. "Donkey . . . ," he whispered hoarsely. "*Donkey.*"

"Sheesh," said Danny. "There's no need to be so rude. I'm trying to help you, you silly old fool."

"Na . . . aaaah . . . Don . . . *key*. I put a donkey hair in the Wraith's flask. As a safety valve. It . . . it won't attack a donkey . . . we need . . . to get to the . . ."

"Donkey. Okay. I get it. We'll go find the donkey." Summoning every ounce of strength, Danny slowly dragged Hagos across the cobbles toward a stable door by the cart. He felt as though he was walking through an invisible blizzard deep inside a hurricane, and he had to fight for ground every bone-chilling step of the way.

Exhausted, Danny at last reached the stable door and leaned back against it. The door flew open, and accompanied by an indignant *hee-haw* from Howard, Danny fell backward onto a pile of straw, bringing Hagos with him. He lay winded for a few moments until Hagos began struggling against his unseen assailant once more. Danny got to his feet and slammed the door shut.

"Poor Howard," Benn whispered. "He's scared."

"Howard will be fine," Nella said. "He's a brave donkey."

"Do you think it's gotten inside his stable?" asked Benn.

"If it has, it won't stay in for long," Nella said with a smile. "Howard will see to that."

Howard did indeed see to that. He watched a boy make a skinny old man comfortable on the straw, laying him on his side so he could breathe more easily. Howard saw gray wisps of Wraith curling around the old man's neck like a snake and noticed how the gray tendrils were coming in under his stable door. Howard didn't like the look of them at all, and he particularly did not like the fact that they were in *his* stable. And so Howard went over to the boy and his bag-of-bones friend, bared his yellow tombstone teeth and let out an unearthly hee-hawing shriek. With great satisfaction Howard watched the Wraith uncurl itself, and then he lunged forward and took a great bite of the gray misty air. It tasted vile, but the Wraith recoiled. As it slithered away like a snake, Howard set about stamping on it, sending it streaming out under the door into the courtyard beyond.

Released from his stranglehold, Hagos sat up, gasping in long, shuddering breaths. The boy looked up at Howard in amazement. "Thank you," he said. "You saved him. *Thank you.*" Howard gave a soft hee-haw of appreciation. It wasn't often that anyone thanked him. For the rest of the night Howard lay across his stable door, guarding his territory and repelling the Gray Walker as only a donkey could.

Much depleted, the Gray Walker turned its attention back to the roundhouse. It spiraled around the walls, climbing upward like ghostly ivy toward the little windows at the top. But as it drew close to them, it felt a fear come over it. The encounter with the donkey had weakened it, and the Enchantment behind the shutters felt young and full of life, honed and sharp like a dagger, and the Gray Walker feared it would be cut to shreds by it. And so it wrapped itself around the roundhouse like a dirty ribbon around a hat; and at the first rays of sunlight the next morning, it dropped into the yard like a shower of old dandruff.

CHAPTER 26

Table Talk

Morning came, as it always did, and Nella was up early with her broom again, chasing Wraith dust into the duck pond, watching the sun climb over the distant pointed roofs of Luma. As she swept energetically past the stable door, it creaked open and Nella—more jangled than she realized—screamed and dropped the broom with a clatter. A wild-looking boy with straw in his hair stumbled out and stood blinking in the sunlight. "Has it gone?" he whispered.

"It?" Nella said, bending slowly to pick up the broom.

"Here, let me help," the boy said, retrieving the broom from the cobbles and handing it to her.

"Thank you," Nella said, the effects of two sleepless nights fogging her brain. "Very kind. But what are you doing in the stable, young man?"

Danny smiled wanly. "It's a long story. And there are two of us. The other one's still in there." He nodded toward the open stable door.

"With Howard?"

"I dunno. Didn't meet a Howard. There's a donkey."

"Howard is the donkey," Nella said.

"Ah. Well, I was wondering if you could help us. Please? The old guy's not feeling too well. If you have any water . . . or anything really?"

"Yes. Of course. I'll make you some lemon-and-honey tea."

"Thanks so much. That is very kind. I'm Danny, by the way."

"Nella Lau," said Nella, peering into the gloom of the stable where she saw what looked like a pile of rags in the far corner. She turned back to Danny, concerned. "Is your friend . . . alive?" she whispered.

Danny nodded. "Yeah. I checked his pulse. He got attacked last night by that Wraith."

"*He* got attacked?"

"It nearly strangled him. He's very weak. You'd be doing us a great kindness, Mrs. Lau, if you would let him rest here a while."

"I'll do more than that," Nella said, feeling solidarity for another victim of the Gray Walker. "Bring him inside."

In the kitchen Nella peered under the cloth covering Mirram's cage. Mirram was curled up like a baby on a pile of cushions, deeply asleep. Gently, Nella trundled the cage from its alcove and pushed it farther along the wall, nearer the door. Then she set about making another improvised bed for yet another waif and stray, and helped Danny lift his bony old friend into a soft nest of cushions under the stairs. The man did not stir, but Nella could see the rise and fall of his ribs, so at least he was still alive, she thought.

She sat Danny down at the table with a mug of hot lemon-and-honey tea and was touched to see he first took it over to his friend and tried to get him to take some. But as Danny was kneeling beside the man Nella saw, with a shock, the outstretched silver wings on the back of his jacket. Like everyone in Lemon Valley, Nella knew very well what a Flyer's jacket looked like. Surely, she told herself, such a caring young man could not be something as wicked as a Flyer? Nella told herself that he must have found it somewhere. The Flyer must have dropped it. She set about making pancakes and tried to put the jacket from her mind.

Nella decided to let Alex sleep on, but the sweet smell

of the pancakes brought Benn downstairs. "We've got guests," Nella said a little unnecessarily. She brought a plate of pancakes over to Danny. "Danny, this is my grandson, Benn."

Benn was shocked. This was the boy from Luma Station yesterday, the boy who Alex said had seen through her Fade. But far worse than that, this was the boy who had tried to kill Alex and Louie halfway up a sheer cliff face. Here he was, flaunting his Flyer jacket in front of them all and *Gramma was feeding him pancakes.* How *could* she?

Danny grinned. "Hi, Benn."

Benn scowled. "So you Fly the Hawke?" he said. "Go around killing people, right?"

"Benn, please!" Nella remonstrated. "I'm sure that's not so."

"It's okay, Mrs. Lau. It's a fair comment," Danny said. "Yeah, Benn. I Flew the Hawke until a few days ago. And then I stopped. I never killed anyone, I promise. I couldn't do it. These are such great pancakes, Mrs. Lau. Amazing."

Benn sat down opposite Danny and glared at him.

"So," said Danny, "you help out on the farm, do you, Benn?"

Benn did not reply.

"He's a great help, aren't you, Benn?" Nella said fondly as she placed Benn's pancakes in front of him.

Benn pushed his pancakes away. He wasn't hungry.

"Don't know what I'd do without him," Nella said, joining them at the table with a mug of lemon tea.

"Big place for just the two of you," Danny said, noisily scraping up the last of the honey and setting Benn's teeth on edge.

"Oh, we get by," Nella said. "I'm very lucky to have such a hardworking grandson." She leaned over and patted Benn's hand, and something in the pressure of her hand made Benn pay attention. "I'm just going up to fetch my shawl. It's chilly this morning."

Benn watched his grandmother hurry up the stairs, and when he heard her footsteps going all the way to his room at the top, he felt very relieved. So Gramma didn't trust Danny either. She was making sure Alex stayed upstairs and hidden.

Silence fell in the kitchen, broken by a sudden snort from the giant parrot cage. Both Benn and Danny jumped. "Your parrot does a great imitation of a snore," Danny said. "Just as good as the real thing."

"Yeah," said Benn, wondering if Danny really thought it was a parrot under there. He could not shake off the feeling that Danny knew more about them than was safe. It was then that he noticed that there was a pile of rags next to Mirram's cage and it was *breathing*.

"That's my boss," Danny said, seeing Benn's expression. "He had a rough night. Your grandmother kindly let him rest up here." Danny pushed the last piece of pancake into his mouth and washed it down with a long gulp of lemon tea. "I can eat those if you don't want them," he said, pointing at Benn's untouched pancakes.

Benn pushed the pancakes across to Danny without a word. He was trying to figure Danny out and he didn't like the conclusion he was coming to. Alex said that Danny had stared after her and had watched where they went. Which meant that, like a sneaky lowdown creep, he must have followed them all the way home and lurked outside in the yard all night, watching them. Hawke or no Hawke, it was obvious that Danny was still hunting Alex. And so, no doubt, was his raggedy boss who was lying in the corner pretending to sleep but listening to every word they said.

He had to get Alex away as soon as he could.

CHAPTER 27
Orphan Out

ZERRA D'ARBO WAS NOT HAPPY. She had just spent the night on the bottom berth of a three-tier bunk in the girls' dormitory in the Luma House of Orphans. That morning Zerra had brushed her teeth with the communal toothbrush and washed her face with the communal sponge and now, wearing the orphan uniform of a pink pinafore dress with matching sunbonnet—Zerra hated pink, she hated pinafore dresses and she absolutely loathed sunbonnets—she was marching at the back of the orphan line on her way to school.

Zerra could not believe how quickly it had all gone wrong, especially as it had begun so well. After she had

Named her Beguiler-loving mother and little brother, not to mention the Beguiler herself, she had had a great time. At long last she had been treated with the respect she deserved: she had been made a Junior Sentinel and given her mother's tenancy of the house. Okay, so she'd had to share it with the sniveling Francina, but she was planning to Name her too, so she figured she'd soon have the place to herself.

That next morning after Francina—who had refused to speak to her—had left the house early, Zerra had decided not to bother with school and have some fun instead. She left her Junior Sentinel jacket at home and hung out with the cool kids in the marketplace, learning how to "borrow" stuff from the stalls without the stupid traders even noticing. All the while she had watched the stage being prepared for the trial: the ramp, the red carpet and the three gold-painted chairs for the judges at the back of the stage. It was only when she saw the small chair put on the edge of the stage that Zerra had begun to feel a little nervous—this was where she, as the Namer, would be sitting. *Ma's going to be really upset with me*, she had thought. But she had quickly replaced the thought with *I don't care. It serves her right*. She'd held that thought in her head for the rest of the afternoon and it had all been fine. Until the trial. And then, just because her stupid foster sister had had the nerve to rescue her mother—Zerra still could not believe it—the Sentinels had blamed the fiasco on her and she had gone from the dizzy heights of Junior Sentinel to the lowest of the low—a Luma Orphan, stuck with all the other kids of criminals.

Now, as she marched along in her pink bonnet, praying that no one she knew would see her, Zerra saw the high white walls of her school come into view and a heavy dread settled into the pit of her stomach. *There is no way I am going into class looking like this*, Zerra told herself. *No way at all.* She glanced back at the large, elderly woman who was policing the end of the line. "Eyes forward, orphan!" the woman barked.

Apparently obedient, Zerra complied. But she had seen what she needed to. In a moment they would be passing the little snicket between the school wall and the head teacher's house next door. It was notorious as the narrowest path in Luma, and there was no way the attendant following her would fit down it. Zerra waited until the dark strip of shadow between the walls was right beside her and then she simply slipped into the snicket.

"Hey, you!" A shocked yell from the attendant, followed by a bellow of, "Orphan out! Orphan out!"

Zerra threw off her bonnet and wriggled sideways along the passage, head turned so she didn't graze her nose upon the rough stone of the wall. It was dark and the walls were slimy, but Zerra didn't care—anything was better than sitting in class wearing the orphan pink pinafore dress. Behind her she heard shouts and then screams of protest from a little one who, it seemed, was being pushed into the snicket to go after her. *Idiots*, Zerra thought, *why don't they just go around to where this comes out?* And then, suddenly fearful that that was exactly what they would do, Zerra pushed herself forward with added vigor, heading toward the bright strip of sunlight at the end. She emerged, scratched and grazed by the stone, covered in slime mold and utterly elated. She was free!

Zerra ran through the alleyways, dodging this way and that, until she was sure that no one was following her. She longed to go home and get rid of the ghastly orphan pink and have a bath to get rid of the slime, but she did not dare. Someone would surely be waiting for her. And so Zerra lurked in the shadows and waited until the market-opening bell was rung, and then she set off for the marketplace. Within ten minutes Zerra had stolen a red silk cloak with a hood, a fancy yellow tunic with a purple sash, orange leggings shot through with green thread, a pair of soft blue-and-gold leather boots and a market trader's pass.

Using her pass, Zerra sauntered into the market traders' bathroom, washed her face and hands, and changed into her new clothes. She shoved the hated orphan pink dress into a bin, and with her long silk cloak swishing behind her, its hood prudently up and hiding her face, she set off, sailing jauntily out through the Sentinel Gate in a cacophony of shimmering red, blue, orange and gold, gaily waving her pass at the very same nasty Sentinel who had marched her off to the orphanage. *And I hope he gets into big trouble when they discover he let me out*, she thought.

It was a long and dusty walk down the winding track to the valley floor, but Zerra didn't mind. She was still savoring her freedom and was increasingly entranced by what she saw below. Lemon Valley didn't look frightening at all; there was certainly no sign of all the Hauntings they learned about in school. The sweet scent of orange blossom drifted up in the warm air and by the time she reached the foot of the track, Zerra was smitten. She glanced back up at Luma and all she could see were its sandy-colored walls and its ridiculously pointy roofs. *What a dusty old dump*, she thought.

At the bottom of the track Zerra headed across to the old platform and the stalls selling parasols, sun visors, iced water, pies and heaped-up piles of orange quarters. Zerra longed for a glistening bottle of water, but she had no money at all—everything had been taken from her at the orphanage. She wandered around the stalls as if choosing what to buy, and it did not take long for Zerra to have a cool bottle of water and a bright yellow parasol stashed beneath her red silk cloak.

Deciding it would be pushing her luck to drink it in full view of the water stall, Zerra sat on the far edge of the platform facing away from the stalls. As she drank the cool water and admired her beautiful new boots, Zerra noticed a steel rail glinting up through the sandy ground. A long-forgotten memory rushed through her like a tidal wave.

It had been early morning, misty and cold. She was sleepy, oh so sleepy, stumbling off a crowded train with Francina holding her hand because her mother was clutching an ugly, bawling toddler that had come from nowhere. She remembered trailing up the steep track behind her mother, she and Francina carrying all their heavy bags because her mother was stuck with the squirming brat. And then they were in the horrible dusty town, full of nosy people staring at them, and they had nowhere to go and the brat was wailing, wailing, wailing. And the nosy people were clustering around the brat, trying to soothe it and giving it candy and oranges to suck and no one was giving her and Francina *anything*, because no one cared about them. Not even their mother.

Zerra finished the water and hurled the stone bottle angrily to the ground. She didn't care if the stallholder saw her. In fact, she hoped he did. She wanted a fight. She wanted to scream and shout and punch someone. But no one noticed. As usual. With the cool water running through her, Zerra felt a sudden surge of energy and optimism. She stood up, opened her purloined parasol, and stepped down from the platform. Then she walked rapidly away—to who knew where—holding the parasol above her head like a glowing sun.

"Hey! You! With that parasol! Come back!" Zerra swung around and stared angrily at the stallholder who came chasing after her. "Give me back my parasol," the woman demanded.

Zerra felt the same sense of calm descend on her as she had when she had Named her mother. "It is not your parasol," she said, very slowly, keeping her gaze steadily upon the face of the flustered woman. "It is *my* parasol. Do you understand?"

The stallholder backed away. "Yes," she said. "It is your parasol. I understand." And then she turned and hurried back to the safety of her own stall. Zerra watched the woman go with a feeling of triumph. She knew she had made the stallholder go away. She didn't quite know how it worked, but it seemed to her that if she looked someone in the eye and said something, they believed her. Feeling buoyed up by her power, Zerra marched along the dusty track, her shimmering silks billowing behind her, her blue-and-gold boots striding ever onward. She was walking into a new life—a new life where she was going to be someone. Someone special.

Then they'd all be sorry.

CHAPTER 28

Hello and Goodbye

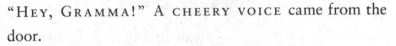

"Hey, Gramma!" A cheery voice came from the door.

"Jay!" Nella said, hurrying over to greet her grandson. "Well, just look at you all. Come in, come in."

Jay—a taller, more carefree version of Benn—came breezing into the kitchen, followed by Francina and Louie. Jay's brown eyes shone with pleasure at being home once more, and Nella forgave him his grease-stained jacket that smelled of soot and his dirt-ingrained hands. It was just good to see him. "Bella asked me to drop these two back, as she's gone to the cavern today. Hope that's okay?" Jay, like Francina, was eyeing the covered parrot cage with some misgivings. "I can take them back to Bella's if it's not," he said.

"It's fine, Jay. We have a few things to sort out, that's all," Nella said. She handed him a hacksaw, saying under her breath, "There's something I need you to do. Neither Benn nor I are strong enough."

Jay caught his grandmother's eye as she glanced meaningfully at the covered cage. "Is that what I think it is?" he asked in a low voice.

Nella gave a warning nod and turned her attention to Francina, who was staring at the covered cage, looking horrified. "Now, Francina. Why don't you take Louie out to see the ducks?"

Francina did not move. "Ma?" she whispered.

"Out we go, out we go," Nella said in her singsong happy voice as she propelled Francina and Louie outside. "Benn!" she called. "Come and show Louie the ducks!"

Benn dutifully appeared and took Louie off to the duck pond, but Francina refused to budge. "Is . . . is that Ma under there?" Francina whispered. "In a cage?"

Nella nodded.

"Why is she still in there? Can't she get out?"

"Come now, Francina, we'll have her out very soon. Off you go into the sunshine."

Suddenly Danny was beside Francina. "There's an

amazing donkey here called Howard," he said. "Come on, I'll introduce you."

The color came back into Francina's cheeks and Nella watched her walk away with Danny. She wasn't sure if she was grateful to Danny for rescuing Francina or annoyed at the way he acted like he owned the place.

Annoyed, Nella thought. *Most definitely annoyed.*

She went back into the kitchen hoping for a quiet few moments with Jay, only to hear the remorseless grating of hacksaw upon metal. The cover was off the cage now and Mirram sat stone still, knees drawn up to her chin, watching intently the hypnotic rhythm of the saw.

Nella had all but forgotten about the occupant of the quilt beneath the stairs when a movement brought him to her attention, and she went to see if he was all right.

"What you got there, Gramma?" Jay asked, looking up, stopping his sawing for a moment to give his arm a rest.

"It's not a 'what' Jay, it's a 'who.'"

Jay looked shocked. "Oh. I thought it was that boy's dog."

"Dog?" came an affronted croak from the blankets as Hagos struggled to sit up.

At the sound of the voice, Mirram looked up. Her eyes widened in surprise as she watched Nella tend to her fellow guest.

Jay resumed his sawing, but Mirram did not take her gaze off Hagos for a second.

Out by the duck pond, Benn was telling Louie how they had rescued his momma. He left out the terror and the nastiness and told him the good parts about the rescue—particularly the pokkle, which made Louie laugh.

Danny and Francina had found a shared interest in Howard, who was grazing at the end of the olive grove. They stood stroking the donkey's neck while Francina gazed into Danny's eyes and asked him every question she could think of about what it was like to be a Flyer and then listened with her head to one side—which her mother had always told her looked cute—while Danny happily answered every one.

Benn preferred the company of Louie and the ducks, but the occasional squeaky giggle from Francina cut through the soft quacking of the ducks and irritated Benn more than it should have.

"Who is that show-off boy?" Louie asked disapprovingly.

Benn liked Louie. The kid had good judgment. "Don't you remember him?" Benn asked—and then thought he shouldn't have.

Louie looked puzzled. "I don't think so."

Benn decided to be straight with Louie. "He flew the Hawke. The one that attacked you and Alex."

Louie looked shocked. "It was *him*?"

"Yeah. Look at his jacket when he turns around. You'll see the Hawke on the back."

"I did see it," Louie said. "But I thought it was just a nice jacket. I don't think it's nice now. I wish Franny would stop giggling at him."

"Not much chance of that, I think," Benn said, watching Francina playfully tugging at Danny's long hair.

Mirram D'Arbo's a strange one, Nella thought. *She's out of the cage with not a word of thanks to Jay for all his hard work—or to me for that matter.* Mirram had not been able to get out of the kitchen fast enough and had headed off without a backward glance.

"She just wants to see her kids," Jay said.

"Maybe," Nella said. But she had the distinct impression that Mirram was more desperate to escape the kitchen than be reunited with her children.

An apologetic cough came from the corner under the stairs. "Ahem. Madam. Excuse me."

Nella swung around to see her remaining guest struggling to his feet. "Hey, take it easy," Jay said, hurrying over to help Hagos up.

"Thank you," said Hagos, his voice still husky. "Would you mind showing me to the, um . . . facilities?"

Jay went to help Hagos upstairs and Nella stopped him. "Outside, in the courtyard," she said brusquely. Nella watched them go and then hurried up the stairs to see Alex.

Alex was already up. She was looking out of the

window, watching the glint of silver from the Hawke jacket at the far end of the olive grove.

"Ah," Nella said, breathless. "You've seen him."

Alex turned to Nella. "He's still hunting me, even without the Hawke. He's not going to give up, is he?"

"I fear not," Nella said. "He's got a very strange, raggedy man with him, some kind of spy, I suppose. I've gotten him out of the way for a few minutes, but we need to get you away while we've got the chance."

Alex took a deep breath to steady herself. It was all happening too fast. "Thanks, Nella. I know I have to go." She slipped her card wallet inside the cover of the *HEX* where it belonged, then she tucked the *HEX* into her waist sash and followed Nella down the stairs.

Hagos and Jay made slow progress across the yard to the outbuildings, where Jay pushed open the door of the outside bathroom next to Howard's stable. He was met by a high-pitched scream. "*I'm* in here!"

"Oh. Sorry," Jay said. Blushing, he closed the door.

A few minutes later Mirram scurried out. She saw Hagos and stopped dead. "*You!*" she said. "I thought it was you. You . . . you lowdown, no good, lying *pig*!" And she turned and ran through the gate toward the duck pond.

Speechless, Hagos and Jay stared after her retreating figure, Nella's loaned dress billowing like a flowery balloon. "Do you know the lady?" Jay asked Hagos.

Hagos groaned. He staggered into the bathroom and closed the door, and Jay heard the bolt being firmly drawn. Thinking his charge too weak to return to the kitchen alone, Jay sat down on the cobbles and leaned back against the warmth of the wooden wall, listening to Louie yelling ecstatically, "Momma! Momma!" *At least he's happy*, Jay thought, *because sure enough no one else is.* At that moment Benn came hurrying back across the courtyard with an anxious expression, and so preoccupied that he did not even notice Jay. *Even Benn's in an odd mood*, Jay thought. *And he's always so calm. Whatever is going on?*

Benn burst into the kitchen, relieved to see his grandmother and Alex on their own. "Gramma! Alex! We have to get out of here while that creepy Flyer is out of the way!"

Nella smiled at her grandson. "Which is why Alex is down here all ready to go and you have a picnic basket and some blankets to carry."

Alex cast a quick, regretful glance around the kitchen and then she was out into the sunlight, being hurried across the courtyard, shielded by Benn and Nella. In the distance she heard Louie laughing and her heart did a little flip of sadness—she couldn't even say goodbye to her full-time superhero.

Jay was opening the bathroom door for Hagos when he saw the oddly rapid procession cross the courtyard. Benn gave him a cheery wave as he disappeared through the arch and Jay waved back. *He's in a better mood now*, Jay thought. *I wonder why?*

CHAPTER 29

Dare

ALEX WATCHED THE ROUNDHOUSE RECEDE as Benn rowed Merry away, heading down the river. She gazed at its mellow stones until they disappeared below the tops of the tall reeds that lined the riverbank. Then she forced herself to turn around to face forward, to see where she was going. *There's no point looking back*, Alex told herself. *I'll never see them again. Not Nella, not Louie, not Francina or Mirram. And soon I'll have to say goodbye to Benn too. And then they'll all forget about me—just like my mother and father did. And I never even got the chance to ask Mirram about them either. Yesterday was just a big waste of time.*

As Benn rowed steadily down the river, keeping a watchful eye for any disturbance on its surface, Alex gazed out at the low, flat fields beyond which sheep grazed and someone was calling out to their dog. Alex saw the expanse of sky broadening out and thought she could already smell the salt of the sea that lay ahead. They were rounding a long, lazy bend when she saw a stark iron bridge crossing the river, beneath which a lone swan drifted. "Bridge ahead," she warned Benn, and he turned around to look. "That's the old railway bridge," he said. "It's still got the rails on it. Jay and I walked over it once. Do you want to stop here for breakfast? I could show you the track."

"Sounds good," Alex said.

Benn pulled up to the stone dock beside the bridge. He tied Merry to a large ring and led the way to a grassy bank by a small thicket of water reeds. Alex sat by the river's edge, watching the clear water dancing over the pebbles and strands of waterweed swaying in the current. The sun sent sparkles glancing off the surface and she was entranced by the sight of so much clear water flowing freely. Why, she thought, couldn't she just follow the river in Benn's boat forever? Why couldn't she stay out in the sunshine with the broad blue sky above, and never have to walk through a dark, deep tunnel through the mountains to a dismal orphanage where she would forever be a stranger? *Why?*

Leaving Alex to her thoughts, Benn unpacked Nella's basket. He set a red-and-white checked cloth upon the grass and laid out Nella's breakfast feast: a flask of orange juice, two slabs of lemon cake, a stone jar of marmalade, slices of dark, seeded bread wrapped up in waxed paper and a pat of bright yellow butter that glistened with pieces of salt.

"That's so nice of her," Alex said.

"She's very sad you have to go," Benn said. He looked up at Alex. "And so am I."

Alex turned away and stared at the river, allowing her gaze to wander to the opposite bank, where a flash of red caught her eye. "Sheesh!" she said, ducking down behind the reeds.

"What is it?" Benn asked anxiously.

"It's . . . it's *Zerra*."

"It can't be."

"It is. Look."

Benn wriggled along the grass and peered through the reeds. "What's *she* doing here?" he whispered.

"Feeding that swan, by the look of it," said Alex.

Zerra had stopped beside the river to eat the oranges she had picked along the way. Her stomach was rumbling and she longed for something more substantial; the orphanage breakfast had been a slick of runny oatmeal in the bottom of a bowl and a piece of dried bread with what the girl sitting beside her had told her were three raisins on top. But they hadn't tasted one bit like raisins, and after she had swallowed them the girl had burst out laughing and said to her friend, "She *ate* them!" Zerra still felt sick at the thought.

She was dabbling her sticky fingers in the river, wishing she had thought to steal a pie, when a swan glided up to her and regarded her with two dark, beady eyes.

Zerra sat back on the bank and returned the stare. "Hello, swan," she said, holding out some orange peel. The swan glided toward her and bowed its head down to her hand; then it disdainfully flipped the orange peel off into the water. Zerra burst out laughing. "You and me both," she said. "I don't want to see another orange ever."

The swan tilted its head to the side and Zerra got an uncomfortable feeling that she was being judged in a most disconcerting, yet oddly flattering way. She caught herself hoping the swan would approve and almost laughed again—what was she doing, seeking approval from something that was nothing more than a swanky oversize duck? But the swan had a presence that Zerra could not ignore. Tentatively she reached out and touched the top of its head. It felt cool and smooth, and the neatly round top of its skull seemed to fit exactly into the dip of her palm. A strange vibration ran through Zerra's hand, like the buzzing of a swarm of bees, and Zerra was suddenly almost overwhelmed by the feeling that, at that moment, anything was possible—anything at all. "Hey, swan," she murmured, "let me fly with you."

The swan looked at Zerra as if weighing up the proposition.

"Go on," said Zerra. "I dare you."

Those last three words changed Zerra's life forever.

Alex and Benn stared in astonishment at the sight on the opposite bank. The swan was rearing up, wings outstretched as though it were about to attack Zerra, but she didn't seem scared at all—rather the opposite. She was gazing at the swan, enthralled. The swan's feathers were rippling with light, but beneath their whiteness a different sheen was now visible—a shimmering greenish black. As they watched, the swan's body grew up from the river, a great pillar of gleaming feathers reaching for the sky. Its long neck filled out, its body grew up to meet it, its head grew broad and flat, and its beak shortened to a cruelly curved twist of gold. Two enormous wings spread out, shook themselves and then settled back against its body. The tools of Enchantment—the Flyer's saddle and its half hood—appeared and it bent its head toward the stunned Zerra.

"Sheesh!" Benn said. "It's the Hawke."

Zerra stared up at the golden beak and the two glittering eyes on either side of it. Fifteen feet to Zerra's five and a half, the Hawke towered over her, but Zerra stood firm and returned the Hawke's assessing stare. Zerra did not realize it, but she was very lucky, because in its transformation to a swan, the Hawke's powers had been considerably weakened, and it was not the predator it had once been. So when Zerra whispered once more, "Let me fly with you. Go on. *I dare you*," its instincts were overridden by its secret name, Dare. It laid its head down upon the bank, bowing to the one who had spoken the words that every new Flyer must. (Zerra had in fact muddled the order of words. They should have been *Dare, let me fly with you*, but they were close enough for the befuddled Hawke.)

Zerra clambered onto the saddle with its stirrups that were just a little too long for her. Then she clung on to the pommel on top of the Hawke's half hood and gasped with excitement—and just a little fear—as the Hawke rose slowly into the air.

Benn and Alex stared in shock at the Hawke and Zerra, triumphant, soaring into the sky. But as the Hawke wheeled over the river, a shout rang out from Zerra: "I see you, Alex! I'm going to get you!"

Benn grabbed Alex's hand, pulled her up, and together they raced for the cover of the railway bridge. Alex peered out and saw the Hawke hovering, waiting for instructions from its new Flyer.

"Hey, Alex. Scared, are you?" Alex heard Zerra's taunt. "Running away like you always do. But you can't run forever. I'll get you one day, you know I will."

"I've had enough of this. I'll show her," Alex muttered.

"No, Alex. Please don't," Benn said, reaching out to stop her.

Alex shook Benn off. "No, Benn. I'm not running away anymore. I'm going right out there and I'm going to do a Fade right in front of her. Just like yesterday."

"But it's not just her, is it? The Hawke will still see you."

"No it won't. I read it last night in my codex. The Hawke needs a Flyer who is Dark to Enchantment, but it hasn't got one, has it? Because its real Flyer is back at your place cozying up to Francina. And now it's got itself a great big fake Flyer!" Yelling out the last two words, Alex shot out from beneath the bridge and stood beside the reeds once more, waving at Zerra. "Come on then, if you're so clever!" she yelled up.

"Get her! Get her!" Alex heard Zerra's yell from above. She looked up and saw the Hawke tip forward into a dive and come barreling out of the sky toward her. Using all her concentration, Alex Faded into the reeds behind her and became one with them. She saw the Hawke pull out of its dive and soar up into the air and she heard Zerra's shriek of alarm at the sudden change of flight.

"I'll get you, Alex!" Zerra yelled. "I know you're there!"

But the Hawke was not coming back down for something it could not see. It was unsettled—it could feel Enchantment all around it and yet it could see nothing, and its new Flyer was not guiding it as a Flyer should. But full of the joy of once more being master of the skies—no longer an unwieldy creature that flew like a bucket making a noise like a rusty gate—the Hawke shrugged off its unease, wheeled around and set a course for Rekadom.

Breathless with a terrified excitement, Zerra clung on, watching the ground move fast beneath her. She saw the patchwork of orange and lemon groves, the winding tracks, and as the Hawke soared ever higher, catching the thermal off the hilltop, she looked down upon the silver-tipped roofs of Luma. She tried to catch sight of her old house and she wondered, with a pang, if she would ever see it again. And then she looked away, out across the vast expanse of the rocky desert in front of them, and longed for the moment she would spot the fabled three towers of Rekadom rising from the dusty horizon.

CHAPTER 30

An Empty Pocket

"All clear," Alex called over to Benn.

Benn crept out from the shadows of the bridge. He looked shaken. "How could your sister *do* that?" he said.

"She's no sister to me," Alex said. "It's friends that matter to me now."

The charm of the picnic spot had faded and they gathered the breakfast back into the basket and set off once more in Merry. Benn rowed slowly, letting the stream carry Merry along. They progressed steadily, passing great expanses of reed beds from which voices of reed cutters drifted, mixing with the rustling of the reeds swaying in the soft salty breezes blowing in from the ocean. Suddenly, Benn spotted an ominous V-shaped ripple in the water heading toward them. "Stinger!" he shouted.

Alex swung around just in time to see the shining, flat head of a giant eel rear up out of the water and then dive back down to become a sinuous shape swimming toward them beneath the water. "It's going under the boat!" Benn yelled. He pulled the oars out from their oarlocks and shoved one across to Alex. "If it comes up, bash it on the head."

"You bet," said Alex.

There was a thud beneath Merry and she lurched alarmingly. Benn lost his balance and, arms windmilling wildly, began to topple out of the boat. As Alex grabbed him and pulled him upright, a great fountain of water and mud hurled itself into the air, in the middle of which she saw the silvery flash of a Stinger Eel, twisting and writhing, its shining, red little mouth wide open revealing a line of long, needle-sharp teeth. With a loud yell of "Get out of the way, Benn!" Alex drew back the oar and with a powerful swing, she swept it across and caught the Stinger Eel just below its head. The oar shuddered as it hit the iron-hard muscles of the eel's body and rebounded, but Alex held on tight, ready for another swing. She did not need it. The Stinger Eel dropped into the water like a lead weight and sank into the depths below.

They sat down in Merry, both shaking. "Sheesh," Benn said as he fumbled with the oars. "I've never seen a Stinger before." Benn looked up at Alex. "These Hauntings are terrible. They are just so *wrong*."

"I know," Alex said.

Shaken, they set off once more. The river was now widening out into an estuary. To the left was a huge expanse of reeds, and ahead Alex could see the vast, brilliant blue of the ocean. How small she and Benn were, she thought, and how tiny Merry was. Benn was keeping Merry close to the reeds, where the water was calm, but out in the middle of the estuary the waters were racing in, churning up the sand below and turning the clear river waters a muddy brown.

Benn was rowing slower now, glancing over his shoulder, and Alex saw a stone dock with a wooden jetty sticking out from the reed bed. "Here we are," said Benn. "Lemon Dock. Where they used to load the lemons onto Big Puffer to take them to Rekadom."

"Forget Lemon Dock," Alex said.

"Uh?" Benn was trying to maneuver Merry closer to the bank.

"I'm not going there, Benn."

"Whyever not?"

"Because there is no way I am going to live in an orphanage in a strange land and never see anyone I know *ever* again. That's why."

An eddy spun Merry up to the jetty. Benn put his hand out to catch hold of it and Alex shouted, "No! I mean it, Benn. I'm not going. Take me somewhere else—anywhere else."

Benn didn't like the thought of Alex going to the orphanage any more than she did, but he didn't see what else she could do. "But where?" he asked.

Alex pointed across the wide expanse of the estuary to a small beach on the far bank. "There."

Benn looked out over the stream of turbulent water churning with the chop of the tide. It would be a tricky row across, but he had always wanted to test Merry in less tame waters, and now was his chance. He turned Merry into the fast-flowing current and, pulling powerfully on the oars, set off into the tide race.

Alex hadn't realized quite what she had asked Benn to do. She hung on to the sides of the little boat, feeling the pull of the currents swirling beneath it, and kept her gaze fixed firmly upon their destination. Merry bounced and skittered across the waves, like a pony wanting to break free, but Benn kept her on course, and at last they felt the tug of the currents beneath them begin to wane and Merry settled back onto a steady course. Benn blew a sigh of relief. "That was a bit hairy," he said.

"Hairy?" Alex laughed.

"Hairy-scary," said Benn.

"You didn't look scared at all," Alex told him.

"I was, just a bit." Benn patted the hull of the boat. "But Merry wasn't and that's what matters. It's when your boat gets scared that you worry."

They pulled Merry up onto the small pebble beach, taking her above the high-water line of soggy reed stalks and seaweed, and settled her neatly behind an outcrop of rock so she could not be seen from the water. The beach was calm and sheltered, the landward side bordered by a wood of small oak trees, known as salt oaks for their ability to grow so close to the ocean.

Benn took Nella's basket out of the boat and followed Alex up to a flat, grassy spot beneath a group of the stunted trees, their trunks twisted and gnarled by the winds. "So," he said, setting the basket down, "what's changed?"

"Me," Alex said. "*I've* changed."

Benn considered this as he opened the picnic basket, took out the checked cloth, and laid it on the ground. "You're right," he said. "You're different today."

Alex took the *HEX* from its place inside her sash. "It's this. I am so grateful to your gramma for giving it to me. It's made me understand that having some kind of Enchantment is okay, and that I have just as much a right to live here as anyone else. It got me thinking that it is so wrong that I have to leave everything I've ever known, while people like Zerra get to do whatever murderous things they want and that's just fine. Why should people like me be so afraid all the time? Why should we be stuck in Luma like we're in prison, or when we go outside, get hunted down by things like the Gray Walker and the Hawke and that horrible Stinger Eel?"

Benn shrugged. "It's awful. But what can you do?"

"I'm going to get rid of the Hauntings," Alex said.

"What, just you? On your own?"

Alex thought Benn was not taking her seriously. "Yes, Benn Markham, just me. On my own. And if you don't believe me, you can leave me here right now and go back to your nice cozy home and be with the lovely Mirram and Francina. Oh, and that creepy old man and his flashy Flyer friend. Go back to them all. See if I care."

There was strained silence and then Benn said, "Louie. You forgot Louie."

"I'll never forget Louie," Alex said somberly. "Louie is a big reason why I don't want to keep on running. I don't want to leave him forever without even saying goodbye. I want to be a proper big sister to Louie."

"You're his favorite sister by miles," Benn said. "He told me."

Alex's face lit up. "Did he really? Well, that settles it. I'm doing this for Louie."

"Doing *what* for Louie?"

Alex flipped open the *HEX* and pointed to the empty T-shaped pocket at the front of the sealed pages. "I'm going to find the thing that belongs here. The Tau. Last night I figured it out—if you have the Tau, you can break the Hauntings. See?" Alex pointed to the tiny writing above and below the shape.

Benn squinted at it, confused. "It's just gibberish," he said.

"At the moment it is. But sit down and I'll show you." Alex knelt on the picnic cloth and Benn sat beside her, watching as she took her Hex cards from their wallet and dropped them into their pocket inside the front cover of the *HEX*. A burst of brilliant blue light shone out and Benn gasped. "It's okay, it always does that," Alex said airily as she turned once again to the T-shaped pocket at the back. "*Now* read what it says," she said.

Benn peered at the tiny letters. Slowly—for the spiky writing was not easy to decipher—he read, "One is One, Two is One, and Tau is Three . . . um . . . and . . . One to make it. Three to break it." He looked up at Alex, amazed to have actually understood the words. "Okay. I get that, I think. The Tau thing, whatever it is, is the Three, right?"

"Right."

"But what is the 'it' that the Tau breaks?" he asked.

"The Enchantment that made the Hauntings, dummy."

"Sheesh. Really?"

"Really. So I am going to find the Tau. And then I am going to use it to break this horrible Enchantment and get rid of all the Hauntings—every single one of them. Gone!" With that, Alex snapped the codex shut and stood up.

Benn got to his feet. "Are you serious?" he asked.

"Yes. I am."

"But how are you going to find this Tau thing?"

"I shall use the cards to ask the *HEX* to tell me where it is," said Alex. "Which is what I am going to do *right now.*"

Alex looked so fierce that Benn dared say no more than, "Okay. I'll go and sort Merry out."

Benn walked back down the pebbly beach, got into Merry and began bailing out the water and setting her to rights. Then he gazed at the estuary waters tumbling out to the sea. Up until now, Benn thought, he'd been like the river—flowing along in his day-to-day life, picking lemons, going to the market and helping Gramma. But now he had met an ocean called Alex, and all the undercurrents that he'd ignored were coming to the surface and everything was being churned up. Right now Benn felt as confused as the brown muddy water out there on the turn of the tide, which didn't know if it was coming or going either.

And what exactly was this stupid Tau, anyway?

CHAPTER 31

Home Truths

"THE TAU IS THE KEYSTONE of the Triad of Enchantment." Hagos, his straggly gray curls washed and tied back in a ponytail, was in full-flow teaching mode as he and Danny walked along the riverbank on the edge of Nella's second-best lemon grove.

"Sounds impressive," said Danny, skimming a stone out into the flat surface of the river. "Or it would be if I knew what you were talking about."

"I've already told you, Danny. You don't listen, do you?"

"My ears are listening," Danny said, "but they're not connecting to my brain."

Hagos stopped and looked warily down at the river. Its waters seemed calm, but he was well aware of all the Stinger Eels his Enchantments had placed beneath them. He took a step back, just to be sure. "Okay, Danny. So, simply, this is how it works. All the Hauntings I made for King Belamus I created using the Tau. It's a T-shaped charm. Lovely thing. Packed full of energy. Brilliant blue. Got that?"

Danny nodded. "Blue. Yep, got that. Do you still have it?"

Hagos spluttered with laughter. "Do you really think I would have spent the last eight years skulking in a forest full of snakes if I did?"

"Fair point," Danny agreed.

"It is much easier to create these malevolent Enchantments than to break them. Don't ask me why. That is just how it is. Okay?"

"Okay. You're the boss."

"So, to get rid of the Hauntings I need not just the Tau but the whole Triad."

"You got any of that Triad thing?" Danny asked.

"No," said Hagos.

"Thought you might say that," Danny muttered.

"Belamus stole the Tau. I think my assistant took the codex, which has the codes to unravel the Hauntings sealed into the last few pages. And then there are the Hex cards."

"Another thing you don't have, right?" Danny said. "Seeing as you gave them to your daughter."

"How do you know that?" Hagos demanded.

"You told me. Despite what you think, I do listen to what you say."

"Humph," said Hagos irritably.

"So this quest of yours is to get that Triad back together again, right?" said Danny.

Hagos gave a bitter laugh. "In my dreams. It's clearly impossible. Don't know what I was thinking." He sighed. "I sometimes wonder what I've done to deserve it all."

"Are you planning on complaining *all* morning?" Danny asked.

"While I'm wearing this abomination, yes, I am," Hagos replied, looking down at the reluctantly acquired pink flowery dress that he was—not entirely success-fully—trying to hide beneath his cloak. Hagos had won the battle for his cloak, but Nella had thrown the rest of his clothes in the laundry kettle and boiled them, leav-ing Hagos with no option but to wear one of her spare dresses.

Danny chuckled. "Pink suits you."

"Very comical," Hagos said. "As soon as I get my things back we're off. This has been nothing but a wild goose chase after a so-called invisible daughter. I don't know why I was so gullible as to even think of believing you."

Danny did not reply.

Hagos took Danny's silence for petulance, but it was not—Danny was thinking. He realized he was getting the measure of Hagos RavenStarr. The man had a childlike peevishness when things did not go his way, and Danny was beginning to understand that it should not be taken seriously. If Hagos was going to act like a sulky brat, then it was up to *him* to be the grown-up and do the right thing. Danny knew he had seen Hagos's daughter. She had looked like a nice kid too. Whatever failings Hagos had, he was her father and she deserved to see him again.

As the high wall of the roundhouse courtyard came into view, Danny decided to try some plain speaking. "Look here, Mr. RavenStarr. You've had a rough night and you're not thinking straight. I know for sure that I saw your daughter in the cart yesterday and I am certain that she came along that track to the roundhouse. So it makes no sense to randomly take off somewhere else, just because you're annoyed about things not going your way. Some of this is your own fault, Mr. RavenStarr. You've been on your own for too long and you've forgotten how to be with people without being rude to them, which means they either don't like you or are suspicious of you. I suggest that you try being polite to Mrs. Lau. It was rude not to tell her your name when she told you hers. You need to introduce yourself properly and tell her you are looking for your daughter. Ask her straight out if she is here."

"Oh, very clever. And you really think she would tell me?" Hagos demanded.

"Yes, I do. If she knows who you are and trusts you, then of course she would tell you. But at the moment she doesn't trust you one bit. Or like you very much either."

Hagos was shocked. "How do you know?"

"I can see it in her eyes. If you ask me, she's hiding your daughter because she thinks you are a danger to her."

"Well, I can't be responsible for what one old woman thinks of me."

"Of course you're responsible for what people think of you. Who else would be?"

Hagos was silent for some seconds while this sank in. And then he exploded with anger. "How dare you talk to me like this?"

"Well, someone has to," Danny told him calmly.

They walked into the courtyard to find Hagos's clothes on the clothesline, blowing in the warm breeze. "All dry," Danny said cheerfully. Hagos was surprised. Danny sounded as if no harsh words had passed between them at all. Hagos liked that.

They walked into the kitchen to find Mirram at the table. She looked up and burst out laughing at the sight of Hagos in a pink, flowery frock. Hagos looked stunned. "So it *is* you," he said. "I thought it was all part of the nightmare, but it really is you."

"Well, thank you so much. I see you're as rude as ever," Mirram snapped back.

"Oh, you can talk," Hagos riposted.

"Do you argue with everyone?" Danny asked Hagos.

"He always argued with me," Mirram said sourly.

"Takes two to argue," Hagos said.

"No it doesn't."

"Yes it does."

"Stop it!" Danny yelled.

A strained silence fell in the kitchen, while from outside came the sound of Louie, Jay and Francina laughing. Danny thought what a cute laugh Francina had. He was sorely tempted to go out and join the fun, but he forced himself to stay in the stormy kitchen. He needed to get Hagos back on track.

After a while, Mirram said in an aggrieved tone, "I thought you might at least want to know about your daughter."

Hagos looked up, surprised. "Who told you that?"

Mirram shrugged. "Just thought you might be interested. But forget it. You never were much of a family man, were you?"

Danny tried to clarify things. "The girl who rescued you yesterday," he said to Mirram. "Do you know who she is?"

Mirram snorted like an aggrieved camel. "Of course

I know who she is. I've looked after her for what feels like *forever*." She pointed a short, stubby finger at Hagos. "She's his daughter. Alex."

"Alex! She chose *Alex*?" Hagos was shocked.

"Who chose Alex? I certainly didn't, I can tell you."

"Her name—her precious name. Is that what she chose, Alex?"

"What are you going on about? Pearl told me her name. When she threw her at me."

"Pearl threw Boo-boo at *you*?"

"To be frank, I didn't want her. But then the train moved off and I was stuck with her. She's not a bad kid. But so *secretive*. I blame those weird cards she had."

"*Cards?*" asked Hagos.

"Wretched things. Oh, I tried to take them off her. Over and over and over again. But she would scream so loud my ears rattled. And then my two would start scream-ing too. You have no idea what it was like. So I gave up in the end. Let her keep the wretched things." Mirram shrugged. "Seemed the easiest way out."

Hagos's eyes were shining with hope. "Does she—Alex—still have them?"

"If she didn't, we wouldn't all be in this mess right now," Mirram said sourly. "Bloody kids."

"So where is she?"

"I don't know. I've not seen her this morning. I expect she's lurking in a dark corner somewhere."

"But she's *here*? In *this house*? Right *now*?"

"As far as I know."

"Told you so!" Danny leaped up and thumped the table in triumph.

The door from the courtyard burst open and Nella came in with a basket of laundry. She stopped and surveyed the scene. Something was going on—again. Nella sighed; she felt as if her kitchen would never return to the peaceful haven it had once been. She decided to ignore whatever petty argument was happening between the spiky people around her table. "All clean!" she said brightly. "You can get changed now. Unless you prefer to stay as you are, of course. Pink does rather complement your complexion." She brought the basket over to Hagos and held it out for him to take.

Remembering what Danny had told him, Hagos got to his feet and tried to smile—not entirely successfully.

Nella looked wary—was the wretched man about to throw up over his clean clothes? She withdrew with the basket to a safe range.

Hagos gave a bow of the head accompanied by a little bob—a politeness that had once been fashionable at the court of King Belamus, but looked to unaccustomed eyes like a chicken preparing to lay an egg. Nella took another step backward. Unwilling to let his mission falter, Hagos stepped forward, and before Nella could turn and run—even he could tell that she was seriously considering it—he said, "Kind lady, please stay. I wish to thank you for taking care of me in such a generous fashion. I am forever in your debt. May I introduce myself properly?"

Danny looked at Hagos with approval. His protégé had learned well.

"I am Hagos RavenStarr, ex-Enchanter to King Belamus."

Nella promptly dropped the laundry basket on his foot.

"Argh!" yelled Hagos.

In the background came a giggle from Mirram.

In a state of confusion, Nella sat down on the nearest chair with a thump. "You? Hagos RavenStarr? I . . . I had no idea. We thought you were some kind of spy. For the Flyer here."

"Madam. I assure you I am no spy."

With a shaky hand, Nella rubbed her eyes. "Sol," she said. "My nephew. He . . ."

Hagos sat down beside Nella. "Sol is your nephew? Oh, what a stroke of luck. Is he here? He has something of mine, which I would dearly love back."

Nella shook her head, finding it hard to speak. "He's gone. The Gray Walker . . . it . . . it took him."

Hagos gave a long, low groan. He had, by proxy, killed his own assistant.

The kitchen fell silent and Nella's hand strayed to the blue cord that she wore around her neck under her baggy frock. She tugged the cord up to reveal hanging from it a small silver compass with a fat sapphire in the middle.

Hagos gasped. "My Manifest!" he whispered. "How did you get that?"

Nella pulled the cord over her head and held the compass in her hand. "From Sol. He gave this to me, but I knew it wasn't his to give." She turned it over and ran her thumb over the engraved name on the back: *Hagos RavenStarr.* Then she reached over to Hagos and pressed it into his hand. "I am glad to return it to its rightful owner at last."

Hagos looked down at the tiny silver compass in wonder. "Dear lady. I cannot thank you enough. You have made all things possible." He carefully placed it around his neck.

"Please tell me about Sol," Nella said.

"With pleasure, dear lady. But may I first ask you to tell me about someone very dear to me?"

"Of course you may," Nella said.

"My daughter. Boo-boo. I mean, *Alex.* I think she came here last night?"

"Alex is your *daughter*?"

"Huh," came a disgruntled snort from Mirram. "What does he care about his daughter?"

"Considerably more than you, so it appears," Nella told Mirram. She got up and walked out of the kitchen. At the door she stopped and turned. "Mr. RavenStarr, you have a daughter to be proud of."

Hagos felt suddenly shaky. *Boo-boo really was here. In this place.* "May I . . . may I see her? Please?" he asked, almost in a whisper.

"Alex left a few hours ago," Nella said.

Hagos looked devastated. "She *left*? But where? Where's she gone?"

Nella smiled. "Jay will take you to her. Please, come with me."

Hagos was on the roundhouse dock with Nella, Danny and Jay. His red Enchanter cloak shimmering with gold thread was wrapped around his now clean black tunic and trousers, and his Manifest hung proudly around his neck.

Nella was busy explaining. "Believe me, I would never have kept you from your own child. We all thought you were helping the Flyer here to hunt her down."

Hagos put a hand on Nella's arm. "Dear lady, you did the right thing. You protected her, and I am deeply grateful. I do not think she has had anyone do that for her for a long, long time."

"Neither do I," said Nella. "Although I imagine Mirram did her best."

"Imagination is a wonderful thing," said Hagos dryly.

"So they say. Now, Mr. RavenStarr, Jay will take you to the cave and you will find Alex there." Nella took Hagos's thin, bony hands in hers. "Please come back and see us when times are better."

"Indeed I will. I shall bring Boo-boo—I mean Alex—with me."

"I do hope so. I wish she could stay here, but it is too dangerous. The Gray Walker came both nights she was here."

"It came for *Boo-boo*?" The enormity of what he had done began to dawn upon Hagos. He had been so preoccupied with the danger he had put himself in, that he had up until now given no thought to the danger he had placed others in—let alone his own daughter.

"We Sealed the house," said Nella. "Luckily I had Sol's old Sealing Cloth—"

"Oh, is that where it went?" Hagos said weakly. "Well, I am glad he took it. You put it to good use."

Nella looked at Hagos. "Was Sol a good assistant?" she asked.

Hagos, with his newfound sensitivity, considered what to say. "I liked the boy," he said. "He had, deep down, a good heart. And he tried his very best. But he was, how do I say this, a little light-fingered."

"I did wonder," Nella said. "Sol came back with so many little trinkets."

A thought came to Hagos. "I wonder, did he by any chance bring my codex? It's a tiny book, very heavy. Has *HEX* stamped on the cover. Bound in blue."

Nella smiled. "He did. And it is in good hands. I gave it to your Alex."

"You gave it to *Boo-boo*?" Hagos felt like yelling with frustration. He wanted to ask Nella what she thought she was doing giving his precious tool of Enchantment away to an ignorant child who would have no idea of its importance. But remembering Danny's wise words, Hagos stayed calm and gracious—or tried his best to. "Well, well. Fancy that. How very . . . nice of you. We must be off at once."

"Yes, of course you must," Nella replied. "Give Alex my love, won't you? Tell her that I hope one day to see her again."

"Yes, yes. Now, let's get going." Hagos looked down uncertainly at Jay's rowboat. It was very small and bobbed unsettlingly in the water. Danny and Jay were already squashed together on the middle seat, each one with an oar. "So where do I sit?" Hagos asked plaintively.

"At the back," Danny told him.

Gingerly, Hagos stepped in and the boat wobbled alarmingly.

"Don't do that!" Jay barked. "Keep your weight in the middle. And *sit down*."

Obediently, Hagos folded himself up like an anxious spider and settled onto the narrow plank across the stern of the rowboat, and then he turned and attempted a cheery wave to Nella. She had been joined by a little boy who was clinging onto her hand. They returned his wave and the little boy pointed at him and said something to

Nella. Hagos looked resolutely forward and tried to imagine what it would be like to meet his daughter. And then two words came into his mind: *Stinger Eels.*

Nella and Louie watched the rowboat with its two oarsmen head rapidly out into the middle of the river. "Is that really Alex's daddy?" asked Louie.

"Yes, I do believe it is," said Nella.

"He's got an Enchanter's cloak," said Louie.

"He does," Nella agreed.

"So Alex *is* an Enchanter's child!" Louie said excitedly, jumping up and down. "I knew it. I knew it!" And then his face fell. "But that means she has to go away and I won't see her again, will I? Not ever."

Nella scooped Louie up into a hug. "Who knows, sweetheart. Who knows?" With Louie still in her arms, Nella turned and walked away from the dock, but not before she had glanced over her shoulder at Jay's rowboat and wondered what Alex would make of its strange cargo.

CHAPTER 32

Blue Bubble

BENN WAS STILL SITTING IN Merry when he saw a small rowboat packed with three people draw up to Lemon Dock on the far side of the river. "That's Jay's boat, I'm sure it is," he muttered. Fumbling with his wet hands, he pulled a small brass spyglass from his pocket and focused it on the rowboat. Shocked, Benn saw the two passengers Jay had brought with him. "Jay," he gasped. "What are you *doing*?"

Benn ran back up the beach, his feet slipping on the pebbles, trying to take in what he'd seen. *Jay was bringing the Flyer to Alex. How could he betray her like that?* Benn kicked up the stones angrily. It would serve Jay right when they got there to find that Alex had never arrived. She'd made a good call.

Benn had left Alex laying out her cards on Nella's picnic cloth beneath one of the twisted oaks. As he reached the edge of the wood he stopped: there, beneath a tree, was a shimmering bubble of deep-blue iridescent light. Inside the bubble, like an embryo within an egg, was a dark, crouching shape. *Alex.*

A cold shiver prickled up Benn's spine—this was the weirdest thing he had ever seen. The brilliant stream of blue light flowing up from the hexagonal shape was so bright that it hurt his eyes. He covered them with his hands and peered through his fingers. Now he could see Alex more clearly. She was kneeling, leaning over the cards as though she were looking into a deep well, her hands braced on the ground as if to stop herself from falling in. Even from outside the bubble Benn got a vivid sense of the void into which Alex was staring, and it felt entirely possible to him that she could fall into the cards and disappear forever.

It was with some relief that Benn saw Alex lean back and, with the strangely birdlike fluttering of her fingers that he remembered so well from the marketplace, pass her hands across the hexagon once, twice, three times. The shimmering blue bubble funneled down into the shining hexagon like water going down the drain, and moments later Alex was just a girl sitting beneath a twisted oak, delicately picking up a few colored cards off a picnic cloth. She looked up at Benn and he saw a dazed, faraway look in her eyes—Alex wasn't quite back yet.

Very quietly, Benn sat down next to her. "Alex?" he said tentatively.

"Oh. Benn!" Alex gave her head a shake to bring herself back to reality.

"You were so right not to get off at Lemon Dock," he said. "Jay's just turned up there with the Flyer. And his raggedy old spy."

"Your *brother*?" asked Alex. "With the Flyer?"

"Yep. I have no idea what he's doing."

"Show me," Alex said. "I want to see this."

They made their way down the beach, keeping close by the rocks, and crouched down behind Merry. Benn handed his spyglass to Alex. "See?"

Alex gasped. "I can see him. There's the Hawke on the back of his jacket. And they're helping someone out of the boat."

Alex passed the spyglass back to Benn. He watched his brother usher the Flyer and the spy along the raised bank that ran between the reed beds and would take them straight to the cave—the very place where he and Alex should by now be waiting. "I'm so sorry," he said. "I don't know what Jay is thinking I really don't. He's betrayed us."

"It's not your fault." Alex watched until the three figures had disappeared into the reed beds, and then she stood up purposefully. "All the more reason for me to get going," she said.

"Going where?" asked Benn.

"To get the Tau."

Benn sighed. "Alex. Please. This is such weird stuff. It's . . . it's not real."

Alex crouched back down beside Benn as you would, he thought, beside a little child to explain something difficult to understand. She seemed suddenly so grown up. "Benn, it is real. I promise you it is. You'll understand one day." She stood up with such a businesslike air that Benn knew there was no stopping her.

Trying to delay her, even for just a few minutes, he said, "Okay. So, um, where is this Tau thing?"

"Oracle Rock."

"*Oracle Rock?*" Benn felt scared. Oracle Rock was right next to Rekadom, and it was not a safe place for someone like Alex to be. "You're going to Oracle Rock?"

Alex grinned. "Yup."

Benn looked out across the water to Jay's boat. He wanted to talk to Jay so badly, to ask his advice about what to do, but Jay was not to be trusted anymore. Just like Alex, he was on his own now. He had a choice to make and only he could make it. "We'll go in Merry," he said.

To his surprise and disappointment, Alex shook her head. "Thanks, but no. You must go back to Nella. She'll worry so much if you don't come home tonight. Especially now that Jay has gotten weird." Alex gave Benn a quick hug. "Bye. I'll come back and see you all when I've done this." And with that, she turned and headed off into the trees.

"Hey, wait!" Benn called out after her. "You don't know the way!"

Alex wheeled around, annoyed now. "Benn, I do know my geography, thank you. I just follow the cliff path and I'll get there."

"If the Xin don't get you first."

"Well, thanks for reminding me." Alex set off at a fast pace up the beach with Benn running after her. At the top of the pebbles, she dived into the wood of salt oaks and Benn followed her as best he could through the closely packed, twisted trunks. But Alex was hard to keep track of; her dark jacket and trousers blended into the shadows just as they had when she had disappeared into the alleyways off the marketplace.

Benn stumbled on, tripping over roots that snaked across the ground, ducking the low-hanging branches, until he realized he had no idea where she was. He stopped and listened. All was silence, but he had the distinct feeling that Alex was not far away—that she was standing very still and listening hard, just as he was. He even thought that he could hear her breathing. But he couldn't see her anywhere. "Alex!" he yelled out. "Alex! Where are you?"

There was no reply. Benn knew what had happened—
Alex had done a Fade. And she had done it to hide from
him.

Feeling wretched, Benn walked slowly back through
the trees. He packed the things away in the picnic basket
and went to sit in Merry. Right then it felt like Merry was
his only friend.

CHAPTER 33
On Lemon Dock

"ALEX! BENN! ARE YOU THERE?" Jay yelled, his voice echoing down the brick-lined tunnel.

Jay was confused. He had expected to find Merry tied up at Lemon Dock; then when there was no sign of her, he supposed that Benn had taken Merry along the old and very overgrown cut through the reeds, which led to a disused and crumbling old dock near the entrance to the tunnel. Jay knew that Benn was protective of his boat and guessed he wanted her moored away from the fast-flowing waters of the estuary. But there was no Merry there either. So where was Benn? And, more to the point, where was Alex?

Jay had left Hagos with Danny outside in the sun. The tunnel had reminded Hagos of the Rekadom dungeons, and so, seeing how spooked Hagos was, Jay had offered to go and find Alex himself. Breathing in the heady smell of damp earth and old soot, he headed into the lantern-lit darkness, following the shining rails to the old engine workshop inside a huge cavern, where the Big Puffer stood on its turntable. This was where the old engine had once, at the end of every day, been turned around to start its run back to Rekadom at the first light of dawn.

As Jay walked into the cavern, a burst of sharp, metallic hammering started up. Jay stopped and looked at the magnificent engine, which sat patient and still as a rock while someone fiddled with its insides. Jay loved the Big Puffer almost as much as he loved his family, and he was determined to bring it back to life once again. He looked up at its huge circular smoke-box door—or face, as he thought of it—and reached up on tiptoe to put his hand on the smooth, cold steel of the bump in the middle, which Benn had once called Big Puffer's nose. "Hello, big guy," he said. "Have you seen my little bro and his friend?"

But Big Puffer was saying nothing.

Passing beside the massive driving wheel as high as the top of his head, Jay made his way to the driver's platform, where he could see the glow of a lantern and from which the intermittent hammering was coming. "Hey, Bella!" he called up.

Bella, disheveled and her face smudged with soot, peered down, clutching a large wrench. "Hey yourself," she said.

"You seen Benn?" Jay asked. "And his friend. Alex, she's called."

Bella pushed a strand of hair back from her eyes and blinked. "No. Should I have?"

"Well, yeah," Jay replied. "He's supposed to be bringing her here."

"Great," said Bella. "We could do with another pair of hands."

"She's not staying, I'm afraid. I was going to be taking her through the main tunnel to the orphanage on the far side."

"Sheesh. Poor kid. She's one of the Enchanter kids, is she?"

"Yeah. So it seems. But now . . ." Jay shook his head. "Well, now I've got her father outside waiting for her. But she's disappeared."

Bella laughed. "Maybe she's just gone invisible."

"So where's Benn? *He* can't go invisible, can he?" Jay sighed. "Why is everything always so complicated with Benn and Gramma?"

The entrance to the old railroad tunnel through the mountain was at the back of the workshop and Jay took a lantern and went to investigate. Perhaps, he thought, Benn and Alex had already gone through, and Bella, busy in the driver's cab, just hadn't noticed. The entrance was blocked by shuttering to keep the drafts out, and at once Jay saw that it had not been touched. Grasping at straws, he went over to the bunkhouse—a small cave off the main cavern where there was a row of sleeping platforms with neatly folded blankets. It was most definitely empty. Concerned now, Jay retraced his steps out of the tunnel toward the semicircle of sunlight where the silhouettes of two figures stood waiting.

He emerged into the sunlight and Hagos turned to him, expectant. The Enchanter's face fell when he saw that Jay was alone. "I suppose she didn't want to see me," he said.

Jay felt sorry for the man. "No, not at all. They're not here yet," he said.

Hagos frowned. "But they left before us."

"I know," Jay agreed. "I don't understand where they can have gotten to."

Hagos paced up and down. "The current was strong. Your brother's boat, was it safe?"

Jay was beginning to have the same worries, but he was not about to admit to them. "Of course it was safe," he said.

"The boy is young," said Hagos. "Maybe too young for such responsibility."

"Benn is the most responsible person I know," Jay said, annoyed now.

"Maybe he had other ideas," Danny said. "Decided to go somewhere else."

Jay didn't like Danny; he seemed like a know-it-all. In Jay's opinion, anyone who proudly carried the image of a murderous Hawke on his back was not to be trusted— especially someone who had tried to kill Benn's first real friend. Jay got nearer to the truth than he realized when he retorted, "Or maybe he saw you following them and decided to keep away. My grandmother tells me you tried to kill Alex."

"I did not!" Danny retorted. "I stopped the attack."

"From what I hear you had a darned good go at it," Jay said. "And how many other poor souls have you killed, huh?"

"None!" Danny protested. "Not one."

Jay's concern about Benn turned to anger with Danny. Somehow, he didn't know how, this Flyer was the reason for Benn's disappearance. Without another word he turned on his heel and walked off toward the river. He was leaving these two weirdos here; they could do whatever they liked, but it was none of his business. His business was to find Benn.

"That went well," Hagos said dryly as he and Danny watched Jay stride away along the path through the reeds.

"This doesn't feel right," Danny said. "I think he brought us here to get us out of the way. Planned it all along." He turned to Hagos. "I'll get the truth out of him." With that, Danny ran off in pursuit of Jay.

"No!" Hagos called after him. "Wait!" But his words vanished in the rustle of the reeds and Hagos sighed. He hoped Danny wouldn't do anything silly, but he rather thought he would.

Danny caught up with Jay as he was getting into his boat. He leaped in after Jay, sending it rocking violently. "Hey!" Jay protested. "Get out!"

"I will not," Danny told him. "*You* get out." He gave Jay a shove, sending him staggering back into the prow. "You tricked us," Danny said, advancing on Jay. "You brought us here to get us out of the way."

Jay struggled to his feet. "Out of the way of *what*?" he demanded.

"His daughter. You don't want him to find her, do you? Or maybe she really is here, huh? Maybe I need to go back in there and check it out myself. Huh? Huh?" With each "huh" Danny pushed Jay farther back, until he was very nearly toppling into the water. On the last "Huh?" Jay had enough. He threw himself at Danny and sent him reeling back, arms flailing. There was a loud splash and Danny was in the river.

To Jay's concern, Danny sank. He leaned over the stern, waiting for Danny to bob up again so he could drag him out of the water and tell him what he thought of him, but all Jay saw was a stream of bubbles rising to the surface. There was no sign of Danny. "Hey!" Jay yelled into the water. "Hey, this isn't funny!"

The bubbles stopped and Jay felt a sense of dread. He knew he had no choice—he would have to go in after Danny.

Hagos arrived just in time to see Jay jump into the river. He took in the empty rowboat and the distinct lack of Danny and a flicker of fear passed through him—both boys were in the river. It was deep and treacherous and they were weighted down with clothes. He was pretty sure too that Danny could not swim. With a sigh, Hagos took off his cloak and jumped into the cold, gritty water. He suspended his breath and sank, blinking with shock at the cold. The riverbed was a dark place and Hagos could barely see his outstretched hand as he swept his fingers over the mud, desperately hoping to find Danny. Long seconds passed and Hagos grew very fearful indeed, but just as he was giving up hope he saw the silver glint of the Hawke lying upon the riverbed, bumping up and down with the tug of the current. He grabbed Danny's belt and struggled up through the swirl and gloom until he emerged, gasping, into the sunlight. With much difficulty, he heaved Danny out onto the wet stones of the dock. Danny lay prone, blue and inert.

A spluttering gasp at the far end of the dock took Hagos's attention and he saw Jay hauling himself out onto the jetty.

"Help!" Hagos called out.

Jay half ran, half stumbled over and threw himself down beside Danny. "Oh, n-no, no, no," he stammered, his teeth chattering with the cold.

"Help me put his head down, over the edge," Hagos said. "Quickly."

Trembling, Jay did as Hagos instructed and watched as Hagos pressed down onto Danny's chest, pushing the water from his lungs, allowing Danny to cough and splutter his way back to life. Then, together, they helped Danny sit up. His face was gray with cold, his lips were dark blue, and it seemed to Jay that the spirit of the river still inhabited him.

Hagos placed his hands around Danny's head and leaned in, whispering words in his right ear. Jay knelt beside them, understanding nothing. After some time, Hagos changed to Danny's left ear and continued whispering. Jay got up and paced the dock, shaking the water from his clothes like a wet dog. When he turned around Hagos was rubbing Danny's hands, trying to get some warmth into them. Danny stared down at his hands, seeming not to understand what they were.

"A fine sight we make," Hagos said as Jay joined him. "Three drowned rats."

"I thought he *had* drowned," Jay said. "He was in there so long."

"You went in after him?" Hagos asked.

Jay nodded. "It was my fault. I pushed him and he fell backward."

"I imagine he gave you cause," Hagos said dryly.

"Will he be okay?" Jay asked.

"He should be," Hagos said. "I've made it possible. He needs to rest now for at least twenty-four hours to allow things to reconnect in his head."

"He can sleep in the bunkhouse here."

"That is kind. Thank you," said Hagos.

"And you can too, of course," Jay said.

"That is most considerate of you," Hagos said. "However, before I sleep again there is somewhere I must go. Someone I need to talk to."

Jay looked at the skinny man who stood dripping and shivering on the dock, his hand grasping the silver compass he wore around his neck. He didn't look in a fit state to go anywhere, Jay thought. "Can I help at all?" he asked.

"Look after Mr. Dark for me until I return."

Jay watched Hagos walk slowly along the dock, and then out to the end of the jetty, where he stopped, raised his arms and looked up to the sky.

He's going to dive in, Jay thought. "No!" he yelled, and ran to the jetty, but by the time he got there, Hagos had vanished. And not into the river, of that Jay was sure.

Jay stood for a few seconds looking out across the river, anxiously scanning the murky water as it tumbled out to the ocean, searching for any sign of Merry's white hull.

Suppose Benn had lost control of Merry and been taken out with the tide? The current was strong here. Benn was a good river sailor, but the ocean was a different beast altogether. Maybe even now he was drifting in the vast blue waters, helpless. "Benn!" he yelled. "Benn! Where are you?"

But the only answer was the distant screech of a gull.

CHAPTER 34

The Thirteen Titans

"BENN! BENN! WHERE ARE YOU?" Voices travel well across water and Benn heard the words clearly. He threw himself down into Merry, hoping that Jay had not seen him. *Don't be silly*, he told himself. *Jay wouldn't be yelling "where are you?" if he could see you, would he?*

Crouched in Merry, Benn could not get the echo of Jay's voice out of his head—Jay had sounded so desperate. *I ought to row over to Jay and let him know I'm okay*, he told himself. *And then I should go home.*

Benn steadied his spyglass on the top of the rock and looked across to Lemon Dock. To his surprise he saw Jay with his arm around Danny, walking with him along the path to the tunnel. Benn sat down with a bump. He watched Jay and Danny wander through the reeds together until he could no longer see the silver glint of the Hawke on the back of the jacket. Then, bubbling with anger at Jay's betrayal, he got out of Merry, dragged her down the beach and floated her upon the water, thinking, *How can I possibly go home when Jay would be there with that creepy Flyer—who was still hunting Alex?*

Benn leaped into Merry, grabbed the mast with its furled sail, and lifted it into its neat step near the prow. Then he pushed off from the beach and rowed as fast as he could along the shallows beside the long sand spit that separated him from the ocean beyond. At the end of the sand spit Benn glanced over to Lemon Dock for any sign of Jay, but there was none. He unfurled Merry's red sail and caught its mainsheet—the rope at its foot. The sail filled with the breeze and Merry slewed around toward the billow of the cloth. Quickly, Benn took his place at the tiller, and Merry settled onto her course, as he knew she would. The little boat slipped into the flow of the outgoing tide, and soon Benn rounded the end of the dunes and, for the very first time ever, took Merry out into the ocean where she belonged. And then they were off, bouncing through the water, riding the little waves as easily as a seagull flies the breeze.

As Merry headed back along the seaward side of the sand spit, Benn found he was laughing with the excitement of it all. Merry sped along faster than he had dreamed possible and soon they were past the sand spit and heading toward the Thirteen Titans—a string of granite cliffs, the edges of which rose and fell like waves themselves. Benn knew that it was along the Titans that Alex must travel if she intended to reach Oracle Rock by land. He glanced up at the first Titan, Baby Titan, the lowest of them all, and wondered if he might catch sight of her. But he guessed not. Anyone traveling through the Titans would go unseen if they possibly could. It was said the Xin that Haunted the Titans had gone feral and were no longer so fussy about their victims—Enchanters or not, it was all the same to them, day or night. But like all Hauntings, they were most powerful at twilight.

Benn kept Merry close to the shore. The water was clear and the cliffs rose up high into the sky and plunged down deep into the ocean. At every new Titan a line of pointed rocks ran out into the sea and Benn kept a wary lookout for any small breaking waves that would show where a rock might be lurking, ready to spear Merry on its point.

But Benn could not help but keep glancing up, looking for Alex. He longed to catch a glimpse of her, to know that she was all right. But the dark, inscrutable Titans gave nothing away. They seemed deserted, home only to wheeling, calling seabirds above and the thriving populations of fork-tailed rats below that lived on their eggs.

The day drew on and the sun began to drop down

toward the horizon. Merry was making a good pace and Benn was level with the last and largest of the Titans now—the thirteenth—which formed a high headland that Merry must now go around. The wind was more blustery here, and although Merry still rode the waves well, like the good sea-pony she was, Benn was chilled from the spray and tired from the constant struggle to keep Merry on course. He was also very hungry. As the shadows lengthened over the water, Benn began to feel anxious too—he needed to get around the headland before nightfall, for there was no shelter for him and Merry here.

The high peak of the thirteenth Titan was dark against the late afternoon sky as Benn and Merry crept slowly through the deep blue shadows at the foot of the Titan. The sea was calmer here in the lee of the wind, but not so very far ahead Benn could see the choppy waters off the headland, and he knew that soon enough they would be in the midst of them.

Then, suddenly, they were. The wind hit Merry like a train and she heeled over so far that Benn very nearly fell out. He let go of the mainsheet and the sail went flapping like a wild thing, but Merry settled herself and Benn managed to turn her into the wind. He grabbed the mainsheet, let the sail out, and he and Merry settled back into balance with the wind once again. They rode the waves around the headland in the most exhilarating half hour Benn had ever spent.

On the other side of the long and pointy nose of the thirteenth Titan the waters became a little calmer and Benn had time to look around. In the distance along the coast, almost on the horizon, he saw the distinctive bell shape of Oracle Rock, bright in the westerly sun, but Benn knew better than to head for that tonight. Instead he took Merry toward a tiny harbor nestling at the foot of the Thirteenth Titan, where a few cottages lined the dockside, which lay dark in the late afternoon shadows. Above the harbor rose a steep hill, and at the very top Benn saw the silhouetted remains of an old station house, with its distinctive pointed roof. The brisk wind was right behind Merry now and it soon blew her past the enclosing wall that wrapped itself around the harbor like a protective arm and sent her gliding into the calm, clear green waters of Netters Cove, where Benn swung her gracefully over to some well-worn steps and tied her to a ring in the wall.

"Hey, Merry, we did it!" Benn sat for a few minutes, savoring the success of their first sea voyage, contemplating the surprising amount of water washing around his feet. He set to work with the bailer, and when Merry was at last dry inside, he plunged his cold fingers into his pocket to warm them—and there he found the silver dollar his father had given him for Gramma. Benn grinned. That would buy supper, at the very least.

And first thing tomorrow he would go to Oracle Rock, and there he would find Alex. It didn't matter if she was still in her Fade, because to get to Oracle Rock she would have to wait for the tide to go out and then cross on the causeway. And even invisible people leave footprints in sand.

CHAPTER 35

A Net of Xin

STINGING, WINGING, ZINGING XIN, PUSH *them off and throw them in!* This line of the Hauntings Song, which they had sung every morning at school in Luma, went around and around Alex's mind as she headed fast along the old goose track that sat deep in the soft, springy turf that covered the Thirteen Titans.

Alex knew where she was going. Like all children in Luma, at the beginning of each term she had had to draw from memory a map of their land—or "The Lands and Dominions of King Belamus the Great," as they had to title it. Every term, up until age sixteen, a little more detail was added, and Alex was glad that for her most recent map she had had to learn about the old goose track to Rekadom. Alex was relieved that the track ran a safe distance from the edges of the cliffs, but even so, she watched carefully for any little flash of light that might warn of a Xin attack.

It was late in the afternoon by now, and Alex was tired. She had long ago let go of her Fade—it took way too much energy—and she was so thirsty that her thoughts were becoming muddled. There were no streams on the Titan tops and she dared not leave the goose track to look for one in case she lost her way. So she forced herself onward, knowing that she must reach the next settlement—which should be Netters Cove—before nightfall.

As Alex had traveled northward she had counted off the sweeping rise and fall of each Titan, its cliff edge stark against the bright blue of the sky, and she was now walking through the lengthening shadows of the twelfth Titan. The sky above its dark curve was turning orange and Alex knew that soon the sun would be setting. Knowing that twilight would soon be upon her, she forced herself on faster, and at last she reached the foot of the steep slopes of the thirteenth Titan.

Just as the tired geese and their drovers must have done before her, Alex stumbled wearily up the long bends of the goose track. At a resting place near the top she found to her delight a long, shallow trough filled with rainwater. Alex didn't care that it was clearly meant for geese—she would have happily grown feathers, a long neck and a snappy orange beak if those were the rules for drinking from it. The water tasted of iron and moss and Alex wondered why she had never known that iron and moss were so delicious. She drank enough to fill up an entire goose and then ran to the top of the thirteenth Titan and caught her breath.

It was exhilarating to be up above the ocean, out in the breeze. She breathed in deeply and looked out across the water to see if she could spot Oracle Rock. The sea looked dark and forbidding, and it was now that Alex realized that the sun had dropped below the horizon. Evening clouds were blowing in and the light was fading fast—she must get off the thirteenth Titan at once. Alex set off at a trot along the goose track, looking for the turnoff that would take her down the twisty little path to Netters Cove. The goose track strayed close to the cliff edge and Alex—who was well aware that Xin pushed their victims off the cliff—kept glancing behind as she ran.

Suddenly, from the corner of her vision she caught a small flicker of light. Alex whirled around but the light had vanished. She ran anxiously on, searching for the path down to Netters Cove that she knew must be somewhere.

But *where*?

And then, above the loud swash of the waves below, Alex heard a series of brittle clinks, like breaking glass. A chill shot through her—this was the Zinging of the Xin.

Alex came to a skidding halt and shoved her hands over her ears. It was unbearable. It felt as if the sharp, pointy noises were boring deep into her brain. As she stood on the cliff she saw a myriad of glittering strings floating toward her like a shower of sparkling rain. As they drew closer together the threads began to join up, crisscrossing over one another to form the eerily beautiful Net of Xin.

Alex stared at the net, watching it float toward her. The Zinging had quieted now and Alex became aware of a soft, soothing humming vibrating through the net. It was, she thought, quite pleasant to listen to. It made her feel kind of . . . happy.

And now, with Alex lulled into an almost trancelike state, the deadly Dance of the Xin began. Bowing and fluttering like an obsequious butterfly, the glittering net swirled around Alex as though, she thought, it wanted to be her friend. Dreamily, she reached out to touch its delicate strands, but it eluded her, always just a little beyond her reach. As the Net of Xin danced and trembled its way toward the edge of the cliff—and the three-hundred-foot drop to the sharp rocks below—Alex followed its mesmerizing, undulating movements, languorously placing one foot in front of the other, walking toward the abyss.

Alex was just one step from the brink when a sudden gust of wind blew up from the waters below and sent her sash flapping. Dreamily, she caught the silk and tucked it back around her waist, and as she did, her fingers touched the cover of the *HEX*. A frisson of warmth flowed up her arm and Alex suddenly saw the terrifying drop only one step away. She threw herself backward, taking the Xin by surprise. Quickly, it recovered and flowed up behind her, trapping her between it and the cliff edge.

With nowhere else to go, Alex hurled herself at the net. Stinging electric shocks like pinpricks shot up her arms and Alex shrieked in pain and fell to the ground. The Net of Xin shot upward and as Alex scrambled to her feet the glittering net dropped down in front of her, trapping her once again, pushing her back toward the cliff edge. In desperation Alex hurled her precious *HEX* into the middle of the Xin. The net gave a tinkling shiver and then, with the sound of splintering glass, it shattered into a shower of needles of light and came raining down. Alex threw her arms over her head, hurtled over to the *HEX*, scooped it up and then ran faster than she ever had in her life. Down the slope of the thirteenth Titan she raced, where she now saw, to her great relief, a small sign saying, "Netters Cove." Moments later she was at the top of a steep path winding down the cliff. She risked a quick glance backward, and to her immense relief she saw nothing but a dull glimmering upon the grass, blown and scattered by the wind.

Alex half ran, half slid down the path, sending loose stones skittering before her. In the gathering darkness she could see the glow of lights in the windows of a few small cottages below, which were spread around a small harbor, and her spirits soared. Breathless, she reached the foot of the cliff and stumbled out onto a wide dock with lanterns set along the harbor wall, throwing a soft, welcoming light upon the old stones. There was no one around, but Alex could see the shadows of people in the lighted windows of their houses, and spicy cooking smells wafted out. Alex's stomach growled with hunger and her relief at escaping the Xin began to evaporate. What should she do now—knock on someone's door and ask for shelter? Or find somewhere to curl up and sleep—if she could—until the morning? She was, as ever, an outsider. Feeling despondent, Alex sat at the top of the stone steps that led down to the water and considered her options.

It was only when her eyes grew accustomed to the darkness of the water below that Alex realized there was a small boat tied up at the foot of the steps. It looked oddly familiar. And sitting in the boat was a hunched-up figure staring out to sea. The figure looked oddly familiar too.

A slow smile broke over Alex's features—her first since she had left Benn that morning. She tiptoed down the steps until she was standing silently beside the little white-hulled boat. And then she took a deep breath.

"Boo!" she said.

CHAPTER 36

A Seeker of Truth

A FEW MILES FROM NETTERS Cove, a light glowed in the tiny stone cottage perched on the top of Oracle Rock.

Inside it, beside a fire of sea coals, Deela Ming, the Oracle, was knitting an octopus. The octopus looked good, but Deela—short, comfortably round, with thick glasses perched upon the end of her nose—did not. Deela was fighting off a cold. Her nose was red and her bushy black hair stuck up in surprised tufts.

Palla Lau, a young woman with long, dark hair worn in a braid that reached to her waist and a serious expression, stood beside Deela. She was holding a steaming mug of something pungent. Deela carefully tied off the seventh octopus arm and regarded the mug with deep suspicion.

"Drink up your seaweed infusion, Deela," Palla told the Oracle sternly. "Just close your eyes and swallow it."

"You mean close my nose," Deela complained. "It smells like a dead starfish."

Patiently, Palla stoked the sea coals in the grate and then sat down beside the fire. "This damp old rock is not good for you, Deela," Palla said. "Every summer you get a fever. Every winter, a quinsy. I think you need to move inland. To somewhere dry."

Deela was indignant. "And then who would do the Oracle?" Palla did not reply, but Deela saw the answer in her eyes. "*You?*"

"I've done it before," Palla murmured.

"I *know* you've done it before. How could I ever forget?" Deela said snappily. "You caused havoc, Palla. Telling the king that he would die by the hand of an Enchanter's child. How *could* you?"

"I told the truth, as the Oracle is bound to do," Palla said, not rising to Deela's taunt. Whenever Palla spoke or thought about the Oracle, a great sense of calm descended upon her.

But not upon Deela. "Nonsense!" Deela said sharply. "The Oracle is bound to keep the peace. That is—or was—the whole point."

"I want to keep the peace as much as you do, Deela," Palla said. "But, unlike you, I cannot lie."

Deela was indignant. "I am not a liar! Everyone knows that the Oracle isn't real. It's just a game."

Palla was shocked. "How can you say that? The Oracle is the gift of truth." She looked at Deela, understanding beginning to dawn. "You mean you *always* make it up? Not just for the king, but for everyone?"

"Of course I make it up. Unlike you, I don't see why one needs to say nasty things when one can say nice ones. I really don't."

The two women sat in angry silence, listening to the spitting of the salt from the sea coals. They watched tiny red sparks arc out onto the rug, filling their nostrils with the acrid smell of burning wool. Unchallenged, the night's darkness crept into the little room in the top of the tower. Normally Palla would have gotten up to close the curtains and light the lantern, but she did not move. She felt affronted on behalf of the Oracle that Deela used it so carelessly. It wasn't right. It just wasn't.

Deela and Palla stared into the gathering darkness, the silence between them like a great weight that neither had the strength to lift. Had it not been for a dull blue light that began to manifest in the middle of the room, Deela and Palla would have gone to their beds without saying another word. But the eerie blue light put a stop to that. "Oh my days, what is *that*?" Deela squeaked.

Before Palla could reply it became very clear what it was—a somewhat transparent, wild-looking man in a red cloak dripping copious amounts of water onto the rug.

"It's the ghost of a drowned sailor," Deela whispered. "Don't upset it. It will go away soon."

Palla watched the figure becoming increasingly substantial. It gave no indication of either being a ghost or going away anytime soon. It walked slowly over to the fire, where it held out its hands to catch the warmth and looked very content to stay just where it was. "Who are you?" Palla whispered.

The figure spun around as if surprised to find anyone there.

"Hagos!" Deela squeaked. "Oh my days. I can't believe it." Deela hurried over to him. "My dear man, you're soaked. Have you been shipwrecked?"

Clasping his silver Manifest in his frozen hand, Hagos looked down at Deela, bemused. His head felt fuzzy and there was a nasty clattering noise inside it, which, he realized with a shock, was his teeth chattering. Hagos had spent many hours of trial and error Manifesting on the wrong rocks in the middle of the wrong oceans, fighting off seabirds, losing his Lightning Lance to an angry walrus, slipping on seaweed and falling into water-filled crevices before he had finally arrived at his intended destination. "It feels like it," he said.

"I . . . I never thought to see you again," Deela stammered. "Not after that"—she glared at Palla—"that *terrible* Oracle. You did get my letter, didn't you?"

"Thank you, Deela, I received your letter. However, I was under arrest and unable to reply."

"Oh, Hagos. I am so, so sorry."

Hagos shrugged wearily. "What's done is done."

Deela felt wretched. "It was not done deliberately, I promise you. I was ill, Hagos. I lost my voice. So little Palla here . . ." She waved her hand at Palla, who was sitting in a low armchair watching the seawater drip steadily from Hagos's cloak and pool around his ice-blue bare feet. "Well, she was little then, only nine years old. Little Palla spoke for the Oracle. Oh, Hagos, will you ever forgive me?"

Hagos sighed. He saw the anguish in Deela's eyes and he knew that he no longer blamed her for King Belamus's cruel expulsion of all Enchanters and their families from Rekadom. And, most importantly, he no longer blamed his old friend for the death of his wife and the loss of his daughter. "I do forgive you, Deela."

Deela felt as though a weight she had been carrying for ten long years had been lifted from her shoulders. "Thank you," she whispered.

Hagos put a friendly but ice-cold hand upon her arm. "Now, Deela. I would very much like a word with the one who spoke that Oracle."

"You mean me?" Palla asked, looking nervously up at the dripping, yet impressive Enchanter. She felt as though his dark eyes were piercing straight into her thoughts.

"Tell me, Palla," Hagos said. "Why *did* you speak those words in the Oracle Bell?"

Palla gulped. "Sir, it was not me who spoke. It was the Oracle."

"Oh, really, Palla," Deela protested. "You were just a child. You didn't know what you were doing."

"Deela," Palla said icily, "I *did* know what I was doing."

"Well then, that's even worse," Deela told her. "To tell the king he would die at the hand of an Enchanter's child *on purpose* is a terrible thing."

"But *I* didn't say it. The Oracle did," Palla protested, not for the first time. She looked up at Hagos, sensing an ally. "I was in a kind of trance, you see. It came over me when I put on the Oracle Shadow Robe. As soon as it slipped over my head I felt as though I was a thousand years old, not just nine. And then, when I stepped into the Oracle Bell and heard the king's question, I knew the answer at once. Here." Palla placed her hand solemnly over her heart.

Hagos could not help but smile. Palla's answer was the very reason he had spent the long, cold, tedious day slipping around on benighted rocks full of spiteful birds and snappy sea lions—to come to Oracle Rock and see if what Danny had said was actually right: that the true Oracle had indeed spoken.

"I spoke the truth," Palla said quietly. "I could do nothing else."

"Indeed. The true Oracle must speak the truth," Hagos said.

"Not *you* as well!" Deela spluttered indignantly.

"Which is why I am here," Hagos continued, ignoring Deela's outburst. He looked at Palla. "I have come to Seek the truth. From the *true* Oracle."

Deela looked from Palla to Hagos and back again. "Well, *really*." She stomped back to her couch and threw herself down on it in a temper. "Go ahead," she said. "Don't bother about me, will you?"

"Oh, Deela, don't be like that," Palla remonstrated. She got up and went over to Deela and gently lifted her fluffy-slippered feet up on the footstool. Then she turned to Hagos. "Sir, I will be more than happy to speak the Oracle, if that is what you wish. But see how you are shivering. And wet through. You are in no state to Seek the Oracle. Please, have my seat by the fire and rest awhile."

Gratefully, Hagos flopped into Palla's seat like a limp rag and sank deep into the soft cushions. It felt wonderful. It had been, he reflected, eight long and lonely years since he had sat in an armchair beside a fire. He closed his eyes and a few seconds later his soft snoring began to fill the room. Palla gently placed a pillow behind Hagos's head and covered him with a blanket. "Sleep well, Enchanter," she murmured. "I am so very sorry for the trouble I have caused you." As she spoke, another set of snores from the couch joined in.

Palla left the sleepers to their dreams and tiptoed out, heading down the cold stone stairs to her little room on the floor below. She sat by her window, watching the darkness of the cliffs opposite topped by the high walls of Rekadom and its sinister lookout posts. She looked down at the outgoing tide and the myriad of little rising moons reflected on its surface as it slowly uncovered the sandy causeway that joined Oracle Rock to the mainland, and she smiled. Palla remembered how Hagos had looked into her eyes and called her "the true Oracle," and she felt the guilt she had carried for ten long years begin to lift. She leaned against the cool stone of the windowsill, and memories of that night when she was nine years old came flooding back . . .

A lantern in her hand, she is running down the precipitous steps that lead deep into the heart of Oracle Rock. Inside the first of the Oracle chambers—the Shadow Chamber—she puts down the lantern and takes off her shoes as she has seen Deela do. Then she clambers up onto the stone bench and takes down the Shadow Robe—a gossamer-fine silvery-gray cloak that hangs from a peg. Only a few days ago she had helped Deela into it and had been afraid of tearing such a delicate thing, but Deela had told her it was woven from spider silk and was stronger than steel.

The Shadow Robe settles over her like a second skin, bringing with it a sense of awe. How different she feels now—taller, quieter, slower, and much, much older. I feel ancient, *she thinks. She pulls the voluminous hood up over her head, just as she has seen Deela do. It flops down over her eyes, but to her surprise, the fabric is translucent and she can easily see through it. Calmly, serenely, she leaves the Shadow Chamber and walks through a narrow opening in the rock.*

Then she steps into the Oracle Bell.

It is a tiny space and it is indeed shaped like the inside of a bell. The floor is worn silky smooth by the footfall of thousands of years of Oracles, and she walks slowly to the dip in the center and places her feet where so many have stood before. She is cocooned by the walls, which are inlaid with mother-of-pearl and shimmer like the inside of a shell. They are incised with long, deep grooves that run up to the top of the Bell, where there is a round opening through which light filters down from the Oracle Chamber above.

Palla has lost all sense of herself. Now, in the Oracle Bell, she is nothing and yet she is everything. She is the Oracle.

As Palla stands in stillness, she hears a loud cough and then the words—spoken with an edge of impatience—"I Seek the Oracle."

From deep within her aura of calm, Palla replies, "Seeker, you have Found." Her words, transformed by the Oracle Bell, sound nothing whatsoever like Palla Lau.

There is silence above for some seconds and then Palla hears the king speak. "Look here, Oracle. I know you keep telling me that everything is all right, but I'm not so sure. I've not been feeling well and I think my Enchanter might be poisoning me. Or maybe it is his foreign wife from across the mountains, with her ridiculous chanting. Maybe she is jinxing me. And I have such headaches. Oh dear . . . Now, I know you will only answer one question, and I'm trying to work out what best to ask you. I . . . yes, that's it. I must be brave this time. I must ask what I really want to know."

There is silence and Palla says nothing. She feels no need, for the Seeker has not yet said the words he must.

At last the king speaks: "Oracle. I Seek to know . . . how I will die."

The question, in all of its enormity, swirls around Palla like the waters of a storm. The normal, everyday Palla would have been thrown into a panic, but Palla Lau, the Oracle, feels a stillness come over her and without hesitation she gives the king the answer that she knows in her heart and soul to be the truth. "You will die by the hand of an Enchanter's child," she says.

The grown-up Palla sighed at the memory. What terrible trouble those few words caused for people. But it was the truth, so how could she, as the Oracle, not tell it? But at least, Palla thought, the person who she hurt the most understood that now.

And with that comforting thought, Palla got into her narrow bed and lay listening to the sound of the wind howling around Oracle Rock like a crazy cat chasing its own tail and the strangely reassuring duet of snores above. She snuggled down gratefully beneath her quilt. This was not a night to be out.

However, there were others that night who had no choice but to be out. In Netters Cove, a little white boat tied firmly to a ring in the harbor wall bobbed and rocked in the wind. Beneath its red sail, which was rigged over the boat to form a tent, the outline of two figures could be seen by anyone who was foolish enough to be on the harborside that night. But no one was, and Alex and Benn had the place to themselves.

They sat on either side of the central thwart upon which were the remains of a supper of bread, smoked fish, crispy seaweed and fruitcake that Benn had bought with half of his father's silver dollar at the door of a cottage on the dock. To his surprise, the fisherwoman had snipped the coin in two with some wire cutters and returned a sharp-edged half to him with a smile, telling him to come back in the morning with the other half and she would give him breakfast.

Benn was feeling good. He waggled his fingers over what looked at first sight like a glowing fire but was in fact a circle of six small hexagons, which glowed red like coals and gave out a small amount of very welcome warmth. "Did you know they could be warm like this before you had Sol's book?" he asked Alex.

Alex shook her head. "I hardly knew anything about them until I had this." She patted the little blue leather book affectionately. "I can't imagine being without it now." She opened the codex and Benn watched a little uneasily as she scooped the hexagons up and dropped them into a pocket inside the book's front cover. He knew it was crazy to be jealous of a book, but he could not help but feel that the scruffy little book that nestled so comfortably in Alex's hands was taking away the friend he had only just found.

As if Alex knew what Benn was thinking, she passed the codex across to him. "You can read it too if you like," she said.

Touched that Alex trusted him with such a precious object, Benn carefully cradled the book in his hands. It felt ridiculously heavy for such a small thing. "It must feel like carrying a brick," he said.

"A very clever brick." Alex smiled. "Go on, open it."

Warily, Benn looked down at the book. "I don't want to end up in a bubble. I wouldn't know how to get out again."

Alex laughed. "Oh, that was using the hexagons. The book just tells you things."

Benn shook his head. "It's a bit too weird for me,"

he said, handing the codex back to Alex. "But thanks anyway."

"But, Benn, I really do want you to understand why I'm going to Oracle Rock," Alex said.

Benn grinned. "Why *we're* going to Oracle Rock, you mean."

"*We?*"

"Yep. We're sailing there tomorrow. Aren't we?"

Alex smiled. "I guess we are."

CHAPTER 37
Zerra Dark

THE MORNING DAWNED GRAY AND blustery. Alex slept on but Benn, woken by Merry's rocking, peered out from under the sail. Beyond the protective arm of the harbor wall, the sea looked dark and uneasy. A storm was coming in, Benn was sure. "We can do it, Merry," he whispered. "I know we can."

Leaving Alex sleeping, Benn wriggled out from under the sail and took the other half of the silver dollar to claim breakfast. At the tumbledown cottage he exchanged the half dollar for two huge crab and lobster sandwiches, a bag of plums and a jug of hot, spiced milk, which he carried triumphantly back to the boat.

An hour later, Merry's sail was up and they were swinging out from the harbor and hitting the chop of the sea. Benn pointed Merry's prow toward the distant bell-shaped rock and, with the wind very nearly behind them, he let the sail right out. "We're flying!" he yelled.

"While someone throws buckets of water at us!" Alex yelled back. She looked ahead to Oracle Rock, dark and unknown against the sky, and was surprised to see a tiny cottage with a lighted window perched incongruously upon the very top. She had imagined Oracle Rock to be deserted and the Tau nestling in a chamber within, just waiting for her to find it. To have someone actually living there made it feel very different. Who were they? And were they, at that very moment, looking out of their window, watching Merry in the distance bounding through the waves toward them? Alex shivered. She didn't like the idea of being watched. It reminded her of the Hawke.

But it was the Hawke, not Alex, that was being watched from the lighted window. From her little room Palla Lau was watching not the sea but the sky. As she had done on so many mornings, Palla observed the dark shape of the Hawke sweeping in, wings wide, wing tips splayed and feet down as it glided in on the last stage of its journey back to Rekadom. The sight made her shiver, and, as ever, she could not help but wonder how many Enchanters or their children had fallen victim to it. Palla was tougher on herself than Deela ever realized. If she saw the Hawke, she forced herself to watch the creature, telling herself, *You caused that to be made and you must face up to it.* A flash of red caught Palla's eye, and to her surprise she saw that the Flyer was wearing shimmering red silks. Palla had watched a lot of Flyers over the years, but she'd never seen one dressed like that. *It must be freezing up there*, Palla thought, and went up to the tiny kitchen to light the stove.

Zerra was indeed freezing. She and the Hawke had spent the night in a roost on the far edge of the Seven Snake Forest. More accurately, the Hawke had happily roosted in one of the enormous ancient trees and Zerra had shivered in the crook of a branch one hundred feet above the ground, terrified of falling out. They had left before dawn and Zerra could no longer feel her fingers or toes. What she did feel was apprehensive—because right ahead were the fabled three towers of Rekadom, rising high into the sky, their tips of pure gold glinting in the rays of the rising sun.

Zerra watched the stronghold of King Belamus grow ever nearer. Beneath its golden pinnacles it looked dark and forbidding. The inner part of the city was shaped like a five-pointed star, the tips of which touched the high outer city wall that encircled the whole of Rekadom. This left five triangular spaces marooned between the outside of the star and the towering city wall, which were dark with shadows. Inside the star was no better; the narrow streets were deserted and weed strewn, and some of the roofs of the gray granite buildings were falling in. Zerra felt a surge of disappointment. She had expected so much from the city of King Belamus the Great—lights, music, finery and people gathered to greet the return of the Hawke and its new Flyer. But the place was a dump. Even Luma was more exciting.

As the Hawke swooped into its descent, the shrill of a whistle pierced the air and Zerra saw a sudden flurry of movement in the triangular courtyard below. Lanterns flared to life, and in a golden archway at the top of a long flight of steps, she saw the slinky shapes of the King's Jackal—Belamus's notorious bodyguards: half-human, half-dog, white-headed creatures with pale yellow eyes that walked upon their hind legs and stood over seven feet tall. They wore long red coats and carried short swords at their waists. There were only six of them now, but there had once been many more. The Jackal had a taste for cannibalism.

Zerra felt a little nervous.

As the King's Jackal came bounding out from the archway, a squat figure ran into the middle of the courtyard waving a long, red-and-white striped pennant. "Dark!" it yelled up at the Hawke. "Where have you been? Get down here at once, you no-good little . . ." The last word was lost in the whistle of the wind rushing past the Hawke's wings, but Zerra guessed it wasn't entirely complimentary.

Its feet down, the Hawke dropped fast toward the ground, and Zerra clung on tight to the pommel on top of the half hood while her stomach did a backflip. But they landed surprisingly gently, and as the Hawke folded its wings, the pennant-waving figure ran up. "Who the bewittance are *you*, girl?" it yelled.

Zerra looked down at the flat, red face belonging to a square-set man in a leather jerkin. She knew a bully when she saw one. "I am the Flyer," she replied. "Who are *you*?"

She saw the man glance anxiously across to the arch at the top of the steps where the King's Jackal were now lined up on either side of the arch. "Get off that Hawke, girl. Right now!" he yelled at Zerra.

Zerra was saved from asking how on earth he expected her to do that—seeing as she was fifteen feet above the ground—by the Hawke itself. Following its normal landing routine, the Hawke walked over to a block of steps that ended in a platform at the exact height of its saddle. Zerra shook her feet out from the stirrups and slipped down onto solid ground, although as she descended the steps she felt as though she was still wheeling through the air. She stopped on the next-to-last step so that she was eye to eye with the red-faced man.

"You'll explain yourself later, make no doubt about that," he hissed at her. "But right now you will conduct yourself like a properly trained Flyer, got that?"

Zerra regarded the man coolly. As he yet again glanced fearfully at the Jackal, Zerra sensed she had the advantage. "Don't you ever speak to me like that again," she told him. "Understand?"

The man looked so stunned that Zerra almost felt sorry for him. A sudden eerie howling from the King's Jackal began and the color drained from his face. "The king's coming," he jabbered. "Tell him you're our new Flyer. And you're back from a *very* successful mission."

"Okay," Zerra agreed. "New Flyer. Successful mission. I got that. So who are you?"

"Ratchet," said the man. "King's Chief Falconer. Now come along. We have to present the Hawke to the king."

Zerra was amazed. In her wildest dreams she had never expected to meet the king.

Ratchet broke into her thoughts. "Here, take this. It's called the jess," he said, handing her one of the long leashes he had clipped on either side of the Hawke's half hood. "At least try to look like you know what you're doing. Walk in step with me. The king can't abide people being out of step. Bow your head when you meet him. Call him 'Sire.' Got that?"

"Got it," Zerra said.

"And whatever you do, don't say the *E* word."

"What *E* word?"

"Enchanter," Ratchet whispered. "Please, please don't say that word. For all our sakes."

"Sheesh," muttered Zerra. "What a total fusspot."

"He's the king. He can be whatever he wishes."

"I didn't mean the *king*," Zerra replied.

Ratchet turned on his heel and went to the other side of the Hawke, where he took hold of the other jess. "Now, right foot forward. Go."

Tempted as Zerra was to fall out of step, she didn't quite dare. And so she and Ratchet reached the foot of the steps perfectly in time, where they halted and bowed their heads in unison. Above them, framed in the archway, surrounded by his restless Jackal, the king stood eyeing up the Hawke and its new Flyer with a mistrustful stare.

Zerra returned the stare. The king had weak eyes, she thought. She also thought the wings on his crown looked silly. His gold-heeled shoes were too high, his legs were too skinny, his red stockings were wrinkled and purple did not suit him. And he was wearing way too much fur. He looked, Zerra thought, a mess.

Fortunately unaware of Zerra's opinion, the king regarded the Hawke and its new Flyer through half-closed eyes, dark with suspicion. "Where's the boy?" he asked Ratchet.

Ratchet coughed nervously. "Er. That one was no good, Sire. This is a better one."

"Name?" asked the king.

Panic flashed across Ratchet's features as he realized he

had no idea what his new Flyer was called. Zerra stepped in and saved him. "Zerra," she said.

"Zerra, *Sire*," Ratchet added.

King Belamus's narrow little eyes regarded Zerra. "Zerra Dark," he said. "I trust you will catch us a few more Beguilers. Hawke knows we still have more to get rid of."

Ratchet nudged Zerra in the ribs. She flashed him an angry look. "I have had a very successful mission," she said, remembering her instructions. "I caught *tons* of them."

"Sire. Tons of them, *Sire*," Ratchet added.

"Tons?" asked the king. "You *weighed* them?"

"No," Zerra laughed. "It's an expression. It means lots. Lots and *lots*."

"*Sire*," added Ratchet.

"Be silent, Ratchet. Let the Flyer speak," King Belamus snapped.

Ratchet, terrified, made a noise like air escaping from a large balloon and Zerra clapped her hands to her mouth to smother a giggle.

"How many did you get?" the king asked anxiously.

"Oh, at least twenty," Zerra said airily. "Although it might have been more. I lost count." She glanced at Ratchet to check that he was pleased with her description of how well the make-believe mission had gone, but he had his eyes closed and the color had drained from his face. He didn't look at all well, Zerra thought. The king didn't look too great either. Maybe they were both coming down with something. She hoped it wasn't contagious.

Suddenly the king wailed, "Oh, where are they all coming from? I thought we were down to the last few. It must surely be RavenStarr's fault. Regenerating others in his own image or some such nefariousness." He threw his hands up in despair and cried loudly, "Oh, will I never be free of this curse?" The king tottered down the steps on his golden heels and headed across the arena for the high walls encircling it. The King's Jackal loped off after him, following their master as he clattered up to the top ledge that ran around the top of the walls. There, he leaned out to look at the ocean that tumbled onto the foot of the cliffs far below.

"Oh, Hawke save us all." Ratchet sat down on the bottom step, his head in his hands. "Whyever did you say that?"

"Because you asked me to," Zerra said.

Ratchet groaned. "And what did you do with the Flyer? With Danny?"

"Nothing," said Zerra. "He wasn't there. And the Hawke was a swan when I found it. So you have me to thank for getting it back. Not your precious Danny."

Ratchet stared at Zerra in disbelief. "A *swan*?"

Zerra did not reply. She was watching King Belamus hurry back across the arena, closely followed by the Jackal. Ratchet jumped to attention and tried not to flinch when one of the Jackal sniffed at him and then let loose a stream of drool over his boots.

"We leave to Seek the Oracle in three hours," the king told Ratchet. "We will be accompanied by the Hawke. Do not feed it. We wish to check that there are no Beguilers on the Rock and we do not want its instincts muddied by a meal. The new Flyer, as she is so remarkably talented, will attend."

Ratchet's stammer, "Yes, Sire, of course, Sire, whatever you wish, Sire," was lost on the king as he clattered back up the steps and disappeared through the golden arch, followed into its shadows by his Jackal. Ratchet waited until the Jackal had slunk away, and then he turned to Zerra. "Well, girl, it looks like you've got the job," he said, a grudging admiration in his voice. "You'll need a Flyer uniform. You'll have to have a training jacket for now. I'll send the Hawke out to find the old one later—and the blasted Lightning Lance. I suppose the Flyer's made off with that too. Dratted boy."

Zerra shrugged. It wasn't her problem what the last Flyer had done, although the Lightning Lance did sound cool.

Ratchet was tapping his foot irritably. "I can't send

you out with the king unarmed," he said. "I'll get you the training lance. It's not the real thing, but it's pretty lethal. But you only get two shots with it. So don't go firing it off at any old seagull just for fun, got that?"

Zerra grinned. "Who wants to shoot seagulls," she said, "when you can kill Enchanters?"

CHAPTER 38

A Knit Octopus

HAGOS WOKE LATE, WONDERING WHERE he was. Deep in the unaccustomed coziness of the armchair and its blankets, he found memories of the night before drifting back. He stretched his toes out to the warmth of the fire— Palla had already tiptoed in and topped off the coal—and allowed his thoughts to turn to the question he would ask the Oracle. The problem was, there were two questions he longed to ask, and yet the Oracle would answer only one. And it was no good storing up the other one for the next day. If you weren't King Belamus, you got one shot at the Oracle every year and a day. Hagos smiled to himself. Of course, King Belamus had only ever had one chance to hear the true Oracle—not that he knew that.

Hagos could not decide what to ask. He sat in his chair, agonizing over the choice: *Boo-boo or Tau? Tau or Boo-boo?* The more he thought about Boo-boo, the more desperate he became to see her. If only he had not come so close to seeing her, he could have put her out of his mind, just as he had—mostly—managed to banish Pearl from his thoughts all these years. But now that he knew for sure that Boo-boo was alive, she had become real to him again. Hagos sighed. But he desperately needed the Tau too, for without it he would never have the power to disenchant all the Hauntings. And while the Hauntings still Haunted, Boo-boo was in great danger.

As Hagos was letting his thoughts torment him, Deela came quietly into the room. "Well, well," she said. "You really are here. I thought it was a dream."

"Nightmare, more like," Hagos said gloomily.

Deela went and sat next to Hagos on the small footstool by the fire. She reached out and laid her hand on his arm. "I cannot apologize for what happened ten years ago. It is beyond apologies. But I do have something for you. I kept it just in case you ever came back."

"That's nice," Hagos said politely. He watched Deela get up and go to the trio of arched windows where a row of multicolored octopuses were lined up along the windowsill, gazing stoically out of the window at the forbidding cliffs on the far side of the causeway and the three towers of Rekadom, the pointed pure-gold tops of which were just visible, rearing up above the city walls. Deela's hand hovered between two red octopuses with multicolored octopus arms. Carefully, she counted the octopus arms and then she picked one up and brought it over to Hagos. "Here you are. I kept it specially," she said and thrust the octopus into his hands.

"That's very nice of you, Deela," Hagos said politely. "I didn't know you knit."

"Oh, I only knit octopuses," Deela said.

"Octopodes." Hagos could not help himself.

"What?"

"The correct plural is octopodes."

"Well, that's nice for them," Deela said, remembering now how annoying Hagos could be at times. "So do you want it or not?"

With Danny's straight talking in mind, Hagos tried to make amends. "Of course I do. It's very kind of you. Indeed, I am very fond of octo*puses*," he said.

"There's some buttons underneath if you want to undo them," Deela said.

"How lovely. An octopus with *buttons*. How very . . . charming. I suppose that is where its beak is."

"It's where *something* is," Deela said mysteriously. She watched Hagos turn the octopus upside down and, with his bony fingers and their bitten nails, fumble at the buttons. At last—and this was the moment Deela had longed for—something tumbled into his hands and the room was flooded with brilliant blue light. "My, that *is* bright," said Deela. "Much brighter than when I put it in there."

Hagos was speechless. He stared at the small, enameled T-shaped charm that had fallen from the octopus. It sat quietly in the dip of his palm, shimmering with a brilliant blue like an iridescent butterfly wing. Hagos looked up at Deela in wonder. "How?" he whispered. "How in the world did you get the Tau?"

Deela looked a little sheepish. "I know I shouldn't have," she said, "but when the king threw it into the Oracle Bell and it hit me on the head, I thought, *Don't expect me to look after your stolen goods for you, you old ratbag.*"

Hagos was affronted. "Belamus threw the Tau into the Oracle?"

"He did. Tossed it in like a piece of junk. He told the Oracle to keep it safe inside the Oracle Bell and to never, *ever*, let it go. Naturally, the Oracle said that she would. As you know only too well, *this* Oracle does not always tell the exact truth. So *this* Oracle took the Tau and left a blue lamp in the Oracle Bell so that the king would not ask any questions. Then I put it in the octopus I was knitting. The Tau is as light as a feather, isn't it? I knit it an extra arm so that I could tell which one."

Hagos looked at Deela with new respect. "You did all that?"

She put her hand on Hagos's trembling shoulder. "To make amends. Because I knew what trouble I had caused you."

"You did not mean to," Hagos said.

"No. I did not mean to. And Palla did not mean to either. But it happened even so."

Hagos felt as though he was coming alive after a long, cold sleep. All kinds of possibilities opened up before him, but he realized that the most important thing was that he could ask the true Oracle about Boo-boo. And at long last he could be with her again—his curly-haired, bright eyed, laughing little Boo-boo. He looked up at Deela. "I thank the Oracle from the bottom of my heart."

Deela felt a little overcome. "The Oracle will be waiting for you," she said. She smiled, admitting at last what, deep down, she had known for a long time. "The *true* Oracle." Then she sat down, picked up her wool and set to work on her latest octopus.

CHAPTER 39

Seekers and Finders

A LEX WAS BAILING MERRY OUT as fast as she could, but it felt as if the whole ocean wanted to be inside the little boat rather than outside where—and Alex felt strongly about this—it belonged.

They had just crossed a wide bay edged with a long strip of sand upon which white-topped waves rolled in, and the dark bell shape of Oracle Rock loomed large now, its granite dark against the white-clouded sky, the curving wall of the harbor drawing ever closer.

And then, at last they were heading into the welcome calmness of the tiny—but famously deep—Oracle Rock harbor. As Merry scudded into the lee of the wind, the sail relaxed and so did Alex, Benn and even Merry herself. Benn took the little boat alongside the harbor wall, jumped out, stumbled up the slippery steps and secured her to the bollard at the top.

Alex threw him up another rope and glanced up at the cottage that sat so solidly high on the very top of the rock. There were three arched windows lit with the warm glow of lantern light, and through the upper ones she glimpsed the shadow of someone looking down at them. Alex shivered. She didn't like being watched. She ran up the steps and took Benn's arm. "Come on," she said. "Let's go find the Oracle."

Palla Lau had just gone into the kitchen to fetch a new lantern when she glanced out of the window to see a small white boat in the harbor and two sodden young ones following Deela's signs to the Oracle. Palla disapproved of the signs. She felt the Oracle should be a mysterious thing, not signposted like a tourist attraction. Palla also thought there should be a lower age limit on Seeking the Oracle. It was not right that kids sometimes turned up asking what they were going to get for their birthdays or what to call their new pet rabbit. Palla had to admit, though, these kids with the boat looked serious—they'd certainly gone to a lot of trouble to get there. She was about to go tell Deela that she had what Deela annoyingly called "customers" when she heard Deela calling for her.

She found Deela knitting a pink-and-green striped octopus. "Oh, Palla," Deela said. "Hagos has gone down to speak to the true Oracle. And we both know that's not me. So I wonder . . . would you . . . would you mind?"

Palla broke into a huge smile. "I would be honored." she said. "Very honored indeed."

"Off you go then," Deela said. "Oh, and pass me the green wool, would you?"

Hagos was sitting on a bench set back into the rock just around the far corner from the opening into the Oracle Chamber. Now that he was so nearly there, the words he would speak to the Oracle felt immensely important. Should he say: *Tell me, pray, where my daughter is?* A little niggle of concern prodded at Hagos—that wasn't specific enough. Perhaps he should say: *Where is the daughter of Pearl and myself?* Or should it be *Pearl and I?* Paralyzed by indecision, Hagos took out the Tau and held it, marveling at its brilliance and the fizzing buzz of Enchantment that flowed undiminished from all those years of being stuck inside a stuffed octopus. He thought about the moment—after he had finished the very last of his Twilight Hauntings—when the Tau had been ripped from his hand by Belamus, who told him he would never ever see it again. And that night Belamus had thrown him out of Rekadom into the nighttime desert to confront the first of many of his own Hauntings—the deadly, giant

Skorpas. Clearly Belamus had not expected his old friend to survive. Indeed, Hagos had not expected to survive either, but luck—and some ancient spirits—had been with him that night.

A tear trickled down Hagos's cheek at the thought of his old friendship with Belamus so lost and betrayed, but he pushed it aside. Things were different now. He had never thought to see the Tau again—and yet now he held it in his hand. He had never dared hope to see Boo-boo again—and now he knew she was alive, and soon he would know where to find her. And as the energy from the Tau flowed through him, filling the empty spaces from which his Enchantment had long vanished, Hagos found that he knew exactly what question he would ask the Oracle. He sat for a few more minutes gathering his thoughts, readying himself.

Alex and Benn were on a precarious path some twenty feet above the waves, buffeted by the wind. They were outside a narrow slit in the rock from which a mysterious blue light shone from deep inside. Above it a sign proclaimed: "Oracle Chamber." And beneath that a smaller sign added: "No Picnicking. Oracle Seekers Only."

"I guess this is it," Benn said. "Will you be okay?"

"I'll be fine," Alex said. "You can go back and check on Merry if you like."

Benn looked relieved—he was concerned that with the tide going down fast now, he'd not left Merry enough rope. "If that's okay?" he said.

"Sure it is. I'll meet you back there."

To Alex's surprise, Benn gave her a sudden hug. "Good luck," he said, and then he was off, striding back along the path. Alex took a deep breath, and then she turned and walked into the soft silence of the Oracle Chamber.

Suffused with an eerie blue light and glimmering with the quartz trapped in the granite rock, the chamber's utter stillness was a complete contrast with the wild wind and water that surrounded it. It was shaped like the inside of a beehive, and in the middle of the floor—worn to a smooth shimmer by thousands of years of footfall—was a conical mound about three feet high with a hole at the top from which the strange blue light emerged.

Alex was wondering what to do until she caught sight of Deela's helpful bullet-pointed instructions—of which Palla greatly disapproved—written on the wall in big, looping letters:

INSTRUCTIONS FOR SEEKERS
- SPEAK THE WORDS "I SEEK THE ORACLE" SLOWLY AND CLEARLY INTO THE BLUE LIGHT.
- WAIT QUIETLY PLEASE FOR THE ORACLE TO RESPOND WITH THE WORDS "SEEKER, YOU HAVE FOUND."

- ASK ONLY ONE QUESTION REQUIRING ONLY ONE ANSWER.
- WAIT FOR THE REPLY.
- NO SUPPLEMENTARY QUESTIONS WILL BE ANSWERED.
- DO NOT SWEAR AT THE ORACLE.
- DO NOT LEAVE CANDY WRAPPERS IN THE ORACLE CHAMBER.
- NO OVERNIGHT CAMPING.
- PLEASE NOTE, NO RETURNS PERMITTED (APART FROM ROYALTY) FOR A YEAR AND A DAY.

Alex took a deep breath and, speaking into the shaft of blue light, she said: "I Seek the Oracle."

Far below in the Oracle Bell, Palla heard a girl's voice drift down. She stood silently for a few seconds, allowing the stillness of the Shadow Robe to seep into her, and then she spoke: "Seeker, you have Found." Palla got goose bumps as she heard her voice drift upward, transformed by the Bell into the voice of the Oracle.

Palla waited. The question took longer than she had expected, but at last it came. "I wish to know the exact place where the Tau lies here on Oracle Rock."

The question almost knocked Palla out of her trance—this was not the usual child's question. She took a deep breath and allowed the serenity of the Shadow Robe to envelop her once more.

Up in the Oracle Chamber, Alex waited nervously. The answer seemed a long time coming. *Maybe the Oracle hadn't heard her? Or maybe the Oracle didn't know the answer?*

A movement at the entrance caught her eye, and assuming it to be Benn, Alex turned around. But when she looked there was no one there.

Palla felt the peace of the Oracle descend upon her once more. She herself had no idea where, or what, the Tau was, but as the Oracle she knew with great certainty. "The Tau waits at the entrance to the Oracle Chamber."

Alex gasped with surprise. Had the Tau come to meet her? "Oh, thank you!" she called down into the blue light, and then she raced over to the entrance, where she cannoned straight into Hagos.

Hagos stared at the girl, who looked like a drowned rat. He'd not expected anyone else to be Seeking, let alone someone so young. "Sorry," he said. "I was waiting for the Oracle."

"I . . . I'm finished now," Alex said. "You go in."

"Thank you. I will." Hagos gave Alex a formal little bow and walked in. Alex stared after him, puzzled. He looked oddly familiar, but she didn't know why.

* * *

Palla had just taken off the Shadow Robe when she became aware of a presence in the Oracle Chamber. This, she was sure, must be Hagos. Once more, she slipped the Shadow Robe over her head and felt the peace of the Oracle settle on her.

"I Seek the Oracle," a voice came down into the Oracle Chamber.

"Seeker, you have Found," Palla replied.

There was a pause, and then came the question. "Oracle, where is my Boo-boo?"

Palla felt no surprise at the question, for the answer settled over her like a soft cloud. "Your Boo-boo is just behind you," she said.

Hagos wheeled around and saw on the far side of the narrow fissure into the chamber the soaking-wet girl who had just bumped into him running her hands over the rock beside it, apparently looking for something. *Surely that wasn't Boo-boo?* His heart pounding, he walked over to the entrance, calling softly, "Boo-boo? *Boo-boo?*"

Alex wheeled around. *Boo-boo.* Why did that make her feel so strange inside? She looked at the man, scrawny, beaky nosed, intense black eyes, and she felt as though all of the life she could remember had disappeared and she was back at the unremembered beginning again. Back to the time before Mirram and Luma. Back to when she did not have to explain herself. When she could just be

Boo-boo and that was enough—*more* than enough. She was back where she belonged.

Hagos looked at the girl, her dark hair in rattails, a green silk scarf wound around it just as Pearl had once worn hers, and her long, thin fingers that fluttered like little bird wings, just as Pearl's had done. And then she spoke a word that Hagos never thought to hear again: "Poppa?"

CHAPTER 40

At the Oracle Chamber

DEELA CAST OFF THE TOP of the pink-and-green octopus and got up to put some more coal on the fire. As she warmed her hands by the flames she glanced out of the window—and gasped in horror. "No! Oh no!" Coming across the causeway, with that terrifying brute of a Hawke flying above, were the king and his revolting Jackal bodyguards. "Go away! *Go away!*" Deela screamed uselessly at the window.

Seconds later she was throwing on her coat and old Wellington boots, and then running down the dark and winding stairs cut deep inside the rock that led to the cottage's front door, set halfway down Oracle Rock. Deela burst out of the door into the shock of the blustery gray afternoon and stood for a moment taking stock. Down in the harbor, she saw a boy fiddling around in a white sailboat. She briefly wondered what he was doing there, but then, with a feeling of dread, she forced herself to look over to the causeway. To Deela's relief, the king was no more than halfway across and, with his heeled shoes sinking into the wet sand at every step, was making slow progress. If she hurried, she could get to Hagos in time.

Anxiously, Deela glanced up at the Hawke, which was being buffeted by the wind, wheeling to and fro. She was close enough to see its Flyer—a new one, she thought— who looked terrified and was hanging on to the pommel on top of the Hawke's funny little helmet. Hoping that the Flyer had quite enough to think about without going looking for Enchanters, Deela raced run down the zigzagging steps to the harborside. She arrived breathless and peered over the wall to the causeway. There she saw the king still picking his way across the soggy sand like a disdainful heron. Deela turned and set off at a flapping run along the King's Path.

King Belamus's private path to the Oracle Chamber was on the opposite side of Oracle Rock from the rather precipitous public path. Although the King's Path took the longer way around the rock, it was much broader and was smoothly paved and easier to traverse—which was essential, given the king's taste for flimsy shoes. Sheltered from the prevailing winds and with a fancy handrail, it was also much safer. Gasping from her unaccustomed activity, Deela sped along the path as fast as she could. She *must* get to Hagos and warn him that the king and his Jackal were on their way. She could sneak him down the secret tunnel to the Shadow Chamber—if only she could get to him in time.

In the entrance to the Oracle Chamber, Hagos and Alex stared at each other.

"Boo-boo, is it you? Is it really you?" Hagos murmured, reaching his hands out toward the small, dark-haired girl who was looking at him as if in a daze.

Alex moved a step back. *Those hands.* The last time she's seen them they had been pushing her away.

"Why did you do that?" she blurted out. *"Why?"*

"Why did I do what?" Hagos asked, confused.

She looked at the bedraggled, skinny old man in front of her, and all she could feel was an overwhelming terror of being abandoned. "Throw me away," she said.

Hagos felt as if he had been punched. "No, Boo-boo. Not throw you away. Never, Boo-boo."

"Alex. I'm Alex now."

They stood, frozen for a few moments, and then Hagos tried again. "Boo-boo, I—"

"My name is Alex."

"Yes. Of course. Alex. I did *not* throw you away. How

could you think that? Look . . . I gave you my cards. My *Hex* cards. That's not throwing away, is it?"

"You mean your cards are more important than me?" Alex felt as if she was falling into a deep pit of anger, and watching the anguish on her father's face, she hated every second of it. But even so, she could not stop.

Hagos was aghast. "No! Of course not. Please. Booboo. Alex. I put the cards in your jacket pocket when you . . . when you went away. To be *safe*. I put them there so that one day you would understand who you were."

A sudden squall of rain skittered in and Alex shivered.

There was a question that Hagos hardly dared ask, but with the Tau sitting deep in his pocket, he knew he must. "So you do . . . you do still have the cards?" he asked.

"I have them," Alex said stonily.

"And my codex? A little blue book with *HEX* on the cover, I hear you have that too now?"

"Yes."

The relief showed in Hagos's voice just a little too much. "Oh, Boo-boo. Thank the stars. They are both *so* important. You don't know how much."

"I *do* know, actually," Alex retorted. "I figured it out for myself. Just like I've done everything else for myself, okay? And just like I will keep on doing, too. Because no one, not even you, throws me away!" With tears rolling down her cheeks, Alex turned and ran off through the cold rain and the biting wind, racing back to Merry and the only person she could trust.

Stunned, Hagos watched her go. He knew he had done something wrong again, but he had no idea what. Where was Danny when he needed him? With the cold rain dripping down the back of his neck, Hagos set off along the precipitous path. "Boo-boo!" he called out. *"Boo-boo!"*

A few seconds later at the very moment Hagos rounded the bend in the path, Deela appeared from the opposite direction and hurtled into the Oracle Chamber. She found it empty. Where had Hagos gone?

After his slow progress across the causeway, Belamus picked up speed along the King's Path, his shoes clacking a fast *tippy-tap tippy-tap* along the smooth stones. As he reached the far end of Oracle Rock, a sudden gust of wind blew him into the blue-lit shadows of the Oracle Chamber. His Jackal followed, but Belamus shooed them outside to wait. In the quietness of the Chamber Belamus cleaned the sand off his shoes and collected his thoughts.

Deela had already slipped into the secret tunnel and made her way down to the Shadow Chamber. There she found Palla sitting quietly on the bench, submerged in the Shadow Robe.

"Palla!" she whispered. "It's the king again. I need to tell him to go away. Let me go into the Bell. Please!"

Deep in the calmness of the Shadow Robe, Palla gave Deela a vague smile. And then, as she heard the clicky-clacky sound of footsteps above, Palla got up and slowly walked into the Oracle Bell. Deela put her head into her hands. *What on earth would Palla tell the king this time?*

Inside the peace of the Oracle Bell, Palla stood in the dip, waiting.

"I Seek the Oracle!" an impatient voice dropped in from above.

"Seeker, you have Found," Palla dutifully replied.

"It's the king here, Oracle. Now look, this is important. There's a sudden rise in the number of Enchanters out there, and I suspect some of them will have wormed their way into Rekadom. So, Oracle, I want to know if there are any Enchanters—or their nasty little brats in particular—anywhere near my royal person. Be specific now, no pussyfooting around like you usually do."

Even from within the serenity of her Shadow Robe, Palla felt annoyed at the king's tone. But the truth flowed through her like a river and she answered: "Yes, all these are here on Oracle Rock."

"*All?*" the king spluttered. "How many exactly have you got?"

Palla heard his question and in her heart she felt the answer—three—which she did not understand. But Palla did not respond. Her duty done, for even the king was only allowed one question at a time, and she left the Oracle Bell.

"Oracle! Answer me! Answer me!" the king yelled.

"Palla," Deela said nervously as Palla emerged from the Oracle Bell and the king's shouts reverberated out into the Shadow Chamber, "what did you tell him?"

CHAPTER 41

Quarry

ZERRA WAS FAST DEVELOPING A fear of heights. The Hawke was rolling and wheeling above Oracle Rock, and the unforgiving harshness of the dark rocks below made Zerra aware of just how dreadful it would be to fall—and of how very possible it would be to do so, sitting precariously as she was, buffeted by the wind, above a giant bird's nasty little flat head with its stupid bonnet with a pom-pom on the top. Zerra was wondering why any bird with self-respect would consent to wear such a thing when the Hawke suddenly changed direction and she very nearly slipped off.

When Zerra had regained control and her heart stopped

hammering, she saw that the Hawke was hovering above two figures who were running along a narrow path at the outward-facing tip of the island. Why the dumb bird was interested in what looked like an old beggar in a scrappy red cloak chasing a girl, yelling at her to stop, Zerra had no idea. Any fool could see the girl wasn't going to stop for him. Silently willing her on, she watched the girl race toward the harbor, where it looked like a boy in a boat was waiting for her. A brief pang of envy shot through Zerra. She wished *she* had a boy in a boat waiting for her instead of being stuck way up in the air on a stupid bird. And then, suddenly, Zerra realized who the girl was. "Alex!" she screamed out.

But Alex, steeped in misery, heard nothing but the rush of the wind in her ears. She raced on along the path, thinking only of how soon she could be back in Merry and sailing away.

"Get her. Get her!" Zerra yelled at the Hawke.

The Hawke, however, had other ideas. It saw below, in a long red cloak, the one who had turned it into a ridiculous long-necked flying bucket with webbed feet. The one who had laughed at it and called it a marshmallow. Now it was payback time. The Hawke tipped forward, put its wings back and went into a dive. Zerra screamed.

Hagos looked up and saw the Hawke heading straight for him. He threw himself to the ground and Faded fast into the rocks around him. Distraught and utterly exhausted, Hagos lay on the path and waited for the Flyer to finish him off. He didn't care anymore. He really didn't.

The Quarry vanished. The Hawke was not concerned—this happened all the time. It abandoned the dive and soared back up to recommence its positioning hover, waiting for the Flyer to flip down its half hood and direct it to its Quarry. But its Flyer did nothing but kick it in the neck and scream at it. A surge of rage ran through the Hawke—what was the point of a Flyer if it didn't do its job? There was something wrong with this new Flyer. It felt more like Quarry than Flyer. It would like to get rid of it and turn it into Quarry. And that, the Hawke decided, was what it was going to do.

Up on the Hawke, Zerra was desperately clinging onto the pommel of the half hood as the raptor twisted and turned, wheeling and soaring, then dropped so suddenly that Zerra's stomach seemed to jump into her mouth. Zerra was terrified—the Hawke was trying to throw her off.

Once again, the Hawke swooped up and then flipped into a rolling dive. As it plummeted, Zerra saw Alex running down the harbor steps to the boy in the white sailboat. The boy had seen the Hawke and was yelling at Alex, but the roar of the wind took his words away. Zerra grinned. This was her chance. She had two shots but there was no way she'd need them—she'd get Alex with the first. One-handed, she pulled the unwieldy training lance from its holster and leveled it at her target—which was easier said than done on the crazy Hawke. Remembering Ratchet's instructions, she pulled back the lever to prime the lance, counted to three—slowly—and fired. In a blinding stream of blue light, the bolt flew into the water just beyond the sailboat, exploded, and sank in a froth of bubbles.

The rebound from the lance sent Zerra rocketing backward out of the saddle. Her feet slipped from the stirrups, and she went tumbling down toward the cold gray waters below—but not for one moment did she consider letting go of the lance.

Alex jumped into Merry, sending the little boat rocking. "Zerra's in the water!" she yelled.

"Good!" Benn said, fitting the oars into the oarlocks.

Alex was shocked. "We've got to get her, Benn."

"You know that's the third time she's tried to kill you?" Benn demanded angrily. "And it won't be the last." But as he was saying that he was untying the rope and pushing Merry away from the wall. No true sailor can leave a person to drown.

It was now Zerra discovered that her despised training jacket was designed to keep her afloat. Gasping with the cold but with the training lance clasped firmly in her hand, she bobbed up to the surface like a cork and saw, to her surprise, Alex and the boy in the white boat rowing out of the harbor, heading toward her. With numb fingers, she pulled back the priming lever once more. This was her last chance to get Alex and this time she was going to make it happen.

From above, the Hawke watched its Quarry floundering in the water. It flew upward to gain height and then, freed by the absence of its Flyer, it went into a stoop— drawing its pointed wings back until they lay along its body and then plummeting vertically down like an arrow. As it neared the surface of the water it took its wings outward once more to slow itself, then it leveled out and dropped its talons down, ready to take the Quarry.

Zerra looked up and saw just what Alex had seen on that cliff face a few days earlier. But unlike Alex, Zerra had a weapon in her hands. She aimed the lance at the chest of the Hawke and shot it through the heart.

CHAPTER 42

Alex RavenStarr

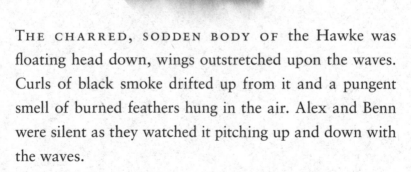

THE CHARRED, SODDEN BODY OF the Hawke was floating head down, wings outstretched upon the waves. Curls of black smoke drifted up from it and a pungent smell of burned feathers hung in the air. Alex and Benn were silent as they watched it pitching up and down with the waves.

But not Zerra. She sat in Merry accepting the rescue as her due. Zerra was euphoric—not only at her survival, but also at the feeling of power in killing such a massive creature. "That was some splash, hey?" she said, laughing. "And I did it *all* for you, Alex. To keep my little sister safe."

"Liar," Alex said. "I saw you point that thing at me first. You'd have shot me if you hadn't had to save yourself. And I am *not* your sister."

As they reached the calm waters of the harbor, Zerra's elation abated as she considered how to handle the death of the Hawke. She wished it would hurry up and sink so she could say it had flown away, but every time she glanced back she saw the horrible thing bobbing around for all to see. How was she going to explain that to the king, who was clearly very proud of his Hawke? Zerra decided that the best approach was to offer a distraction—and that distraction was sitting right here in the boat. Alex.

Benn tied Merry up to the harbor steps, but Zerra seemed reluctant to leave the boat. "Alex," she said. "I . . . I'm sorry about everything. *Really* sorry."

Alex didn't reply, but Benn said, "'Sorry'! Is that all you can manage? You tried to *kill* Alex."

"No, I didn't. I promise." Zerra glanced around. She dropped her voice to a whisper and was pleased that both Benn and Alex leaned in to listen. "I've been taken prisoner by the king," she said. "I *had* to do that stuff. Pretending to shoot you and everything. Because the king is watching me."

Benn and Alex exchanged glances. "You mean the king is *here*?" Benn asked.

"He's come to Seek the Oracle. He's in there right now, which is why I could get away and kill the Hawke. I meant what I said, Alex. I did it for you. To keep you safe."

"Yeah, yeah," Alex muttered.

"And . . . now I'm scared. Because the king's going to be *so* angry about the Hawke. I—I don't suppose I'll see you again. I'll be in a dungeon forever. Which is why I wanted to say . . . well, I'm sorry, Alex. I'm sorry about Naming you, and I'm sorry I tried to get you at the river. And I'm sorry for being mean. Tell Ma and Franny and Louie I love them. Please." Zerra forced out a sob. "Goodbye, little sister," she said, and then she jumped out of Merry and ran up the harbor steps.

Alex watched the bedraggled Zerra walking away along the harbor wall, her shoulders slumped. A pang of pity shot through her. *Zerra looks so defeated*, Alex thought. *And she called me "sister." Zerra has never, ever said that before.*

Alex got to her feet. "We can't let her spend the rest of her life in a dungeon. She could come back with us. Back to Mirram."

"But, Alex, she tried to kill you," Benn said. "I saw it."

Alex shook her head. "She said 'sorry,' Benn. And I believe she meant it." With that, Alex jumped out of Merry and ran up the steps after Zerra.

"Alex!" Benn yelled. "Leave her. Come back!"

But Alex took no notice. Benn leaped out of Merry and ran after her.

At the end of the King's Path at the top of the causeway steps, Zerra reached her destination and stopped. There was no sign of the king—*where was he?*

Breathless, Alex caught up with Zerra. "Zerra, you don't have to go into a dungeon. Come away with us. Please."

Zerra turned to Alex, making sure she had tears streaming down her face. She wished the king would hurry up. Alex was such a pushover, but she couldn't keep this up much longer. And the boy from the boat was heading their way. He was trouble, she could tell.

"Alex!" Benn said, skidding to a halt beside them. "Leave her. We need to get out of here."

At that moment, to her relief, Zerra heard the clicky-clacky sound of gold heels and saw the swirl of purple silks rounding the end of the King's Path. "It's the king," she said. "Alex, go! Don't . . . don't bother about me," she said, managing to gulp back a sob.

"Do as she says, Alex," Benn said urgently.

Alex hesitated as King Belamus came into view, his white-headed Jackal close behind. "Zerra, please," she said. "Come with us."

Belamus, extremely agitated by what the Oracle had just told him, had rounded the last bend of the King's Path to see his bedraggled Flyer—*where was the Hawke*—arguing with two kids. He stopped, fear running through him. He already knew he was on Oracle

Rock with an unspecified number of Enchanters and their brats, one of which, one day, was going to kill him. And there, right in front of him, were two of them. King Belamus tiptoed uncertainly forward and then stopped, horrified—*his precious Hawke was floating facedown in the sea.* Dead. Anger overcame the king's fears. The Hawke was his pride and joy and now it was lying in the water like a mangy old seagull. His heels tapping fast upon the stone, he marched up to Zerra and asked a surprisingly reasonable question: "What have you done to my Hawke?"

Zerra took hold of Alex's arm, and Alex recognized the confiding way Zerra always had when she wanted you to do something for her. Still cultivating her tears, Zerra turned to Alex, pleading, "Alex. Please. Tell the king it wasn't my fault. *Please.*"

In her wildest dreams Alex had never expected to meet King Belamus, let alone be asked to speak to him. There was something about standing in front of the king so close that she could see the grease stain on the front of his furry vest that made her slow to react. It all felt so unreal. And then, suddenly Zerra's grip tightened around her forearm like a vise, and Alex began to feel just a little scared.

"Sire," Zerra was saying, "this is my foster sister, Alex. She is an Enchanter's child. She possesses cards of

Beguilement and she uses them against you. I Named her in Luma and she escaped. I now Name her again. *She killed your Hawke. Sire.*"

"Jackal! Arrest the Enchanter's child!" Belamus yelled. Teeth bared, drool dripping, the six creatures sprang forward and surrounded Alex.

"No! No!" Benn shouted.

"Arrest that boy too!" Belamus barked. A Jackal broke away from Alex and grabbed Benn. As he fought and kicked against its clutching claws, Benn felt something push past him and an invisible kick took away the hind legs of the Jackal. The creature toppled over and fell, howling in fear, into the deep waters of the harbor below. As it hit the water, steam hissed up and it sank in a stream of bubbles.

Benn withdrew a few paces, watching warily for another of the Jackal to come for him. But none did—they were all occupied with Alex. Suddenly, out of nowhere, Benn saw a skinny man in a red cloak appear next to Alex. He was shocked to see it was the Flyer's spy and yet, oddly, Alex did not seem afraid of him.

But King Belamus did. "RavenStarr!" The king's voice trembled with fear. "What . . . what the Hex are you doing here?"

The old spy made a low, rather formal bow and doffed an imaginary hat. "I come to offer myself in exchange for this child," he said, indicating Alex.

"I don't need an exchange," the king said. "I'll have you too. Jackal, take him!"

But the spy raised his hand and a blue light shone out from it so bright than Benn scrunched up his eyes. "Take me in exchange for her and you will have the Tau," the spy said. "This is worth more to you than any child. You know that, Belamus."

The king laughed. "So how about I have you, the brat *and* the Tau, eh, RavenStarr?"

"You shall not. I shall throw the Tau into the water. You know how deep this harbor is. The Tau will be gone forever."

Confused, Benn watched Alex. She was shaking her head. As if she didn't want the spy to give himself up. But the king was persuaded. "Very well. Jackal, let the child go. For now. We will return later." The Jackal let go of Alex, but to Benn's surprise she did not move. She just stood, watching as the Jackal took hold of the unresisting spy.

"The Tau, RavenStarr," said the king. "Hand it over."

"Not until she is out of your way," said the spy. He whispered something to Alex and she nodded, and then walked slowly past Benn, unseeing, with tears streaming down her face. Benn set off after her. "Alex," he called softly. *"Alex."*

Alex did not hear. All she could think of were the words her father had whispered to her: "Go with the boy in the boat. Go now. Poppa will come and find you, sweetheart. I promise." And as he spoke them, Alex had felt abandoned all over again.

At the top of the harbor steps, Alex stopped. With Benn standing silently at her side, she watched Poppa handing over the precious Tau to the king, who shoved it greedily into his pocket. She saw Poppa, surrounded by the pointy-eared Jackal, being hustled down the steps to the causeway in the wake of the king—with Zerra trotting after him like a little dog—and then she lost sight of him behind the wall.

"Alex," Benn said, a little louder.

This time Alex heard. She turned to Benn. "Poppa," she said. "That was Poppa. My father."

Benn could not believe it. "But he was the spy. With the Flyer."

"And when I saw him through the spyglass I never even knew," said Alex. "Why couldn't I tell he was my father? All I did was run away from him."

Benn slowly shook his head, trying to work it all out. "So that's why Jay came after us. He was bringing him to meet you. I . . . never thought of that."

"I wish I'd known," said Alex quietly. "He had the Tau, Benn. He had the precious Tau and he gave it away to save me. He did that all for me."

"Wow . . ." Benn tried to imagine his father giving away something even half as precious to save him, but he couldn't.

"Come now," said a soft voice behind them. They turned to see a small, wild-haired woman wearing yellow Wellington boots and a long coat in the pocket of which appeared to be a multicolored knit octopus. The woman put her arm around Alex and said, "He is a good man, your father. A very good man. But look at you both—soaked to the skin and shivering. Let's get you into the warm, shall we? I've got a nice fire going and Palla will have the kettle on by now."

Alex allowed the woman to guide her up the long, winding steps up Oracle Rock. At every turn that faced the causeway she stopped to watch her father, surrounded by the Jackal, walking away from her, drawing ever closer to the dark granite cliffs beneath Rekadom.

At the top of the steps was a small door set into the rock. While the wild-haired woman in Wellington boots fiddled with the latch, Alex watched the fluttering of her father's red cloak as it disappeared into the dark mouth of the tunnel at the foot of the cliffs.

When he was gone, the softly spoken woman broke the silence. "Come in, dears," she said, pushing open the weather-beaten door. "I'm Deela Ming, by the way."

"I'm Benn Markham," said Benn, "and this is . . ." He stopped, feeling it was not right for him to speak for Alex.

Alex smiled at Deela, and for the first time in her life she spoke her real name. "I'm Alex. Alex RavenStarr."

Later that afternoon . . .

LATER THAT AFTERNOON AS THE light faded, Alex gazed out the window over the heads of a line of woolly octopodes, as her father would have called them. The clouds had blown away, leaving the sky clear, and the gold tips of the three towers of Rekadom were shining in the orange light of the setting sun. Alex thought about her father and the danger he had willingly walked into, just for her. She made a promise to herself. Next time, her father would not have to find her. Next time, *she* would find *him*.

She would set Hagos RavenStarr free, and the Tau, and then together they would rid the land of the Twilight Hauntings. Forever.

Also by
ANGIE SAGE

"An exciting tale full of double blinds, double crosses and unexpected family connections." –*Wall Street Journal*

KATHERINE TEGEN BOOKS
An Imprint of HarperCollins Publishers

www.harpercollinschildrens.com

More books by
ANGIE SAGE

SEPTIMUS HEAP

TODHUNTER MOON

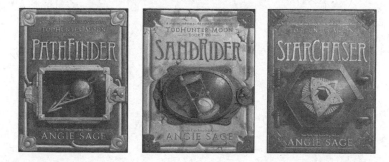

 KATHERINE TEGEN BOOKS
An Imprint of HarperCollins Publishers

www.harpercollinschildrens.com